Taken from reviews of the

Mossy Creek Hometown Series

"Delightful." — *Marie Barnes, former Fir~ ~ ~f Georgia*

"Mitford meets Mayberry in *th~* ~ ~ve and warmhearted new series — Cleveland Daily Banne~

"MOSSY CREEK is as much ~ ~..ion; like sipping ice cold lemonade on a hot ~ ~ afternoon. Hire me a moving van, it's the kind of town where everyone wishes they could live."
— *Debbie Macomber,* NYT *bestselling author*

"A fast, funny, and folksy read. Enjoy!"
— *Lois Battle, acclaimed author of S*toryville, Bed & Breakfast, *and* The Florabama Ladies' Auxiliary & Sewing Circle

"SUMMER IN MOSSY CREEK takes you to a land that time has not forgotten, but has embraced."
— *Jackie K. Cooper, WMAC-AM, Macon, GA*

"Colorfully and cleverly portrayed. A wholesome story."
— *Harriet Klausner, Amazon.com's top reviewer*

"The characters and kinships of MOSSY CREEK are quirky, hilarious and all too human. This story reads like a delicious, meringue-covered slice of home. I couldn't get enough."
— *Pamela Morsi,* USA Today *bestselling author*

"[MOSSY CREEK] is a book you will not lend for fear you won't get it back."
— *Chloe LeMay,* The Herald, *Rock Hill, SC*

"These southern belle authors have done it again, even better this time." — *Bob Spear, Heartland Reviews*

"In the best tradition of women's fiction, MOSSY CREEK points to a genuine spirit of love and community that is our best hope for the future."
— *Betina Krahn,* NYT *bestselling author of* The Last Bachelor

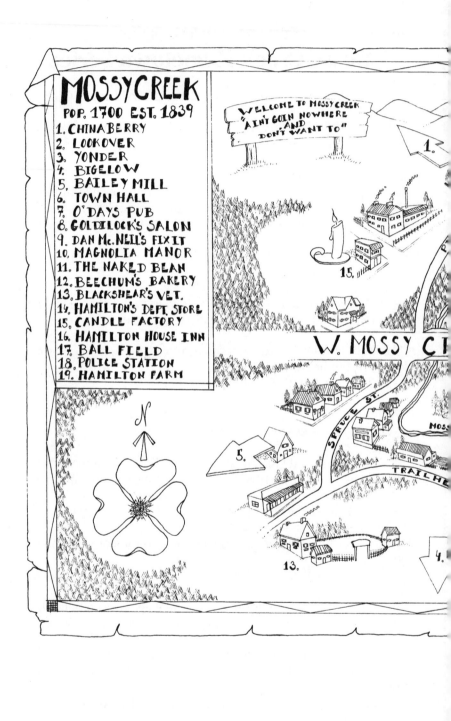

MOSSY CREEK

POP. 1700 EST. 1839

1. CHINA BERRY
2. LOOKOVER
3. YONDER
4. BIGELOW
5. BAILEY MILL
6. TOWN HALL
7. O'DAYS PUB
8. GOLDILOCK'S SALON
9. DAN Mc. NEIL'S FIX IT
10. MAGNOLIA MANOR
11. THE NAKED BEAN
12. BEECHUM'S BAKERY
13. BLACKSHEAR'S VET.
14. HAMILTON'S DEPT. STORE
15. CANDLE FACTORY
16. HAMILTON HOUSE INN
17. BALL FIELD
18. POLICE STATION
19. HAMILTON FARM

WELCOME TO MOSSY CREEK
"AIN'T GOIN NOWHERE
AND
DON'T WANT TO"

W. MOSSY C[...]

DEDICATIONS

This book is dedicated to all the furry, finned and feathered friends that have touched our lives with their love and companionship.

Sandra Chastain dedicates her story to Rosie
(Pomeranian) who loves everyone,
Baby (cat) who stops traffic by walking on a leash
with Rosie, me and Weople (wild Yorkshire Terrier).

Martha Crockett dedicates her story to Marvin,
a beloved Cairn "terror" who died just a few months
before this book went to press.

Debra Dixon dedicates her story to Sweetie,
who showed up at precisely the right time.

Susan Goggins dedicates her story to Longjohn,
the best dog-in-a-cat's-body in the history of the world.

Maureen Hardegree dedicates her story
to the tortoiseshell calico who taught her
that she could love a cat as much as a dog.

Michele Hauf dedicates her story to the cats
in her house, Maxwell and Toast,
and with loving memory to the best cat ever, Sebastian.

Kathleen Watson Hodges dedicates her story to Simon,
the loudest, stinkiest, most obnoxious bird on the planet
that stole her daughter's heart
and thus earned a place in hers.

Everyone gets one great dog per lifetime.
Carolyn McSparren's was Bruin,
a big, black part-Labrador foundling.
She also acknowledges Gamby and Katie, the two
Bouviers who collaborated on *Louise & the Marauders*.

Deborah Smith dedicates her story to a
palomino barrel horse named Reb's Buck,
who shared her teenage years with loyalty and patience.

Critters of Mossy Creek

A collective novel featuring the voices of

Deborah Smith, Sandra Chastain
Martha Crockett and Debra Dixon

with

Susan Goggins, Maureen Hardegree,
Michele Hauf, Kathleen Watson Hodges
Pam Mantovani and Carolyn McSparren

Memphis, Tennessee

BelleBooks, Inc.

ISBN 978-0-9841258-2-1

Critters of Mossy Creek

Published by:
BelleBooks, Inc. · P.O. Box 300921 · Memphis, TN 38130
We at BelleBooks enjoy hearing from readers. You can contact us at the address above or at BelleBooks@BelleBooks.com

Visit our website— www.BelleBooks.com

First Edition September 2009

10 9 8 7 6 5 4 3 2 1

Cover art: © CALLALLOO Canis - Fotolia.com
Book & cover design: Martha Crockett
Mossy Creek map: Dino Fritz

Critters of Mossy Creek

Odd Places & Beautiful Spaces
A Guide to the Towns & Attractions of the South

Mossy Creek, Georgia

Don't miss this quirky, historic Southern village on your drive through the Appalachian mountains! Located in a breathtaking valley two hours north of Atlanta, the town (1,700 residents, established 1839) is completely encircled by its lovely namesake creek. Picturesque bridges span the creek around the turn-of-the-century town square like charms on a bracelet. Be sure to arrive via the scenic route along South Bigelow Road, the main two-lane from Bigelow, Mossy Creek's big-sister city, hometown of Georgia governor Ham Bigelow. (Don't be surprised if you overhear "Creekites" in heated debate about Ham, who's the nephew of longtime Mossy Creek mayor, Ida Walker.) You'll know when you reach the Mossy Creek town limits — just look for the charming, whitewashed grain silo by the road at Mayor Walker's farm. Painted with the town's pioneer motto — *Ain't goin' nowhere, and don't want to* — the silo makes a great photo opportunity. The motto perfectly sums up the stubborn (but not unfriendly) free spirits you'll find everywhere in what the chamber of commerce calls "Greater Mossy Creek," which includes the outlying mountain communities of Bailey Mill, Over, Yonder, and Chinaberry.

Lodging, Dining, and Attractions: Shop and eat to your heart's delight around the town's shady square. Don't miss *Mama's All You Can Eat Café*, *Beechum's Bakery* (be sure to say hello to Bob, the "flying" Chihuahua), *The Naked Bean* coffee shop, *O'Day's Pub*, the *Bubba Rice Diner*, *Hamilton's Department Store* (featuring the origami napkin work of local beauty queen Josie McClure Rutherford), *Hamilton House Inn*, the *I Probably Got It* store, *Moonheart's Natural Living*, and *Mossy Creek Books and What-Nots*. Drop by town hall for a look at the notorious Ten-Cent Gypsy (a carnival booth at the heart of a dramatic Creekite mystery). Stop by the town jail for an update on local shenanigans courtesy of Officer Sandy Crane, who calls herself "the gal in front of the man behind the badge," Mossy Creek Police Chief Amos Royden (recently featured in *Georgia Today Magazine* as the sexiest bachelor police chief in the state). And don't forget to pop into the newspaper offices of the *Mossy Creek Gazette*, where you can get the latest event news from Katie Bell, local gossip columnist *extraordinaire*.

As Katie Bell likes to say, "In Mossy Creek, I can't make up better stories than the truth."

Lady Victoria Salter Stanhope
The Clifts
Seaward Road
St. Ives, Cornwall, TR3 7PJ
United Kingdom

Hey, Vick!

Spring has finally broken through
the winter here in Mossy Creek!
And we're plumb glad to see
it come. The buttercups have
already come and gone, the
azaleas are in their prime and
the dogwoods and rhododendrons
are just around the corner.

You know, one thing I've never
asked you about is pets. Do you
have a dog or cat or anything
furry and warm to cuddle up to on
cold winter nights?

Creekites have all kinds of
critters in our barnyards . . .
and our backyards, too! Mostly

cats and dogs, you know, like the rest of the world. Although we can get a little exotic. Coons and possums and even a beaver or two have come and gone over the years. One Eagle Scout a few years back nursed a wounded eagle back to health. How's that for irony? The whole town watched him set it free. It flew off, purty as you please, right back to Colchick Mountain. We even had a dancing bear a few months ago.

I don't know why, but for some reason I picture you with one of those little lap Spaniels. Write and set me straight!

Your azalea-sniffin' correspondent,

Katie

"Dogs are not our whole life, but they make our lives whole."

—Roger Caras

The Mice that Roared

Part One

Jayne Reynolds

Odd, isn't it, how things and animals and people come into your life.

While it's happening, it seems rather random. You make love to your perfectly healthy husband and a month later, he dies of an aggressive cancer. Yet somehow you wind up pregnant. You feed a poor, pitiful cat that shows up at your door. You unwittingly start a feud with the owner of the bakery next door to your new coffee house the first day you open.

The next thing you know, you have a pet for the next twenty years, you have your husband's son, and you wind up buying the bakery and hiring the owner who has become a dear friend.

It seems to me that when you look back over the years, you can see how all the pieces of your life's puzzle fit together and you get the distinct feeling that each event was meant to be.

Looking forward, life may be a box of chocolates, as Forrest Gump's mother purported. But when you look back, you realize life is a mosaic. Though you think you're making random choices with each piece you place in your life's work of art, in the end you have a complete picture, and you understand that each one of those pieces was

3

destined to be in just that spot.

Take my moving to Mossy Creek a few years ago, for instance. At the time, I was operating in a fog of grief over my husband's death, and I didn't much care where I was. I just couldn't stay in the place where he and I had spent so many happy years. Yet, what I thought had been a knee-jerk reaction turned out to be one of the main themes in my life's mosaic.

I've found a true home in Mossy Creek. I've been accepted for who I am. Am loved for who I am. And while I still miss Matthew, it's almost as if I'd been living another life back then.

Now I feel as if I'm adding jewels to my mosaic, not just dull-colored pieces of tile.

Oh gracious. Listen to me, waxing all rhapsodic. I guess I just have mosaics on the brain.

Tiles, anyway.

Which one? Which one?

I picked up my top three choices and took them over to the fading spring light of my shop's window to see if that would help me make up my mind.

The Naked Bean's front door opened. "Jayne?"

I glanced over see Ingrid Beechum holding the door open with her back as she wiped her hands on a dish towel. Her dog, Bob, stood patiently at her feet, looking up at me because that's what his beloved mistress was doing. The Chihuahua's sight had gotten so bad, I doubted he could actually see me. The white apron Ingrid always wore was missing, so I knew it was time to close up shop.

"That time already?" I asked.

"Hmmm," she said. "Since you're the boss now, I thought I'd check in before I locked the door . . . for the last time."

We grinned at each other. We'd begun our relationship as mortal enemies, but were now partners . . . of a sort.

Several months ago, Ingrid had a health scare about the

big "C. Turned out everything was fine, but it put the fear of God in her, and the upshot of that was, she decided to sell Beechum's Bakery to me.

It made good business sense for me, because what complimented gourmet coffee more than bakery goods? And since the bakery shared a wall with The Naked Bean, it wasn't going to take much to make the two shops into one. Or so Dan McNeil, our town handyman, promised me.

From our truculent beginning, Ingrid and I'd had a tacit agreement that I wouldn't sell baked goods, and she wouldn't sell coffee. That meant, of course, that customers had to go from one shop to the other to get both, and many of them did. When the portal was finished, however— hopefully before the weekend was over—they'd no longer have to go outside.

Ingrid and I weren't technically partners, of course, since I owned both places, but I wanted to think of it that way, and I wanted her to think of it that way.

Ingrid still worked at the bakery, but now she had a tidy little nest egg in case something really did happen, and she didn't have to worry about the managerial aspects of running a business, which she never liked anyway, and I loved. Now all she had to do was create her wonderful pies and cookies and cakes.

She was happy. I was happy. Our customers were going to be happy. It was a win-win situation all 'round.

Which brought me back to the tile.

Dan McNeil's crew started work tomorrow. Dan said it'd only take a few days to join the two shops, then he'd start work on my apartment upstairs. All of this renovation had been approved by the landlord, Mossy Creek Mayor Ida Hamilton Walker. She and her relatives own major portions of the town but are, thankfully, open to innovation.

With my son Matt approaching three years of age, I needed more room than the tiny, one-bedroom loft over

The Naked Bean, in which he and I had been living. Now that I owned the bakery, I was going to expand our living quarters into the bakery's long-unused second floor.

"Come help me decide which of these to use in the master bath," I said to Ingrid.

"Ingie!"

Ingrid bent to catch Matt, who'd launched himself at her from the children's play area in the corner of the shop.

She'd been looking for him, so she caught him deftly.

He laughed and planted a loud kiss on her cheek. He giggled at the noise he'd made and pushed up his goggles from his Bob the Builder Power Tool set. Ingrid had bought the toy for him to encourage his interest in the upcoming construction. Not that she had to. Matt had shown an early interest in building and engineering. Tinker Toys, Legos and old-fashioned Lincoln Logs were his favorite toys. Just like his father.

"You haven't helped Mama pick out her tile?" Ingrid asked Matt as she came up beside me, Bob the Chihuahua at her heels.

"I like the tav'tine," he said with definite decision.

Ingrid looked over the selections I held up and nodded. "I think you're right, Matt. I like that, too."

I'd been surprised that Matt picked the same tile that I was leaning toward. Kids usually went for flash. "So do I. Josie gave me two conservative choices, knowing I'm not too exciting, and one 'decorator' choice. This blue-green glass combination here."

"You're just as exciting as the next person," Ingrid countered, letting Matt down to play with Bob. "The blue tile is too vivid. I think you'd get tired of it pretty quick. But you can live with the travertine for years and years. It's so earthy. Like you."

I held the tile in the weak sunlight. "Yeah. Josie says I have a double dose of earth, since I'm a Capricorn-Ox."

"Humphf." Ingrid made no secret about her skepticism regarding Josie's astrological observations.

"Hey, you're the one who made the 'earthy' comment," I countered, then changed the subject. "Ready for a long weekend off?"

"Weekend off?" Ingrid archly raised her brow. "You mean we're not taking cookies and coffee to the soccer game on Saturday?"

"Yes, of course we are. I meant days off from manning the shops," I said. "Four whole days, and when we come back Monday morning, we'll have an honest-to-goodness full-service coffeehouse." I felt decadent. I hadn't taken more than a day off since I'd opened The Naked Bean, other than the month after Matt was born, and I'd hardly call that a vacation.

"We should've done this two years ago." Ingrid bent to pick up Bob, who'd settled happily in Matt's lap. Matt was gently stroking Bob's head, like Ingrid had taught him.

"We're doing it now, and that's what—" I frowned at my son, who held Bob tight, turning so Ingrid couldn't get him. "Matt, let Ingrid have Bob."

"Bob stay with us tonight."

Thinking of the last time Bob had "slept over" at our house and the puddles I'd had to clean up, I sighed and knelt beside Matt. "Bob is much happier with Ingie." I pried the Chihuahua from Matt's chubby little fingers and handed him to Ingrid.

Matt didn't cry. He rarely cried. But the look he gave me could've melted Colchick Mountain.

I raised my brow at him, and he looked away.

"The boy wants a dog, Jayne," Ingrid said.

I stood, "And I want a million dollars to pay for this renovation."

She stuck her chin in the air. "A boy needs a dog."

"He has a cat."

Ingrid "humpfed" again. "Not the same thing."

"Thank God," I murmured as I locked the door behind her.

The world is roughly divided into two pet camps: cats and dogs. True, a small percentage of the population opts for more exotic pets like snakes or ferrets or parrots, but by and large, it's a race between cats and dogs.

I'd always been firmly in the cat camp. My husband, Matthew, had shown dog tendencies early in our relationship, and little Matt had obviously inherited his father's dog-lovin' genes.

Well, I had set his father straight. I could do the same for my son.

I bent and picked him up. "Come on, little darlin'. Let's go upstairs and fix our supper."

🐾🐾🐾

The next afternoon, I stood in the gaping hole between The Naked Bean and the bakery. It was about six feet wide, uneven and ugly. On either side, it showed an old brick wall that had been sandwiched between two-by-four studs and drywall. In places, I could see down to the basement and up to the attic.

Dan's crew had hung heavy plastic from the ceiling on both sides to keep the dust to a minimum. Even so, dust had crept through to coat the tables in both the coffeehouse and the bakery.

"It'll look better tomorrow evening," Dan said, a bit defensively.

I smiled into his square-jawed face. "I know. It's just that telling yourself there's going to be a mess is one thing. Confronting the mess is quite another."

"How's it going?"

I turned as my good friend and psychic advisor, Josie Rutherford, pushed through a seam in the plastic wall.

"Wow," she exclaimed as she looked at the same gaping hole I saw. "This is great."

I chuckled at Dan. "I guess beauty is in the eye of the decorator."

"It'll look completely different this time tomorrow," she said. "Right, Dan?"

I chuckled again. "Is there an echo in here?"

Dan chuckled, too, and gathered his tools. His two workmen had already gone for the day. "I'll see you early in the morning."

"All right," I said, and saw him to the door. Then I turned to see Josie watching me like a mother robin watches her babies returning from their first flight. "What?"

"Did I see a spark between you and Dan?" she asked with what could only be excitement.

"Me and Dan? A spark?" I blinked in startled surprise, then recovered. "I sure hope not. All this dust would go up like kindling."

"You sure? He's verryy good-looking, and that workman's body . . ." She sucked in a rapid breath. "Oooh la la."

I laughed out loud. "Oooh la la??? What are you, French today?"

"Harry says when I kiss I'm Fr—"

"Hey hey hey! Keep it clean." I pointed to the other side of the plastic curtain where Matt was drawing pictures of houses in the dust.

Josie studied me for a long moment, then said, "You're not worried about Matt. You're jealous."

"And you're nuts." I briskly pushed my way through the plastic. "Dan? The hunk who every single—and some not so single—women in town pants over? That Dan?"

Josie rolled her eyes as she followed me. "Yes, that Dan. And he is a hunk, isn't he?"

I shook my head at her. It seemed as if everybody in

town had tried to pair me up with Mossy Creek Police Chief Amos Royden, and both he and I had taken that in stride. But Dan McNeil had never crossed my mind. Dan. Hmmm. He did have very nice . . . shoulders—

"No. Are you crazy? I'm the mother of a toddler and a small business owner who just doubled the size of her business loan. I don't have time for such things."

Josie snorted. "You're a healthy, thirty-six-year-old, flesh-and-blood woman. It's been three years since your husband died. Even Confederate widows put away their 'widow's weeds' after a year."

I stopped and thoughtfully regarded what I could see of the front door through the thick, dust-covered plastic. "Dan?"

Josie moved in for the kill. "Why not? He's a Scorpio, true, and they can be a tad moody, but he's got enough Ox to overcome that. And I've never known Dan to be moody, have you?"

"Well, no, but—"

"Ssshhhh!" Josie grabbed my arm. "What was that?"

"What was wh—" Then the skittering sound registered. "Oh no. Not—"

"Mice," she breathed. "The construction must've stirred them up."

I ran to the door at the back that hid the stairs up to my apartment and screamed up them for my cat. "Emma! You have a job to do!"

"The Voice Of The Creek"

Good morning, Mossy Creek! This is Bert Lyman, as always, of WMOS-FM and its sister station WMOS-TV, local cable access channel 22, bringing you breaking news of greater Mossy Creek on this fine day in early springtime.

Spring means love is in the air, and love is for critters as well as for human beings, and so . . . that means new puppies! And new kittens! And new hamsters! And new parakeets! And new you-name-it!

So get yourselves down to Bigelow, where our own Mayor Ida Hamilton Walker is helping to dedicate the new Bigelow County Humane Society this morning and take home a new something-or-other that's messy and furry and has fangs, even if it looks too much like your mother-in-law.

Excuse me while I turn to my wife, Honey Lyman, and tell her I'm just kidding about her mom.

*"Thousands of years ago, cats were worshipped as gods.
Cats have never forgotten this."*

—*Anonymous*

Peggy and the Curmudgeonly Cats

Peggy

My daughter, Marilee, was against it, although she started me thinking in the first place.

She and her husband Claude and my granddaughter Josie live down in the big-little city of Bigelow, seat of Bigelow County. I live up in Mossy Creek in a turn-of-the-century mock Tudor on a lot the size of three football fields. My husband Ben and I bought it when we both retired. He wanted the land to garden. I wanted the inside of the house for books.

After he died on me—I have never forgiven him for that, by the way—I was forced into gardening. I've grown fond of it and even fonder of my friends in the Mossy Creek Garden Club, but I needed a new challenge. Gardening was never really my thing, but I couldn't remain locked in the house reading murder mysteries until I mummified.

Marilee is afraid that's what will happen. She says the yard is too much for me. It is, but I have help. The house is too big for me. It is, but not for my books. I am not even seventy yet, and here she wants to shove me off into a condo in Bigelow, where she can keep tabs on me.

I don't think so. I'd rather be mummified, especially now that my original cat, Dashiell, has become four cats with the adoption of Sherlock, Marple and Watson. I don't think they'd take to mummification, however much the ancient Egyptians extolled the virtues of spending eternity with their felines.

Those condo places have rules about animals, and since I much prefer my four cats to most of the human beings I know, that is not acceptable.

Besides, this house is paid for. Even if I could sell it in this market, I'd have to spend a fortune to live somewhere else, and with condo fees, I'd never be free of monthly payments.

Again, I don't think so.

I've told Marilee all that, but she continues to fidget. "Those condo units are quite spacious," she said.

"The complex only takes people over fifty-five."

"Are you saying you don't qualify?"

"I'm saying I intend to stay here until somebody carries me out to the funeral home."

"What if you break a hip?"

The way she fixates on my aging joints, she seems to think I have as many hips as a brown recluse spider.

"What if a burglar breaks in and kills you? Or worse?" she added.

"That would be the fate worse than death, I assume."

"This is not a joke!"

"I'm not laughing. But I'm not moving, either. Those condo people—they're a way-station on the way to a nursing home—will only allow me to have a single cat. That's like saying you have to pick one of your children and put the others into a sweat shop. Unacceptable."

I think Claude, her husband, puts her up to it. He's a Bigelowan. Need I say more? They are born messers-around in other people's lives. Bigelowans have been trying to control Mossy Creekites for more than a century.

This spring I put my mind to how I could forestall interference from my family, and after some consideration and a great deal of planning with my financial advisers, I came up with a plan. I did not discuss it with Marilee and Claude. Claude is a master of what I call 'the civil service No.' No matter what you ask him, his instant reply is 'No.' He never even hears the question. He may be talked around to grudging agreement, but it's hard slogging. Marilee isn't as bad, but she gets worse the longer she lives with him. I am attempting to keep all the negativity from slopping over into Josie's character. So far I have been successful, but she's barely five and spends more time with her parents than with me, so I am not sanguine.

Back to my plan. Built on a steep slope front to back, my living space is only one story with an attic, but because of the slope, there is a gigantic double garage and a concrete, walkout, floored cellar beneath the house, that Ben intended to turn into a shop for his garden. He never got around to it. It's dry and looks out onto the back yard.

The basement was built with a small toilet, electricity and gas lines. I had no idea why anyone would want a toilet in the basement, until Ben told me that in the early days of the twentieth century, when the house was built, the separate toilet would have been used by servants and gardeners. My family never could afford servants, so I'd never run into anything like that. Amazing. Separation of classes (and probably races) even in normal bodily functions. Maybe we have made a tad of progress. Like many proud, small-D democratic Appalachian mountain towns, Mossy Creek has never been a place where a few people lord it over the rest.

I decided to turn the cellar into a garden apartment with French doors looking out on the yard and a patio under my deck. I might rent it to some nice elderly widow. We could check on one another to monitor our descents into decrepitude and dementia, plus I'd have some extra income in the meantime.

Mossy Creek has only a few apartments, largely because the population isn't that mobile. Still, a college student might move in and commute to the community college down in Bigelow. Bigelow rents are much higher, and the drive isn't bad except during ice and snowstorms, when anyone in his right mind stays home anyway.

I called my friend Louise, who endured the tortures of the lowest circle of hell redoing the Queen Anne she inherited from her aunt. I took her to lunch at Mama's All You Can Eat Café to pick her brain and came away with a dizzying list of permits, contractors, architects and suppliers of everything from concrete to upward-flushing toilets.

Louise terrified me, but she did tell me that, in the end, her renovation was worth it. She also agreed to act as my unpaid consultant.

I decided against hiring an architect. I knew what I wanted. I didn't need some fancy young man to turn my cellar into Rubik's Cube. I wanted an all-around small contractor. I had two choices, Dan McNeil, who might be the obvious choice, but there was a new game in town—young Arturo Sanchez. Since he'd been adopted by Opal Suggs, along with his two sisters, Arturo had become Mossy Creek's second go-to fix-it guy.

Dan McNeil may be the contractor of choice by dyed-in-the-wool Creekites, but since I'm new relatively new here, I thought outside the box and decided on Arturo. I liked the fact that he worked alone, although he occasionally called on his sisters for help when he needed them. They're both very young, but they seem to be able to do anything he needs help doing.

Another reason I chose Arturo was because I hoped to keep even the slightest hint of what I was considering from leaving the city limits of Mossy Creek and sneaking down to Bigelow and thus into Marilee's ears. Dan McNeil is *not* known for his closed mouth.

Did it work? You don't know Mossy Creek.

Two days after I talked to Arturo, I got a call from Marilee. "Have you lost your mind, Mother? That old house must be falling down around your ears. I warned you . . ."

"Knock it off," I said. "The house is not falling down around my ears, my mind is still largely intact despite your assaults on it, and everything is going splendidly, thank you."

She actually does mean well, but mothers and daughters have this dynamic going that no one else can understand. At some point the daughters want to become the mothers and treat us like the daughters. That may happen to me some day, but I'll have to be running around the neighborhood naked and thinking I'm living in 1810 with Napoleon before I relinquish control to Marilee.

After I told her what I planned, she said she'd have Claude call to talk me out of it.

"You cannot have some stranger living in the basement of your house, Mother Caldwell," Claude said. He has always called me Mother Caldwell. I loathe it. I've told him a million times to call me just plain Peggy. 'Mother Caldwell' sounds either like liver capsules or the head of a cloistered order of nuns who's bucking for sainthood. I am neither.

"You will spend a fortune. These things always go over budget. Don't you watch This Old House?

"Indeed I do, although I would never let Norm Abrams within a country mile of my house. The man could find carpenter beetles in the Metropolitan Gallery of Art." Come to think of it, there probably are carpenter beetles there, but that's not the point. If I have beetles, I intend to live with them. Let my heirs deal with them.

Claude tried with mounting exasperation to change my mind. In the end we agreed to disagree. I think he sees every dime I spend as one less that Marilee will inherit.

The morning Arturo's truck drove down my driveway

for the first time, all four cats flew into the cabinet under my sink in the master bath. They are not used to strangers, particularly male strangers with heavy boots.

Louise discovered that because I did not intend to change the footprint of my house, but only to upgrade existing areas, I didn't need permits. She said that was probably the only good news I was likely to hear until the job was finished, but she can be a downer, so I ignored her.

With few exceptions, the work would take place completely downstairs and away from my daily living areas of the house, except when utility and telephone connections had to be made, but Arturo planned to check in with me every day to report progress.

Piece of cake.

As if.

🐾🐾🐾

Dashiell, Cat Extraordinaire

Peggy calls me Dashiell after some mystery writer person who drank himself to death before I was born. Hardly a recommendation. I must intervene to tell the real story of our home's invasion.

I can no longer levitate from the floor to the top of the library shelves without thrusting off the back of the wing chair. I still, however, maintain order, decorum, quiet and command in my household and intend to do so until I depart for my next incarnation.

My adopted family—acquired through no fault of my own, by the way—demands constant supervision. The logistics of our lives, such as food, water, cushions and a clean litter box, are maintained by our staff human, Peggy, of whom I am inordinately fond, or as fond as any master can be of an admirable servant. She also provides mental stimulation, not that the others have enough intellect to appreciate the books she reads. I have read over her shoulder since I discovered at six months that I could understand the scratchings on the paper when she read aloud to me.

The three kittens—Sherlock, Marple and Watson—that came to live with us after the lamentable affair of the misplanted catnip, are now adults in body, if not necessarily in mind.

I consider myself pleasantly portly. Sherlock, however, is monumental. One suspects his mother had an unfortunate liaison with one of the bobcats that occasionally traverse our property. What he provides in avoirdupois, however, he lacks in mental acumen. He must be coached to cough up a hairball.

One makes allowances for his lack of brains because of his inherent gentleness. Peggy's granddaughter lugs him about like a handbag. I would never permit such liberties.

Watson is much smaller and a born sycophant. He lacks any dignity when either petting or food is on offer. It is a mistake to allow "them" to think we can be seduced by a tummy rub. They get ideas well above their station in life. Unfortunately, he is devoted to bright toys.

Marple, the only queen among our quartet, is nearly as intelligent as I, sleekly beautiful, extremely vain and holds grudges. Once Peggy's friend Carlyle, a man we generally admired as he always brought us treats, accidentally trod on Marple's tail, then left his shoes in Peggy's bedroom. I will not put words to what Marple did in his shoes. I was disgusted with her, but she was unrepentant.

We live exclusively inside Peggy's admirably comfortable house. Since my one foray outside, I have come to agree with her strictures. Constant dangers lurk outside for felines.

Inside, however, one expects to be completely safe, peaceful and content—cosseted, in fact.

Even mild discomfort is intolerable. Under ordinary circumstances, I complain to Peggy (whom we call Staff), who then cleans the litter box, replenishes the kibble, fills the water dish, plumps up the cushions, and does whatever other small service I might require, with admirable dispatch.

This time, however, Peggy was, please forgive the modern idiom, totally clueless. There are times when none of "them" can understand what we tell them, no matter how many times we repeat ourselves. Exasperating. I put up with the disruptions as long as I could. If Peggy could not fix the problem, it was up to us.

The young man who arrived much too early one morning and made too much noise seemed pleasant enough, but one doesn't like to take chances, so I shooed my brood into the bathroom cabinet. If he were merely temporary, I couldn't be bothered to discover whether he liked cats.

Unfortunately, it seemed he not only planned to return, but to take up semi-permanent residence downstairs, where we are never allowed, since it is reached only by going outside. Not only that, but he intended to make a great deal of noise. I informed Staff I was not pleased. She stroked me and gave each of us a treat, but did not offer to send the noisy one away. Each morning he returned to sit at the kitchen table with Staff, pore over sheaves of papers, then repair downstairs to make more noise.

I deduced that she was creating a new nest downstairs to be occupied either by this noisy one or by a human who was not a member of our family. We learned to put up with Staff's friend, Carlyle, until he moved away, and with her family, of whom Josie is the only acceptable member, but to introduce a perfect stranger into our lives?

I assembled my troops to discuss a plan of attack.

🐾🐾🐾

Peggy

My big old cat Dashiell is as fat as a barbecue hog and has been known to slip off the top of the hutch in the dining room and crash into the silver service. He never hurts his body, but his pride demands that he act as though he had intended to crash. Then he grumps about for the rest of the afternoon. I'm afraid he'll break a leg or a hip. He already hates going to the vet. He'd never forgive me for coating parts of him in plaster of Paris.

He's been spending too much time lately scaling his own private Everests. I think the other cats are fraying his nerves. They are much younger, and with the exception of Sherlock, commonly referred to as Lard Ass, more active. They want to chase things and play fight. Much above Dashiell's dignity. He takes it just so long, then he holds down whichever of them—Watson or Marple—has bitten his tail and washes their faces for them. That, in cats, is a sign of dominance.

I hope he maintains his pre-eminence. So far I think the only one of them with the power to hold Dashiell down is Sherlock, who would never consider demanding dominance. A. A. Milne called Pooh "A bear of very little brain." Substitute "cat" for "bear," and you have Sherlock.

That's one of the reasons the present situation is worrying. All cats are inherent thieves, just like magpies. If they can pick it up in their teeth or bat it with their paws and if it appeals to them esthetically, a cat will hide demitasse spoons under the Kirghiz rug or bury your great aunt Sophie's silver filigree pin under his canned salmon. Dashiell did that one time. Took me hours to clean it once I found it, and I've never been able to wear it since. I swear it still smells faintly of fish.

The first thing to disappear was my great-grandmother's antique cloisonné snuffbox, that she swore came over with the first settlers. The cats didn't steal it, surely, after this long. It has sat on the piecrust table in the living room as long as I've lived in the house, and they've never bothered it.

The second item was my antique gold thimble, inherited from my other great-grandmother. Again, not the cats. It has sat in my sewing box forever. They never bother my sewing.

Cats are not assessors of real value. They're as likely to cherish a plastic ring off the top of the milk bottle as they are the Hope Diamond. If they hide a 'precious,' they tuck it under the sofa cushions or behind the television. I checked the likely hiding places with no success.

The latest item to disappear is the emerald and diamond ring Ben's mother left me when she died. The stone is the size and color of the bottom of a Coke bottle. I never have occasion to wear it. I should have put it into the lock box at the bank, but it's on an insurance rider, and I never got around to it. It's always kept in the jewel case on my dressing table. Even if the cats knew it was there, they couldn't possibly have lifted the lid of the case to get it out.

I worried and stewed and searched most of the afternoon I discovered it was missing. I planned to leave the ring to Marilee and then to Josie, so I was feeling guilty that I had in some sense shirked my responsibility to Ben's family.

If I couldn't find it in a reasonable time, I'd have to make a police report to Amos. The insurance company would demand it. I definitely did not want to do that.

When the snuff box disappeared, I reluctantly called Ida. Our mayor is good for any emergency, civic or otherwise. Her definition of her mayoral duties is broad. "I'm afraid she's at it again," I said.

"Who?" Ida Walker, a fiftyish bombshell of womanhood, speaks with the crisp Southern drawl of an army general.

"Millicent."

Millicent Hart is who I want to be when I get old. Well, older. Tough, feisty, believes that the best defense is a good offense. And takes things. I have never known her to take anything of real value, however. "I don't want to accuse her falsely," I told Ida. "As a matter of fact, I don't want to accuse her at all. I simply don't know how to go about finding out if she took my snuff box and get it back."

"When did you lose it?" Ida asked.

"The Garden Club met here last week, despite the dust from downstairs. What should I do?"

"I'll check around."

"How are things with you and Amos?" I am incorrigible when it comes to gossip about Ida and the Chief's romantic life.

"Who?" she said grimly, and hung up. Not a woman of talkative instincts.

Then the thimble went missing. None of the Garden Club members, including Millicent, was in my house during that period. So I couldn't blame Millicent, then.

The other possible solution to the thefts was one I didn't even want to contemplate. Arturo Sanchez came into my house for coffee every morning before he started work, and I'd given him a key to my house the first week so that he could access utilities and breaker boxes when I wasn't home. Arturo is a fine young man and to the best of my knowledge, his family is squeaky clean.

Arturo is a Hispanic newcomer not only to the United States but to Mossy Creek. I simply could not accuse him or his sisters without ironclad proof. I consider myself a good judge of character. I liked Arturo and did not believe him willing to jeopardize his new status by stealing something as identifiable as my humongous emerald ring, a thimble or a cloisonné snuff box. I couldn't even ask him without making him feel I suspected him. At best we'd both be uncomfortable. At worst, he'd quit and leave my basement half-finished.

He really didn't need money, although he claimed he did. We'd become friends over coffee, and he told me that the economy was cutting into his construction business. Still, his adopted mother, Opal Suggs, had a very healthy bank account, according to rumor. No one knew how she kept it growing. "Investments" was all she'd ever say. The rumor mill had her betting on NASCAR races, but I never believed that. I'd never known anyone who considered gambling as a steady source of income.

But even though Opal had money, the machismo inherent in most Hispanic males kept Arturo too proud to rely on it. I admired him for making his own way in the world.

"Consuela, my sister will have her *Quinceanera* in a few years," he told me one morning. "You know, the party that is traditional when a Latino girl becomes fifteen."

Apparently it's a combination debutante ball, Bat Mitzvah and non-marital wedding reception rolled into one.

"My sisters want a big party with music and much food and decorations and a band for dancing." He sighed, the way Ben had sighed when I talked about Marilee's wedding. "Everyone must have new clothes. My sister must have a very beautiful dress. It all costs a great deal of money."

"I hope what you're doing downstairs will help with the expenses," I said.

He brightened. "Oh, yes, senora! The apartment will be beautiful. We will finish very soon."

Good. No matter how carefully one tries to keep out the dust from construction, somehow it filters into the rest of the house, even when it's on a different floor. And although Arturo was careful, he did track mud and dirt in every morning.

"I thought you had cats," he said one morning. "I have never seen them."

"They're not really into strangers," I said.

"I am sorry. I like cats. You do not have a dog?"

"The cats are plenty for one woman." I had not seen so much of the cats myself since the construction started. They stayed as far away from the noise as possible, and Dashiell stalked around in a simmering rage until evening when the Arturo left for the day.

So, Arturo and his family needed money. I hated the idea, but I decided to drive into Bigelow and check some pawn shops. There aren't any in Mossy Creek.

I had never been in a pawnshop in my life, but I pulled out the Yellow Pages and made a list. I've been to Thieves Markets in Paris and Rome, and I know that many people who have items stolen routinely go to the markets to buy back their own goods for a fraction of their value. I was willing to do that so long as the fraction was a tiny one, although the theory enraged me.

Dashiell

The noisy one should be gone by now. "They" don't like thieves. Neither do I. One's food and toys should be sacrosanct. Even Sherlock with his insatiable appetite knows better than to attempt to eat out of my dish. His left ear is still ragged from the bite I gave him when he was a kitten. He is much larger than I now, of course, but he doesn't realize that. He still sees himself as the frightened little scrap he was when he came to live with us. Good.

The selection of items was initially simple to acquire. I have often heard Peggy tell visitors about her thimble and snuffbox and how precious they are to her. The green ring thing, however, required skill. At length after several tries while Peggy was out shopping, Marple managed to insinuate her small paw under the lid of the jewel case and open it far enough so that Watson could insinuate his larger paw inside and open the lid, then he took the thing, probably because it was the shiniest object in the box.

I had difficulty making him put it into our hiding place. He wanted to play with it and refused to understand when I explained that if Peggy found him batting it about, she'd simply put it back and lock the case. He is still grumpy.

Although Peggy and I have lived in this house for a very long time, she has never discovered my hidey hole under the bathroom sink. Oh, she knows we all disappear inside the cabinet, but not that there is an aged mouse hole in a back corner that we have enlarged over the years and now use as a cache for things we do not want her to find. Needless to say, the mouse that carved out the hole and his descendants have long since been dispatched to mouse heaven. One does one's job when one can.

Reluctantly, Watson shoved the green thing inside our cache to join the little box, the thimble, two blue circles from the top of milk bottles, a ball of aluminum foil, two small bells (which I loathed and got rid of as soon as I could after Peggy put them on my collar) and a plaster bear Sherlock detached from last year's Christmas tree. Since the hole decants onto the tile floor beneath the bottom shelf, it is quite commodious and could hold more booty should it become necessary.

Surely Peggy will send the noisy one away now. She must believe that he is a thief. In the event that she does not, however, we four are scouting for other possible items to steal and hide.

🐾🐾🐾

Peggy

For obvious reasons, the Bigelow Pawn shops are in seedy areas. Claude swears there aren't any seedy areas in Bigelow. As if a background of luscious Appalachian mountains erases all possibility of ordinary urban crime. Hah! I dressed as casually as I could without actually looking like a bag lady, parked my car and began my quest.

Before I'd finished speaking to the small man who looked after the first shop, I felt my eyes begin to tear. So many dreams pawned! How could a musician give up his guitar? Or a woman her wedding ring? Not all of the wedding rings displayed could have come from victims of nasty divorces. I say I would never pawn the ring Ben gave me, but what if I were starving? What if my children were starving?

All of the shops had lists of items that had been stolen and swore they kept a weather eye out for them. But of course I hadn't yet reported my thefts, not even to Amos Royden, Mossy Creek's very able police chief. The pawn shop owners were amazingly nice, however, and promised to keep an eye out for the items I described, particularly the ring, especially after I offered a sizeable reward.

After three hours, I was exhausted and miserable. I had not told Marilee I'd be in Bigelow. She'd demand to meet me for lunch and would see at once how upset I was. I couldn't take the chance of having lunch at any decent restaurant in Bigelow for fear I'd run into her.

I decided to drive home and eat a bacon, lettuce and tomato sandwich. As I was walking to my car, I looked in the shop windows along the way. A shop that recommended I get a tattoo and have some unusual portion of my anatomy pierced sat beside a shop that advertised old LP disks for bargain prices.

I had no idea what the next shop sold until I read the small sign over the door. Spies R Us. No merchandise of any kind in the windows, just discrete gray drapes.

On a whim, I took a deep breath and went in. There was very little merchandise on display inside either. A tall, incredibly thin young man with bad skin and a scraggly beard looked up from the graphic novel he was reading and smiled at me.

"Do you have nanny cams?" I asked.

"Sure." He closed the magazine and laid it on the counter. "How big and how expensive?"

"Small and not very." I hesitated. "And I'd like to be able to install them myself."

"With or without audio?"

"With audio."

"To run, say eight hours? While you're at work?" He came around the counter. "Who you checking up on? Nanny, husband? Caregiver?"

"Caregiver for me?"

"Or your husband or whoever. None of my business," but he smiled so that I didn't take offense. He really meant it was none of his business.

I had been prepared to spend a small fortune, but I was amazed at how inexpensive the equipment was. And teeny! I settled on two cameras, one for the bedroom and one to cover the library and kitchen. We considered one for the downstairs construction area, but I figured that the thefts were taking place upstairs and that with construction going on downstairs, the possibility that they might be discovered was much greater. If Arturo was not guilty, the last thing I wanted was for him to know that I had suspected him.

The instructions had obviously been written by a demented Mongol who spoke only Tibetan, but my new friend Archimedes—not his real name, he told me—spent the next hour showing me how to set the things up and play them back. He offered to drive to Mossy Creek if I got into trouble, for an extra charge, of course. I said I'd try to muddle through on my own and call him if I needed him.

I was ravenous by the time I got home. Since it was well past lunchtime, Arturo's truck sat at the lower end of my driveway. I could hear the banging and bumping before I got into the kitchen. Dashiell glared at me.

"He's a nice man," I said. "He's going to help me make

some extra money. Get over it."

Then I set about installing the cameras. The house has elaborate ceiling molding, so I was able to set up one of the cameras in a corner of my bedroom so that it covered the bedroom door, my dressing table and dresser, and the door to the bathroom. I tested it and was elated when it worked perfectly.

The one in the living room wasn't so easy. I was halfway up the ladder when I heard Arturo clomping up the stairs. I nearly broke my neck getting down and hiding the camera and appurtenances under the sofa cushions before he came in.

"Hey, Senora Peggy, you should not be on a ladder. What you need? I will fix it for you."

"Uh, no thanks, Arturo. I was putting a book on top of the cabinet. I'm all through."

"Me too," he said with a broad grin. "Maybe not through-through, but close. A couple of days, then we walk through, do a punch list, I finish up and it will be complete."

"Great!" He'd be out of my house, I'd have my key back. Assuming he hadn't made one while he had mine. I felt guilty, but relieved as well. "You think I can start advertising in the *Mossy Creek Gazette* and the Bigelow paper next week?"

"Senora Louise has the furniture for the apartment?"

"In Charlie's workshop, waiting to be picked up."

"Then I think you can put an ad in the paper Sunday after this Sunday."

I hugged him.

Then I set a trap for him.

Over our coffee the next morning I told him that I'd be spending the day shopping for things like wastebaskets and towels for the apartment, so if he needed to get in to the house to connect anything, he'd have to use his key.

I was waiting at the door to the bank when it opened. I

don't have a great deal of good jewelry, but for our twentieth anniversary, Ben gave me a lovely platinum chain with one of those journey pendants—the ones with the diamonds in a squiggly row. These were fairly large diamonds and first quality. He'd gotten a big bonus that year.

It was also on an insurance rider, but since Ben put it into the lock box before he died, it wasn't loose in my jewelry box the way the ring had been. I took the necklace and pendant home and laid it conspicuously on my dressing table.

I turned on the nanny cams and went off to spend the day with Louise.

When I got home at four, Arturo had already left. I prayed the necklace would still be where I had left it. Eventually I forced myself to look. My heart sank. No necklace. No one but Arturo had been in my house all day.

I sat on the bed and burst into tears. After I ran the day's accumulation of camera stuff I'd be forced to call Amos, as much as I hated the idea. Not only would Arturo lose his green card and possibly go to jail, he'd be deported and never allowed back into the United States.

"Arturo, you idiot!" I yelled. "I'd have lent you the money!"

I took the tape from my bedroom into the den and plugged it into the television the way Archimedes had shown me. I was prepared to wait through hours of fast-forward. I was very tired, but I'd never be able to nap until I knew.

I nearly missed it. I had to back up the tape and re-run it to be certain. At first I thought it was a bad spot on the tape, it was so small.

Then it moved. A single gray paw lifted over the edge of my dressing table and patted around blindly as I watched in fascination. The gray paw belonged to Watson.

But he had an audience. Sherlock, Dashiell and Marple

sat behind him watching him avidly.

After at least a minute, the paw hooked the chain on my diamond pendant. Slowly he inched it over to the edge of the dressing table until it fell. All four cats jumped back.

They inched forward to sniff the necklace, but Watson brooked no interference. He stole it, so he owned it, he seemed to say. He tumped over on his back and kicked it into the air, then rolled over so quickly that he found himself wrapped in the chain. He left out a bleat of terror. Dashiell pressed a paw into his chest and held him down while Marple carefully teased the chain from under him. Sherlock watched, confused as usual.

They played for a good ten minutes with the necklace before Dashiell called a halt. He picked it up in his teeth as delicately as a courtesan nibbling an ortelan and trotted off through the bathroom door with it. I heard the door under the cabinet open, and all four cats disappeared. A couple of minutes later, I heard the door shut again and they walked out in single file like an army column. They looked like the proverbial cats who had swallowed a whole flock of canaries.

I laughed until I cried. Literally. Relief, I suppose.

I found all four cats asleep in the library. Butter wouldn't melt in their mouths.

I didn't even acknowledge them. I simply shut them out of the bedroom and went down on my hands and knees on the bathroom rug. My knees cracked, but I was too excited to notice.

The single shelf under the sink was completely empty. I know they like to hide there, so I've never filled it up with extra toilet paper or cleaning supplies.

No necklace. I fetched the big mag light I keep in my bedside table, managed to get my arthritic knees down on the floor again and went over that cabinet inch by inch.

Still, it took me over five minutes to find the hole and

even longer to enlarge it so I could reach in with a couple of fingers. I hoped I wouldn't encounter a mouse, and I didn't.

The first item I brought up was the last hidden. The necklace. Next came a silver demitasse spoon I didn't even know was missing from the silver chest, a couple of small bells—I knew Dashiell had removed them, but didn't know he'd hidden them—several other small items and then the emerald ring. I couldn't get the snuffbox or the thimble, but I could feel them.

I sat back on my heels. "Now why on earth did you rapscallions do this?" They couldn't possibly have known how much danger they'd put poor innocent Arturo in. Cats weren't vindictive.

Were they?

I remembered how long it had taken them to warm up to Carlyle. They never did like him to spend the night. He'd asked me to marry him and move to Seattle with him after he retired. I think he was glad I declined. We were fond of one another, but we weren't in love. No way could I pull up stakes, leave Marilee and Josie, and discommode the cats.

Had they seen Arturo as another threat to their well-being? He was here often enough. He made noise and tracked in dirt. They always hid when he showed up.

Could cats reason well enough to frame an innocent man?

Actually, I wouldn't put it past Dashiell. The others would follow his lead.

The next morning, I asked Arturo if he'd replace the shelf under the bathroom sink—no mouse hole and plywood too thick for their little paws to dig through.

Dashiell didn't speak to me for three days.

🐾🐾🐾

Dashiell

Our plan did work. We got caught and our hidey-hole was closed, but that noisy man left us alone only a few days after we stole the necklace. I've already found us a new hidey-hole. I refuse to tell anyone where it is. I hope we won't need it in the future.

But we may. This afternoon we were all snoozing in front of the fire when the doorbell rang.

Peggy opened it. There on the stoop stood a very tall human with gray hair like Watson's. I started to run to the bathroom, but something stopped me.

He smelled fascinating. An animal odor. Not dog nor cat. Pungent. I liked it. So did Marple. She ran over and rubbed her body against his ankles. He bent down, courteously offered to allow her to sniff his fingers first, then scratched her ears.

Humph. Watson was next. Then Sherlock. Finally, I meandered over. He smelled heavenly. And he liked cats.

🐾🐾🐾

Peggy

I certainly didn't expect an answer to my ad for the studio apartment the same day I put it in the paper. I assumed I'd get a few calls before someone actually wanted to see it.

Instead, just after lunch the very Sunday I put it into the paper, I answered the door to find a tall, slim, gray-haired man with Paul Newman eyes and Clint Eastwood looks smiling down at me.

"Sorry to just barge in like this," he said, "But I was afraid to wait. I've just bought a farm outside of Mossy Creek. Has a great barn, but no house. I can't keep staying in a motel in Bigelow, so I'm looking for a place to live. Could you show me the apartment?"

"Let me get my coat and the keys." I'm no fool. I shut the door. No stranger walks into my house uninvited.

He waited for me on the porch in the misty cold.

"We have to walk down the driveway. It's a garden apartment—more like a studio. But everything's new."

"I don't need much. I spend my days and most of my nights out at the farm."

An enormous white crew-cab pickup truck sat in the driveway. It had North Carolina plates.

There's not much arable land around Mossy Creek. I asked him if he was a cattleman.

"No, ma'am. I'm a horse trainer. I train and drive carriage horses and restore carriages."

That was a new one.

He looked at the apartment and liked it. We discussed terms. He agreed to a one-year lease, wrote me a check for the first and last month's rent and gave me the telephone numbers and addresses of people he'd worked for who could vouch for him.

He was as old as I was, though in better physical shape. He was also sexy as the dickens. The widows of Mossy Creek would be all over him like a frog on a June Bug.

"I'd like to move in as soon as you check my references and my check clears," he said with a smile. "I've lived in too many motel rooms all over the world to like living in them for very long."

"That's fine." We shook hands. He climbed into his truck and backed out with a wave.

And that's the way Hiram Lackland became my tenant and my friend.

Little did I suspect how that friendship would turn out.

The Mice that Roared

Part Two

Jayne

"Anudder one!" Matt cried happily as yet another mouse skittered along the wall in our living room two days later.

Emma, my seven-year-old calico, lifted her head from a desultory job of licking her paws and watched the mouse disappear into a hole in the wall so small I'd never noticed it before. Then she calmly went back to her paw-licking.

"How can you look at yourself in the morning?" I asked Emma, who sat on the coffee table in front of me.

She regarded me with feline disdain, then turned her paw over and studied it as if she were Zsa Zsa Gabor admiring her rings. I could just hear her little kitty voice saying in a Hungarian accent, *You get* your *paws dirty if you want to, but I'm not touching one of those things.*

"And you call yourself a self-respecting cat. This is your job," I said in disgust. "Matt, please don't play over there where the mice have been. They're nasty."

A boy through-and-through, Matt was fascinated by the small gray creatures. He'd tried to catch them as they flew across the hardwood floors, but so far hadn't managed to even get close to one.

Thank goodness.

"Come on, Matt. Let's get out of this mice-infested place and go help Ingrid with the cookies for the game tomorrow."

He held my hand as we walked down the narrow steps leading below. At the landing, one set of steps led to the back door, but I turned down the steps to the shop.

The work on the doorway connecting the bakery and The Naked Bean was just about done. Dan and his crew had finished framing the doorway and were painting it and the walls on either side. They'd cleaned up most of the mess they'd made, but I'd already hired Betty Halfacre, Ingrid's full-blooded Cherokee Indian assistant, to scrub both shops from top to bottom on Sunday. Betty was stocky and sour-faced and I'd never see her blink, but she was a rare find—a hard and trustworthy worker. This job was big enough that she'd enlisted the aid of some of her family members, but I didn't care. Neither I nor Ingrid were involved. I'd already made it clear to Ingrid that she wasn't to set foot inside the shop until Monday morning.

"Ingie not here!" Matt exclaimed after pulling away from me and bolting past a worker into the bakery side of the shop. My son was too accustomed to having the run of both shops. He was as certain of his welcome in the bakery as he was in my shop. He and Ingrid had bonded as close as any grandparent and grandchild, though Ingrid was not related to us.

By blood, she would always correct me.

Smiling at the warm fuzzies my relationship with Ingrid always gave me, I held out my hand to Matt. "Come here, please. We need to stay out of the way. Ingie is at her house. You know that. We're going to see her over there."

"OhBoyOhBoyOhBoy!" He used my hand as a lever to aid his bouncing. "See Bob?"

"Yes, of course, little darlin'." But under my breath, I said. "As if Bob ever leaves Ingrid's side."

Dan peeked around the molding of the new door. "Afternoon, y'all off for a walk?"

I nodded. "I have to get away from the mice for awhile."

He shook his head and repeated what he'd already told me. "Sorry about that, but I've seen it happen more often than not, especially in these old buildings. When you don't disturb the walls for years at a time, no telling what you're going to get when they're opened."

"I'm not blaming you, Dan. It's just, well . . ."

"Your cat still not chasing 'em down?"

I snorted, "No. They bore her."

"Not a mouser," Dan said with sympathy. "People think all cats will kill their mice, but some cats just won't. Those mouse traps not working?"

He'd brought her several of the snapping traps yesterday afternoon.

"I don't know. Emma tripped one trying to get the peanut butter, and Matt tripped the other one."

"Did he get hurt?" Dan asked.

"No," I admitted. "Neither did Emma. But it's just a matter of time. Besides, I . . . "

Dan smiled. "You'd have to take out the dead mice."

"Well, yes." I sighed. "What can I say? I'm a girl."

"Yes, you certainly are."

Our eyes met and held. I was so surprised by his comment that it took a moment for me to comprehend that he was flirting with me.

"I'll figure something out," I said, then glanced down at Matt. "You ready to go, little darlin'?"

"Yes'm."

"Are you going to the game tomorrow?" Dan asked quickly.

It took me a second to realize he meant the soccer game. "Yes, we are. That's right. You're on the team, aren't you? Yes, Ingrid and I are setting up a table with coffee and cookies. Proceeds going to the new football stadium, of course."

"Peanut butter cookies?" Dan asked hopefully.

"I don't know what Ingrid's planning, but probably. Peanut butter is one of her staples."

"Be sure and save me a couple."

"Will do. See you there."

As I held open the door of The Naked Bean for Matt, I caught sight of Dan's muscular back disappearing into the bakery side of the shop.

Dan. Hmmm. Maybe Josie was right.

Mossy Creek Gazette

Volume VII, No. One Mossy Creek, Georgia

The Bell Ringer

Mossy Creek Men Prepare to Play with Their Feet

by Katie Bell

The world is changing faster than your teenager's iPhone uploads a Jonas Brothers' video from YouTube, and so . . . get ready to watch a new kind of "football" as the Mossy Creek Men's Community Soccer Team takes on the Bigelow Men in a pre-season opener at the site of the future Mossy Creek High School stadium.

Rob Walker, Mossy Creek team captain and owner of Hamilton's Department Store, says he's lined up an exciting new mystery player for the Mossy Creek team.

Word on the street tells me, your town gossip columnist, that we may have to call the "police" to keep Creekite females away from this mystery man, "chief" among them a certain public official of the "Mayor Ida Walker" variety. . . .

"The greatness of a nation and its moral progress can be judged by the way its animals are treated."

—*Mahatma Gandhi*

The Rabbit Stops Running

We never forget the moments that wise us up about life's disappointments. The men who done us wrong. The great job that went to someone less deserving. The strapless prom dress that proved why prom dresses need straps.

Or, to use a more specific example, the bitter disappointment when Mother and Dad cut short my seventeenth birthday summer backpacking trip through Europe because my sister Ardaleen heard through informants that I'd gone wild in Paris and gotten a tiny peace symbol tattooed above my navel.

I should have known she'd rat me out. This was back in the Jurassic era of hippies and flower power, when only sailors and Hell's Angels had tattoos. Mother sobbed. Dad said I was scarred for life. My friends from Mossy Creek High started a prayer chain for me.

Elderly Grandma Ida, my namesake and mentor, hooted and applauded. Cousin Ingrid thought it was "groovy."

But Gran Ida and Ingrid were in the minority. At the Mossy Creek town pool I was asked by the Mossy Creek Parks and Rec supervisor, Boneeta Truman (mother of Dwight Truman, which explains a lot), to "cover that Communist symbol." I stuck a giant Band-aid over the tattoo and my navel. I refused to give up my flower-print bikini

41

with the little red bows on the hips. So I looked like a red-headed Barbie with a missing belly button.

A few years later, after coming home from college, I rescued Jeb Walker when his small plane crashed in our fields, and I fell in love with him instantly. In our first intimate encounter, he stripped off the Band-aid and kissed my tattoo. That's one reason I loved him, and still do.

Rest in peace, my tattoo-kissing man.

Back to the story. The tattoo bust was hardly the first time Ardaleen betrayed me.

In my clan, the Hamiltons, the sad truth we never forget the most is that even family can stick a knife in your back. Romeo and Juliet. Hatfields and McCoys. Godzilla versus Megatron. Appalachian Southerners feud with their kinfolk because that's what we've always done, going back to the tribal Scots and Irish who battled each other for control of the mountains, the English, the French and the Cherokee Indians, before all of the above intermarried and began sharing bourbon recipes. Drinking together makes us forget our differences just long enough to load the shotgun for the next round.

Which brings me again to my sister, Ardaleen Hamilton Bigelow, and a moment in my life I will always rank among the Top Five Truths I'll Never Forget.

Ardaleen, who was sixteen when I was five, wanted to kill me.

"Pokey likes to be petted," Ardaleen insisted, grinning her fiendish, Maybelline-over-freckles grin as she pointed through the slatted boards of the stall at Hamilton Farm. Inside, blowing hot air softly through his huge nostrils, stood Pokey, the farm's giant champion Guernsey bull. He was not called Pokey because he was slow or because his main job in life was to inseminate cows, but because he had a pair of ten-inch horns, which he often swung like calcified joisting sticks.

Ardaleen aimed her mood-ringed finger underneath Pokey's thick, golden belly. "Pet him right there. On his . . . fire hose. Go in and give it a good hard slap, Ida. He really likes that."

I looked up at her earnestly. I was still trusting of my big sister—I hadn't yet realized that Ardaleen was a sociopath. "But Grandma Ida says that's his wee wee. And she says it's not polite to pat boys on their . . ."

"Bulls like being petted on their . . . I call it their tummy," Ardaleen oozed. "You're not a scaredy cat, are you? Little Miss Ida, the scaredy puss. Grandma Ida will be embarrassed. You're a disgrace to her name if you don't go in this stall and pet Pokey on his tummy. Baby. Chicken. Cluck cluck cluck. Why, oh why do I bother trying to teach you anything? Some days I am so ashamed to call you my baby sister."

My eyes welled with tears. Being unwanted by my big sister seemed like the end of the world to me. "Don't be ashamed! I'll do it! I'm not scared."

She smiled like a shark. "Good."

The universe of children is defined by their innocent devotion to cold-hearted idols. At that age we want to believe in angels, but we learn quickly that life is filled with nasty little devils, many of which share our family name.

To make a long, turning-point story very short, I crept into Pokey's stall, gave him a hearty smack on his euphemistic 'tummy,' and he horned me in the ass like a Spanish bull tossing a pint-sized matador. I hit the plank wall hard enough to stick splinters in my forehead.

For two weeks I limped around the farm with a welt on my head and a deep purple bruise on my right buttock. I was smart enough to tell Grandma Ida, Mama and Daddy that I fell on a tree stob.

Ardaleen threatened to smother me in my sleep if I confessed the truth to anyone. She even added insult to injury. "Baby Sister," she drawled, "I was a honeymoon baby. Mama and Daddy wanted me. But you were just an accident of nature after Mama and Daddy got reckless in their old age. You aren't supposed to be here."

Ahah. Ardaleen hated me for taking away her Only Child status, for being doted on by Grandma Ida, for being pampered as the Miracle Menopause Baby of the Hamilton princess line.

No surprise, then, that Ardaleen felt disappointed by her reduced status in the Hamilton family. She grew up determined to reject and punish everything in our heritage, which included Mossy Creek. She moved to the fancy south-end of our mountain county, married a pompous, hated Bigelow and bore my nephew, Ham Bigelow, who at forty years of age is only ten years younger than me but is the governor of the great state of Georgia, God help the State.

Ham has long been a sharp thorn in my paw, along with Ardaleen. I don't trust him, I don't trust her and I admit that poison ivy grows on the dark side of my family tree.

Some truths are more painful than others.

🐾🐾🐾

As usual, I was trying to control my temper. If you take your oath of office a bit too personally, being mayor of a small town can turn you into a fat, stressed-out wino with anger management issues. Despite two rambunctious decades at the mayoral helm of Mossy Creek I'd managed to escape obesity and alcoholism, but my struggle with my red-headed temper was known far and wide. So it surprised me that Ardaleen was brave enough to turn her back on me that morning in the chilly spring sunshine.

"And so, speaking to you all as Governor Hamilton Bigelow's proud mother . . ." Ardaleen said proudly and loudly, her cigarette-stained voice forming a crust in the cool air around the microphone. She bobbed her red-with-blonde-highlights-to-hide-the-gray head. ". . . I welcome you here today to be with me at this lovely event."

Be with me. Not be with 'us.' Not be with the town of Bigelow, the town of Mossy Creek, or Bigelow Countians in general. In Ardaleen's world, Ardaleen was the only person worth being with. One heavily diamond-ringed hand with perfect French nails stroked the lapel of her blue Dior dress suit. At sixty-one my sister looks and sounds like a deep-fried Dixie version of Bea Arthur on The Golden Girls, only without the humor and charm. "I'm so pleased to lead these dedication ceremonies for yet another fine project built under my son's leadership . . ."

I coughed loudly into my hand. The cough sounded suspiciously like "Bull."

Ardaleen's shoulders stiffened. Oh, yeah, she'd heard me. ". . . with contributions from the citizens of our fair city of Bigelow . . ."

I coughed again. Louder. This time it sounded like Sheet.

Sounded like being the operative words.

Ardaleen and I stood on the bunting-draped stage in the freshly poured parking lot of the sleek new Bigelow County Humane Society facility, a state-of-the art adoption center that had been built with a big dollop of money donated by Mossy Creekites, not to mention that our vet, Dr. Hank Blackshear, was a driving force behind the project. Also, ninety-nine percent of Mossy Creek's 397 registered voters voted in favor of the county-wide special tax that funded the center. The Creekite vote put the tax referendum over the top.

So we had plenty to be proud of, even if no one in Bigelow, city of, or Bigelow, county of, wanted to admit it. Mossy Creek is the little sister Bigelow keeps trying to push off the swing set. Boy, howdy, I could relate to that metaphor.

Ardaleen cocked her head slightly to the right, eyeing me sideways, the way a frustrated zoo chimp eyes a tourist standing within dung-slinging range. I resisted the urge to waggle an imaginary banana at her.

She scowled at me one more time then gave her note cards another try. ". . . yet another fine project . . . with the assistance of our neighboring town—" the snark-level rose in her voice "—dear little Mossy Creek, which may be small, secluded and far less blessed than we are, here in Bigelow, but whose well-meaning citizens held nice little bake sales and car washes to raise an adorable contribution for the new humane society . . ."

I held up a finger.

No, not that one. My forefinger.

One hundred thousand, I mouthed widely, making sure the cameras caught every syllable. We raised one hundred thousand dollars.

Nikons flashed. Video cams swiveled from Ardaleen at the podium to me, standing behind her.

I wiggled my finger, mouthed the amount again and shifted just enough to give a little sass-bop with one hip. Lessons I'd learned in two decades of public troublemaking: wear dark green suits to make my green eyes stand out for the cameras, a touch of red to match my hair and keep my skirts tight enough to talk.

I smiled at Ardaleen and gave another little hip toss.

Ardaleen clenched the podium with both hands. I could see her wrinkled knuckles turning red. A woman's hands tell her age, and Ardaleen's knuckles were a loudspeaker begging for liver spot removal. Not that her advancing age—fifteen years older than my fifty—made me gloat. I spent a lot of time looking at my own hands, these days.

More camera flashes. I lowered my finger and smiled innocently, reassured by my still youthful and willowy knuckles. Yep, I'd make the six o'clock local news and CNN. too, again. The Atlanta media always sent crews to cover every public event featuring me and my sister, or me and my nephew, the governor, or me and the arresting officers, or all of the above.

". . . I'll now introduce . . ." Ardaleen finished between clamped teeth, "my baby sister, Ida Hamilton Walker, my son's colorful aunt and the mayor of Mossy Creek, a town that prides itself on a tradition of—"

"Independence," I inserted, before she could say something less flattering.

"Rebellion."

"Patriotism."

She couldn't top that.

Thinking I'd won today's round of insults, I stepped forward, smiling. But Ardaleen's pink-lined, collagen-filled lips drew back from her blindingly whitened capped teeth in a final, victorious sneer.

She leaned into the mic and added in the sugary, *Bless her heart* drawl which Southern women use to gut their enemies, "I'm so proud of my baby sister. She's been working so hard lately to prepare for Mossy Creek's new high school, which opens in the fall. Sixteen-hour days can really take a toll on a woman my sister's age. But just look at her: Gorgeous." Ardaleen smiled at me. "What is that term a younger man calls a woman your age, baby sister?"

The crowd went on high alert. They knew what younger man she meant, but until now no one had had the bull muffins to mention him in public. I clenched my fists. Breathe.

Focus. Think calm thoughts.

I had an image to uphold for the sake of Mossy Creek. I'm a public servant. Ardaleen is not, despite her public bragging. Ardaleen has never run for any office. She sees her job as breeding Bigelow politicians, like the mother monster in the Aliens movies. I think Ham came out of her as a thirty-pound, soft-shelled egg with mouth tentacles, ready to suck the life out of the nearest campaign donor.

Breathe. Stay calm. Down in front of us, my granddaughter, Little Ida, the third-generation namesake of the glorious Big Ida, my grandmother, gaped up at me and her great aunt Ardaleen. Her freckled hand held her phone high.

Ten years old and trying to score a video she could upload on YouTube. What a hustler. I love her the way Grandma Ida loved me. Independent spirits stick together, irony be damned. Little Ida did what her fellow spectators did, all two hundred of them. She held her camera phone up and thumbed Record.

"What's the term for older women who like to have younger men at their beck and call?" Ardaleen repeated loudly, smile-grimacing at me. "Cougar?"

Cougar. Okay, she could call me that, I didn't care. Cougars are sleek and dangerous.

I laughed as if this were all just some good-natured joke. "I prefer 'Your Highness.'"

Some in the crowd hooted and applauded. But others wisely angled their cameras closer.

Ardaleen put her mouth nearer the mic. "Oh? Did Chief Royden call you that before or after you made out with him? Was that before or after your boyfriend caught the two of you?" She looked out at the crowd solemnly. "For those of you fine folks who haven't heard, my sister recently cheated on her boyfriend, now her ex-boyfriend, Bigelow business-man Del Jackson, a retired army officer and a decorated hero. And the object of her unethical behavior? Her own police chief, who is much, much younger than she."

Camera phones clicked, regular cameras flashed, video cams whirred. Little Ida jerked her phone down and began text messaging madly, her little thumbs moving at warp speed, probably alerting her parents to drive out to Hamilton Farm, quick, and change the lock on my gun cabinet.

And me? I just stood there, my smile frozen, speechless for once in my life. She had gotten me with a one-two punch: the Amos reference followed by the low blow about Del. I would always feel guilty for hurting him. Was merely kissing Amos "cheating" on Del? Yes, in my code of ethics, it was.

Suddenly I felt as if I were five years old again, hitting the wall as Pokey tossed me with his curving brown horns. An eerily familiar sound filled my ears.

Ardaleen, laughing.

Then, and now.

🐾🐾🐾

"Nana," Little Ida said solemnly, holding up at a sympathetic cupcake with white icing and a Chihuahua's face outlined in orange sprinkles. Cousin Ingrid had donated dozens of "pup cakes" from her bakery in Mossy Creek. Little Ida waved the pup cake at me. "You got punked by Great Aunt Ardaleen."

I glared at her. We were hiding in a propane-heated corner of the reception tent outside the humane society's kennels, where a caterer was serving the themed cupcakes along with pimento cheese sandwiches cut in poodle shapes and something called Pet Punch, which was strawberry red with dog-bone-shaped ice cubes floating in it.

Looked like watery blood with ice turds, to me. I was in a bad mood. I wanted a stiff bourbon instead.

"Drop the subject, hon," I said grimly. I kept checking my watch. Five more minutes of mayoral duty then I was out of there. Our fellow citizens smiled nervously at me then sidled away

Little Ida gnawed the cupcake. "Daddy told Mama you and Chief Royden might as well get it out in the open. He says it'd be less fuel for the fire that way. Are you planning on setting something on fire, Nana?"

"Just your Great Aunt Ardaleen." I hesitated. "You didn't hear that. Don't repeat it."

She grinned and made a lock-and-key gesture over her heart. "You gonna start dating Chief Royden? Like a real girlfriend and boyfriend? Can I tell my friends on Facebook?"

"The Chief and I are still just friends. Despite what anyone says. Be quiet. Eat your cupcake."

"But you kissed . . ."

"Friends kiss."

"Not on the lips, and not in a way that made Colonel Jackson quit dating you and go back to his wife."

"Ex-wife," I corrected. I took the cupcake from her. "Too much sugar makes children talk too much. Go eat a carrot."

She chortled.

Ingrid hustled up to me at that point, her graying red hair like a dusty rose and her green eyes snapping above her quilted vest with the embroidered Chihuahuas.

Bob, her non-embroidered Chihuahua, glared at us from a tie-dyed baby sling that was belted across my cousin's considerable boobs. "Trouble in the parking lot," Ingrid announced. "You better intervene, Ida."

"Why?" I grunted. "People want more embarrassing pictures of me?"

"As a member of the Humane Society's board. Come on."

I arched a brow. "There are ten board members. Including you. Can't you take care of it? I've donated my official pound of flesh to Ardaleen's claws and now I'm off-duty." I looked at my watch again. "Plus I promised to get Little Ida back to Mossy Creek in time for her dad's soccer game."

Ingrid smiled wickedly. She fooled people into thinking she was a kindly, middle-aged chick who ran a small bakery and pampered an incontinent dog with a penchant for mishaps, that she was just a doting godmother to Jayne Reynolds' little boy, that she was a harmless star pitcher on the Mossy Creek 50-and-up co-ed fast-pitch softball team.

But I knew better. She bared her teeth at me like a wily Betty Crocker plotting to open a can of whup-butt on the Pillsbury Doughboy. With my help. "So you're just going to let Ardaleen abuse a desperate man with a sobbing little boy and a truck full of miniature livestock that needs a good home? Did I mention the little boy's crying because he has to give up his pet rabbit?"

Little Ida squealed, "A rabbit!" and headed for the parking lot. The child has a pony, two cats, three dogs, some kind of South American lizard, two parakeets, a family of hermit crabs and a pair of ferrets named Mickey and Minnie. She loves critters like Shriners love parades.

"Ardaleen wants the kid's rabbit," Ingrid added darkly.

Oh, hell. Did I mention that Ardaleen's favorite roasted meat, other than human hearts, is rabbit?

I squared my shoulders. "Lead the way."

A rusty old pick-up truck, its bed outfitted with tall wooden sides and a high gate to hold animals inside, sat at the edge of the Humane Society's parking lot, beneath a massive oak just beginning to dapple the concrete with the shadows of its spring leaves.

A small, frowning crowd of Humane Society officials

stood around the truck's open driver's door, with Ardaleen at their center, shaking a finger and talking in a low voice to the truck's owner. He was a grim, skinny, rough-skinned young man with his NASCAR cap in his hands. Inside the truck, his little boy clutched a mound of white fur and cried, burying his face in the neck of a lop-eared rabbit. The rabbit peered out at us with deadly pink eyes. Who could blame him? Little Ida hung on the open window of the passenger door, looking in sadly at the boy and his rabbit. She put a hand on the rabbit's droopy ears. Mr. Bunny's nose twitched in warning. My throat clenched.

But the toxic-eyed bunny sniffed her, decided she was a friend and gently nibbled her fingers.

"Wampa likes you," the boy said brokenly. "He don't like very many folks. Can't you give him a home?"

"You bet," my granddaughter told the crying boy, her voice breaking too. "My Nana won't let anybody hurt Wampa."

Wampa? Wampa? I searched the pop culture lobe of my brain. When you've got a thirty-year-old son and daughter-in-law and an eight-year-old granddaughter, and you grew up on Star Wars movies yourself, you know these things.

Wampa. The rabbit was named after the murderous, white-furred, Yeti-like creature that tried to turn Luke Skywalker into a piñata. I watched our version of a Wampa swivel evil pink eyes toward Ardaleen. Apparently his personality matched the name perfectly.

"Mr. Boggs, we told you to go elsewhere with your farm animals," an official said.

"The sign says this is the humane society," Boggs replied. "I want to talk to somebody humane." He jerked his head toward the menagerie in the back of his truck. There was misery in his eyes. "These here are my son's pets. I've lost my job; had to give up our home. We're moving in with my brother south of Atlanta for a while. No room for critters. I work construction. Got to report to a new boss on Monday. I got no choice." His voice broke as his son's sobs filled in the silence. "I got to find a home for my boy's critters today."

"I said I'll take the rabbit," Ardaleen said. She stepped forward, stony-faced. "Be grateful for small favors. I can place the rabbit in a good home."

In the meat section at Bigelow Gourmet Foods, I thought.

"Grilled, with a side of brussel sprouts and a glass of wine," Ingrid whispered to me. Bob ducked down inside his sling and growled.

"Miz Bigelow, I sure appreciate that, but what about my boy's other pets?"

In the bed of the truck, staring at me through the slats, were a pair of goats, a miniature pig and a spindly brown burro. The goats made unhappy chuckling sounds, the pig grunted anxiously and the burro let out a high-pitched bray that sounded like a four-footed cry for help.

Ardaleen didn't even blink. "This is not a facility for livestock."

"They ain't livestock, they're his friends. Since his mother died, they mean the world to him. He talks to them. I swear, sometimes I think they talk back."

"Nonsense. They're animals. Farm animals. This is a facility for household pets. I'm sorry. Leave the rabbit."

"Wampa," the little boy moaned, hugging the white rabbit harder. Little Ida mewled.

Ardaleen remained stony. "You should have planned your finances better. This society is run by the taxpayers. We can't be bailing out everyone who makes a poor choice."

"Sir, I'll adopt your pets," I announced loudly. "All of

them. Especially the rabbit. I love rabbits." A lie, but for a good cause.

"Yay, Nana!" Little Ida yelled. To the boy she said, "See I told you. We'll take all your critters to Nana's farm. And after you move to some place where they can live, too, you can have your critters back."

The boy smiled at her through his tears.

"Is that true, ma'am?" the man said, looking at me urgently.

I nodded. "Absolutely. They'll be safe and well-cared-for at my farm."

"Thank you, ma'am. God bless you."

Ardaleen turned toward me, her lips twitching with anger. "I. Will. Take. The. Rabbit," she repeated, biting off every word. She was determined to spite me. "I've already claimed the rabbit. I'll. Give. Him. A. Good. Home. Discussion. Closed."

Before I could lob a verbal grenade at her, the boy climbed out of the truck and ran to Ardaleen, Wampa jiggling unhappily in his arms. "Lady, I have to find out if Wampa likes you."

Ruh roh.

Wampa looked huge, fluffy and pissed off.

Ardaleen held up her be-ringed hands. "I don't want to pet him. I'm sure we'll get along merrily."

"Just let him sniff you, ma'am! I can tell right away how he feels about you."

He thrust Wampa at her.

Wampa took a big sniff of Ardaleen Essence and wisely identified her as one of Satan's hungry handmaidens. His pink eyes turned red. His powerful hind feet dug into the front of the boy's camo t-shirt.

Wampa launched himself at my sister, his mouth open and teeth bared. It was surreal. He straight-out flew. If you've ever seen the bunny attack in Monty Python and the Holy Grail, well, that's what it looked like.

Ardaleen screamed and lunged backward. Wampa hit her between the boobs and she sprawled on the hard black asphalt with the rabbit on top of her. His jaws snapped shut on her defending hand. A pinprick of blood sprouted on her little finger.

Ardaleen bellowed, "He bit me! Kill the little bastard!"

Wampa shot away at a fast hippety-hop. Little Ida and Little Boggs chased him across the parking lot. My heart clenched when Little Ida scooped the homicidal bunny into her arms, but Wampa huddled harmlessly inside her hug, glaring back at Ardaleen, his bunny mouth making chew-motions as if he were determined to spit out the taste of her.

Little Ida looked at me worriedly. "Can I still have him?"

I nodded and gave her a thumbs-up.

I suddenly loved Wampa.

Ardaleen's minions surrounded her, bowing and scraping, clamping tissues to her tiny wound, helping her sit up. Our eyes met. Hers, a livid, defeated green. Mine, a glowing victorious green, I'm sure.

"I want that rabbit put to sleep," she yelled. "He's a menace."

I looked down at her without a shred of sympathy. The old Pokey memory welled up inside me, fresh and raw but finally in its rightful place. That chicken, as they say, had come home to roost. And he'd taken a big dump on Ardaleen.

I pivoted toward Jess Crane, husband of Mossy Creek's Police Officer Sandy Bottoms Crane and a part-time reporter for the *Mossy Creek Gazette*. Nowadays he also carried a video cam in hopes of scoring a piece for Mossy Creek's local access cable TV show, or maybe a YouTube hit. "You got all this on tape?" I asked Jess. "Including the part where she yelled 'Kill the little bastard?'"

He grinned widely as he kept aiming the video cam at Ardaleen. "Oh, yeah."

I looked down at my sister, again. The shock in her eyes made me happy.

"The rabbit goes home with me," I said. "Discussion closed."

Her lips flattened, her face reddened even more and she began ordering her much-abused staff to get her car and call her doctor.

I'd won. Jess was still filming.

Beside me, Ingrid started laughing so hard that Bob jiggled in his sling. "Can rabbits spread rabies?" she asked between guffaws.

"I hope so," I said.

"Every boy should have two things:
a dog, and a mother willing to let him have one."

—*Anonymous*

Amos and the Soccer Mom

The station clock's hands landed on 11:38 a.m. by the time I'd sorted out the paperwork we needed for the annual state audit of the police department. My officer-cum-manager Sandy Bottoms Crane would have done it, but Mossy Creek's next mother-to-be looked a little green in the gills and I thought she needed rest and a weekend to herself. Jess, her husband, had taken me aside to let me know she was feeling really queasy these last few days. I could work with queasy, but I was terrified of what would happen when the nesting hormones kicked in.

The boys and I were in for some rough times ahead. Best case scenario was a little wall paint. Worst case scenario was a whole new filing system and God help any of us if we screwed it up. I didn't want to give Sandy any ideas about improving the office while she was feeling the effects of having a baby-on-board, so I'd volunteered to sort out paperwork this Saturday morning. Next week some official bean counter would arrive and make sure our ticket books, fine receipts and deposits all matched. They'd look at our files and certifications. They'd make absolutely sure we conducted ourselves, in our tiny little town, with impeccable professionalism, and then declare us good-to-go for another year.

Another year.

That made me sit up a little straighter in Sandy's chair. Time doesn't fly, but it will strap on rocket boosters and hurtle itself past you. I didn't intend that to happen to me. And it would unless I hauled time to heel like an exuberant dog. When dealing with time, I'd figured out that you either jerked its chain or it jerked yours. Sort of like Ida.

That made me smile; probably wasn't a friendly smile. It was about time to jerk our mayor's chain again. I'd given her space after Valentine's. Given her enough time to absorb her newly unattached state now that Del Jackson had thrown in the towel and gone back to his ex-wife. Once Ida didn't have him to hide behind, she found yet another way to delay the inevitable. She'd launched herself into a frenzy of preparation for the changes coming to Mossy Creek. Next fall we'd have a football team settled in their very own stadium again. That meant the high school needed a coach and Booster Club and probably a million other details. Mayor Ida Hamilton Walker had been busy, busy, busy.

Or as I liked to think of it: running, running, running.

Tweedle chirped his agreement as if he read my mind. When he chirped again, I realized my 'keet wasn't showing masculine solidarity but asking for a treat. Sandy kept some special seeds in her desk. I had no idea what they were other than expensive, but—pound for pound—I had an equally expensive coffee bean habit so I couldn't say much. We doled the seeds out a few at a time. I dutifully reached into the drawer trying to remember when Tweedle hadn't been my responsibility. I felt that whole time-rushing-by thing again.

I didn't mind Tweedle so much. He was, oddly, good company. He'd settled into life at the station, settled into all our lives as if there had always been a bit of space waiting to be filled by a bird brain. We'd put wheels on his cage and rolled him into the big room during the warmer days, if it wasn't too drafty. He chatted up citizens, repeatedly did his bird-with-no-neck impression and walked sideways around the cage walls as if he prepared for an Indy run.

The phone rang before I could deliver the seeds. I tossed the first through the wire of his cage and grabbed the phone. "Mossy Creek Police."

"Amos!" Win Allen sounded relieved. "I need to talk to you."

I wasn't really happy with Win at the moment, but I did try to sound solicitous. "Oh, no. Is the clown back?" (I knew how he felt about clowns, especially since one had burned down his cooking show set.)

"Oh, for crying out loud! Would you stop with the clown bit?"

"I'll call truce if you will."

Win is captain of the Let's-Needle-Amos-About-The-Kiss team. At least I think he is. It could also be Hank or Mac. They'd all pretty much taken every opportunity to point out that I hadn't closed the deal with Ida. To say they were disappointed in me would be an understatement. I'd somehow become the poster boy in Mossy Creek's battle of the sexes and they hated the thought Ida might be winning.

Me? I had no problem letting Ida win the battle as long as I won the war.

I heard whispering through the phone and what sounded like exasperation. I had the impression of several people crowded around the receiver. "Win?"

"I'm working on it!" he hissed. Yep. Hissed. He wasn't talking to me, because I'm pretty sure he wouldn't hiss at me. Next I heard Win hiss, "You wanna do it? Do you? I told you to ask him to begin with." Big sigh, then, "Amos, you still there?"

"Yeah. Confused but here."

"We've got a little problem."

I flipped a second seed into Tweedle's cage. "Define we."

"The men's soccer team."

This would be interesting. They'd formed a team a

while back and excluded me. All the guys on the team were younger than me, some a lot; some just a little. Regardless, someone had drawn a line in the sand, and I'd ended up on the "old guy" side. Not that I could convince Ida of that. She thought I was too young for her. "What can I do for you boys?"

Win's snort was audible on the phone. "We're short a man."

"You were short several men last time I looked." I flipped the last seed at Tweedle. To Win's credit he had lobbied for my inclusion on the team. His vote wasn't enough to tip the scale. Rob Walker had been the driving force behind organizing a men's team. At the time, he'd had issues with my pursuing his mother. I think we've made peace, but I still wasn't on the team. I'm living with that, not happily, but quietly.

"Amos, do not make me beg. Today's the first game of spring pre-season and we're playing Bigelow as a warm-up. I know you can play."

I wasn't going to make him beg. Ida Hamilton Walker never missed one of her son's soccer games. She could watch me run for a change.

❦❦❦

Officer Mutt Bottoms agreed to come in and cover the rest of the day at the station. I stopped by home, grabbed some gear, and headed for the makeshift soccer field that would eventually become our new football field. A couple of risers on the sidelines stood empty. I had no idea from where they'd managed to scrounge those. Maybe the Booster Club was getting a head start.

The crowd wouldn't be showing up for another hour, but Win wanted to run me through some of their offense. There was a nip in the air—a spring nip which made the temperature bearable. At least it would be bearable until we had to strip down to shorts. Right now we all had on sweats.

Both Win and Rob waited midfield. I'd be a liar if I said I didn't enjoy the pained expressions on their faces. Eating crow will twist your face up for sure.

"Howdy, Rob. Win."

Unexpectedly Rob flipped the ball up with his foot and passed it gently to me. Smiling I dropped the bag in my hand and moved to stop the ball with my body and catch it on the edge of my foot as it fell to send it back.

"Told you he could play." Win beamed. "We'll be fine."

"We'd better be." Rob was actually angry with Win. "If we lose to Bigelow because you got into a pissing match with Dwight, you'd better start shopping in Bigelow because you'll be barred from every business in town."

Win fired right back. "Don't get your panties in a twist, Robbie. We don't need Dwight. Dan will move to goalie and Amos can sub in as forward. Done. All fixed."

Before they could argue more, I whistled. "Someone want to fill me in on the crisis while we warm up?"

They spread out, moving the ball between us, as Win explained.

"Dwight is trying to cheap-out on the new football coach. He's told the search committee to consider only the candidates willing to work for the lower end of the salary range."

I intercepted a sloppy pass to Rob and rerouted it. "Dwight can't be that stupid. The town has been waiting years to get its football team back."

"He's that stupid," Rob said and gave Win a pointed look. "But this morning wasn't the day to tell him. It could have waited. Until after the . . . game."

"Well maybe I'm sick of always treating Dwight like the second coming of Elvis. We gave him a bike in appreciation for his service but that doesn't give him a free pass to make decisions carte blanche without telling anyone. I'm tired of hearing him talking about making the tough decisions and being the go-to guy for Mossy Creek. He's full of himself and something else as well."

Thwack. This time there wasn't anything sloppy about the solid way Win's foot connected with the ball. Win was channeling anger all the way down to his toes.

As we moved further away from each other talking ceased and they got down to the business of making sure I remembered my way around a soccer ball. It's a pretty simple game. Run hard, don't use your hands and kick it in the net. Even an old guy like me could remember that.

The rest of the team filtered into our group, putting me through my paces. When Rob was finally satisfied, he produced a uniform. I changed in my Jeep, then hit the bench, decked out in my new uniform shorts and went over some of the plays with Rob quick-drawing them on his clipboard.

"Daddy!"

Rob looked up. Little Ida came jogging over, carrying a stadium blanket and a really big canvas bag . . . that was undulating. "Momma said to tell you that she'll be here before the half. She forgot to get your oranges."

"Thank you, sweet pea. Whatcha got?"

"Wampa." When Rob leaned over to peer in the tote bag Little Ida dropped the blanket and pushed him back with her free hand. She looked a little like a Supreme doing a dance move. "Stop! They told us he had abandonment issues. Aunt Ardaleen said that's why he's mean as a snake. He doesn't bite me. But you should have seen him take a chunk out of Aunt Ardaleen." She giggled.

Little Ida shares her grandmother's troublemaking nature. I bit my lip to keep from saying anything about the apple not falling far from the namesake-tree. Didn't help. Rob made the connection all by himself. A couple of white fluffy, fuzzy ears peaked out of the top of the tote back. I leaned over to Rob. "Hey, Elmer, I think they've been wabbit hunting." I shook my head slowly. "This can't end well."

Rob snorted then turned to his daughter. I admired the boy's grasp on his temper when he asked, "Where's your grandmother?"

Little Ida pointed back over her shoulder. "I'm going to get us the good bleacher seats. And we need extra room for Wampa because of the biting."

Rob and I both swiveled. Ida was about twenty feet away. Deep in conversation with Jayne Reynolds, who pushed her son Matt in a stroller with one hand and pulled a wagon with coffee paraphernalia, including an industrial-size pot, with the other. Jayne was the single mom/businesswoman, never-leave-home-without-everything type.

Right next to her was my type—Ida Hamilton Walker, who never left home without an opinion. She'd pulled back her auburn hair, thrown on a pair of old soft jeans and a black long-sleeved t-shirt. Just your average soccer mom come to watch her kid play soccer. She looked so pretty and harmless.

A new crowd gathered around Matt. Ida touched Jayne's arm and said a quick goodbye. She took a couple of steps, scanned the crowd around the field and spotted Rob. Two more steps and it dawned on her who the new soccer player was. I waved. She stared at my legs and . . . other parts. I like to keep in shape, and soccer shorts are really thin material. Wasn't my fault a breeze was blowing in my direction.

Rob said, "Oh, for God's sake!" and walked away. Apparently his wabbit-issues could wait. I laughed. It was an uneasy truce between us, but he was trying. Before Ida could decide how to dodge me or detour to her son, I met her halfway, dropping my gaze to the words on her t-shirt. Already against the next war.

"Nice slogan."

"Don't start."

"Start what?"

That snapped her head up and squared her shoulders. "Please. You and I both know that if I give you any opening at all, you'll manage to take the old peace anthem about making love, not war and turn it into something intimate about us."

"If the slogan fits . . ."

"And you wonder why I avoid you."

A half-second too late she realized what she'd just admitted. Her face scrunched in the classic, "Oh Crap" maneuver. I leaned in and whispered, "Lucy, you got some 'splainin' to do."

When she opened her eyes, I thought I saw surrender. I tucked a stray lock of hair behind her ear. We were about to have a moment. A very public moment. And that was fine by me.

But then the screaming baby happened. Or yelling toddler. Almost three, Matt was much too old to be called a baby. He was standing in his stroller yelling right at me. Not just in my direction, but clearly yelling for me to come get him. "Daddy! Daddy! Here!"

The actual air temperature dropped a degree. Or that's what it felt like as I watched the words register on Ida's face. She backed up a step, put a respectable distance between us, and a wall came clanging down. I hung on to my temper. "He calls everyone Daddy. He picked it up at Mother's Day out. It's a phase. He sees me every day when I go by Jayne's shop for coffee. Don't make it anything more. I know what you're thinking, but it's just a phase."

She sucked in some indignation. "You think I don't know that? I've had a child. You're the one who hasn't."

"I don't remember wanting one. You don't get to decide things for me, Ida, unless you're in my life. Unless you care about me. Are you? Do you?"

We were still on the verge of a moment, but this wasn't one I wanted to have in public. The chaos of pre-soccer drifted past us as I waited.

Almost too quietly for me to hear, Ida finally said, "I've got no business in your life. But someone like Jayne does. Wake up and smell the coffee shop, Amos."

Before I could answer, Win joined us, jostling me out of position in front of Ida. "You look pissed. I guess Amos is filling you in, but you should know that it wasn't my fault. Rob says it is but I don't think so. Someone had to do it."

Ida looked from him to me, not sure how to tell him we weren't discussing the city. I shouldn't have, but I saved her the awkwardness by throwing her a lifeline disguised as advice to Win. "Dwight isn't thinking clearly if he's trying to cheap-out on the football coach, but telling him he's a cheapskate and should be voted out office wasn't the way to get him to reconsider the salary budget."

In the background, Matt hollered again. Win shoved me. "Amos, go get Matt before he has a cow."

Ida just looked at me. Dared me to dispute the fact that even Win knew Matt was intent on me and no one else. The kid liked me but that didn't mean I wanted to date his mom. But someone had to or I'd never win this argument with Ida. Truth be told, it was probably that very moment I decided to throw Win under the bus. He could take one for the team.

The Rabbit
Stops Running
Part Two

Me, Little Ida and Wampa The Maniacal Rabbit were still feeling a little twitchy when we arrived at Mossy Creek's new high school stadium for the pre-season community-league soccer game. Mossy Creek vs. Bigelow. Our Men vs. Their Men. Our way of life versus, etc. A perfect analogy for the day so far. Maybe Wampa could be our team mascot.

The spring morning had warmed up enough for me to change into a long-sleeve black tee and jeans. My tee bore the slogan, Already Against The Next War. Not that the words were readable at the moment. Too much fur. A black t-shirt isn't the smartest thing to wear around a big, white rabbit. I looked like a giant lint roller.

"Don't let Wampa out of the tote bag again," I warned Little Ida. "He'll clog every vacuum in town."

She grinned up at me and hitched the plaid tote higher on one shoulder. Only Wampa's head showed above the top of the bag. His floppy ears swung gently as we climbed the bleachers. He nuzzled Little Ida's arm. Tufts of his white fur decorated her blue sweater. A breeze shifted some down to her jeans.

"Nuh uh, stay back," I warned as people went "Awww," and tried to pet Wampa. "He's lethal. I'm planning to rent him to the military as a secret weapon."

After Wampa gnashed the air a few times, displaying inch-long bunny teeth, no one tried to pet him again. Go figure.

We stopped on an empty spot with lots of protective space around Wampa. I kept my back to the field as our men strode onto the grass for warm-ups. Ardaleen's jibes about Amos still rang in my ears, reinforcing every doubt I had about proceeding down the path to romance, couple-hood, and me pretending that our thirteen-year age difference no longer mattered.

"Bunny!" I heard behind me. I whipped around just as Jayne Reynolds innocently strollered Matt, her toddler, right up to Wampa.

"Cute rabbit," Jayne said, unsuspecting.

"No, no, Matt," Little Ida yelled, trying to swivel Wampa away from him. But Matt lunged out of the stroller seat and grabbed both of Wampa's ears. "Easter Bunny!"

Wampa stared at him. I grabbed Matt's hands and began prying his fingers loose. "Let go, Matt, let go."

He held on tighter. "Easter Bunny!"

"Let go, Matt," Jayne ordered. She tugged backward on the stroller, but Matt pulled Wampa's ears harder, I pried faster. Wampa was about to take a section of Matt's blond-brown scalp.

Abruptly, Wampa stuck his nose in Matt's hair, took a big sniff, wiggled his pink nose . . . and nibbled the soft brownish locks as if they were sweet grass.

Matt let go of Wampa's ears and burst into giggles. I exhaled a long, relieved breath. Jayne looked upset and bewildered. I decided not to explain. She reached down to pull him back from the rabbit. "Matt, honey, don't . . ."

"He's all right," I soothed. "The rabbit's just giving him a mohawk."

After Jayne calmed down, she fished a paper cup from

the wagon she was hauling and tapped the commercial coffee pot she'd strapped onto it. The aroma of gourmet coffee wafted through the spring air. "Only fifty cents. I'm selling them for the Booster Club."

As owner of The Naked Bean, our coffee shop, she was doing her part to raise money for the new high school. I took the cup from her while she rolled Matt out of Wampa's tasting range. That didn't stop Matt from reaching out for the rabbit again. Little Ida quickly swiveled Wampa away.

I nodded toward the field. "Why don't you take Mr. Haircutter down and introduce him to your daddy? Be sure and tell your daddy I called your mom and she approved the rabbit. And tell him I said Wampa is housebroken."

Little Ida bit back a smile. "Okay, but that's what you told him about the ferrets and the iguana."

"Well, it's a good story and I'm sticking with it."

She trotted down the steps. "Easter Bunny, here!" Matt implored.

Jayne shushed him. "He'll be back soon, honey. Play with some of that hair he left on your sweater. Isn't that nice? You've got Easter Bunny hair all over you." Matt gaped at his sweater front, where poofs of white fur mingled with a cupcake embroidered with the words, Grandma's Boy. Ingrid had given it to him.

"Easter Bunny," Matt said, awed. He began plucking the white fur off his sweater, studying it as if it might turn into a Cadbury egg or marshmallow Peep.

I dropped two quarters in Jayne's hand and sipped the coffee. "I need this."

"I heard what happened this morning down in Bigelow."

I looked at her grimly over my swig of imported joe. Pretty, curvy, pleasant, smart, likable, young Jayne. The sunshine glossed her long, brunette hair. "Everyone's heard?"

"Can't grind a bean in this town without everyone sniffing the aroma."

Which was town lingo for: Of course everyone's heard. This is Mossy Creek. Unofficial town motto? If you want to keep a secret, go live somewhere else.

"Everything? The whole sordid story?"

She nodded. "From the moment you coughed the word 'Bull' until the rabbit sucker-punched your sister in the parking lot."

I sighed. So she and all the other Creekites knew about Ardaleen's Amos remarks. "No wonder so many people in these bleachers craned their heads when I showed up. I was hoping they were all just scared of my killer rabbit."

"If it's any consolation, I expect Amos hasn't heard about it yet. He's been pre-occupied all morning."

"Oh?"

She and Amos are friends. I knew that. Amos is friends with lots of women, older, younger, in-between. Women adore him. He's the town's most eligible bachelor.

And Jayne would be perfect for him.

I like Jayne, I approve of Jayne, I want Jayne to be happy and find a new man. Her husband died while she was pregnant with Matt, and she was a fractured soul when she moved here to open the Bean. Jayne deserves a great new man. Amos would be that for her. Great.

But at the moment I pictured myself happily smearing carrot juice on Jayne and locking her in a room with Wampa. I'm soooo not a good person. I have my sister's dark side.

"Preoccupied? How?" I asked, invisible hackles rising.

She didn't notice. "Getting ready for the game."

"What? This game?" It was a widely known fact that Rob and Amos had some edgy issues. My son has never been subtle about disapproving of Amos's interest in me. So Amos, who dearly wanted to play soccer, had kept his distance from Rob and the team.

Jayne grinned. "Rob finally invited Amos to join. He's playing in today's game."

I stared at her. Was this a sign? Was my son trying to give us his blessing? Jayne cut her eyes toward the field. "Take a look," she said with a hint of I-dare-you. "See you later. I see Ingrid's got our table set up. I need to go relieve her. Come on, Matt."

"Bunny," Matt repeated. As Jayne rolled him away she reached down just in time to stop him from eating a tuft of Wampa's fur.

I swung my gaze to the field. I immediately spotted Rob, my tall, handsome but humorless son, who at the tender age of thirty was only seven years younger than Amos. Rob was bent over Little Ida and Wampa, frowning.

And next to Rob, looking down at the bunny with his trademark, irresistible, just slightly sardonic smile, was Amos.

Amos Royden, Mossy Creek's chief of police.

Who had kissed me when he was sixteen and I was a grieving young widow. Who had come back to Mossy Creek a few years ago, giving up a big-city police force career to fill the over-sized law enforcement shoes left by his father, Mossy Creek's legendary Battle Royden.

So.

Amos Royden, the skinny, earnest, gentle teenager, had now grown into a broad-shoulder man with George Clooney eyes, Hugh Jackman lips and . . .

Legs.

He had legs.

Great legs.

Of course I've always known Amos has legs. I'd watched him stride around town on them. Like all women in the vicinity, I love to watch him walk. But I'd never seen his legs in shorts before.

And not just any shorts. Soccer shorts. Silky. Thin. Clinging. Ruffling in the sudden breeze.

Ingrid showed up beside me. She'd left Bob and his sling at home. She took one long look at what I was looking at and let out a low whistle. "I think Chief Royden just answered the 'boxers or briefs' question. And several other questions women like to ask. Wow."

An understatement. Amos waved. I didn't wave back. Our eyes met and locked. His smile faded into an expression so focused and intense I began to tingle from the top of my head to the soles of my feet. His gaze roamed down my body. The surge of energy traveled along my spine as if he were a long-haul trucker racing to deliver precious cargo. Amos stopped for coffee and a donut at a few particular spots on the route, revving his engines, heating my pavement.

Ingrid jabbed me with her elbow. "Every person in these bleachers is now staring at you staring at him and him staring at you. Don't just stand here, do something."

"Where's Harry Potter's invisibility cloak when I need it?" My voice was a low growl. I felt breathless.

Thank goodness, Rob broke the tension. He straightened from Little Ida and Wampa, frowning harder, and glared at me.

Mother, he mouthed reproachfully. I always got the blame for his child's adventures.

"Go, go," Ingrid urged, pushing me. "Rob needs to talk to you. That gives you an excuse to walk out on the field. I'm headed to the ladies, then back to help Jayne. We're booster-ing today."

I gave up and headed down the steps, straightening my shoulders and lifting my chin, aware of the stares, the whispers. I turned into Scarlett O'Hara shimmying defiantly into Melanie's party after being caught snuggling Ashley at the lumber mill.

Yes, I'm a cougar. Watch me prowl.

Unfortunately, about the time I set foot onto the grassy playing field Rob tossed up both hands and walked away, with Little Ida following him.

Thanks, guys. Now I was just walking toward Amos, alone.

He met me halfway.

"Nice slogan," he said, the sardonic smile returning beneath his very serious eyes, which went from my face to my breasts and back to my face.

"Don't start."

"Start what?"

My electric tingle turned into a security fence. "Please. You and I both know that if I give you any opening at all, you'll manage to take the old peace anthem about making love, not war and turn it into something intimate about us."

"If the slogan fits . . ."

"And you wonder why I avoid you."

Right after the last word left my mouth I realized I'd confessed something. From the satisfied look on Amos's face, he knew it, too. He angled his head close to mine. I shut my eyes against the effect he had. He whispered, "Lucy, you got some 'splainin' to do."

His voice was soft, deep, and his breath brushed my cheek. I opened my eyes with a helpless sensation whirling through me. He studied my hypnotized expression. Damn. I couldn't look away, couldn't hide. He reached out one brawny hand and curled a loose lock of my upswept red hair behind my ear. I leaned closer to him and tilted my face up.

He had me. He'd won. I was going to kiss Chief Royden in front of God, country, my town, its soccer team and a homicidal rabbit.

"Daddy! Daddy! Here!"

Matt's voice. Amos's expression darkened. He pulled back and his gaze shot past me, to the bleachers.

Dazed, I pivoted slowly.

Matt stood up in his stroller. "Daddy!" he yelled again. His arms reached out.

Toward Amos.

I backed away from Amos quickly, froze my face in a mayoral expression of neutrality, but cut my eyes at him fiercely. Wampa had nothing on me. I could go all red-eyed and threatening at the drop of a carrot.

Amos chewed his lower lip, one of the things he does when he's totally exasperated. "He calls everyone Daddy. He picked it up at Mother's Day out. It's a phase. He sees me every day when I go by Jayne's shop for coffee. Don't make it anything more. I know what you're thinking, but it's just a phase."

I lied to keep my dignity. "You don't think I know that? I've had a child. You're the one who hasn't."

Yet, I implied. I kept reminding him that a future with me was a future with no kids of his own.

"I don't remember wanting one," he tossed back. "You don't get to decide things for me, Ida, unless you're in my life. Unless you care about me. Are you? Do you?"

I started to yell it at him: I was about to kiss you in front of everyone in this town. There's not another man on this Earth who could provoke me to stand in the middle of a soccer field and almost kiss him.

"Non-players off the field!" a ref yelled. The Mossy Creek men trotted past and now the Bigelow players were on the field too. All were trying hard not to gawk or be too obvious about trying to overhear our conversation.

Win Allen, stretching his handsome neck to catch our drift, got hit in the head by a soccer ball.

I looked up at Amos sadly. "I've got no business in your life. But someone like Jayne does. Wake up and smell the coffee shop, Amos."

Win chose that moment to wobble over, rubbing his head. He stumbled against Amos then stepped between us. "You look pissed," Win said. "I guess Amos is filling you in, but you should know that it wasn't my fault. Rob says it is but I don't think so. Someone had to do it."

I looked from him to Amos, wondering what Win was talking about. Amos deepened the mystery by shifting his gaze away from my scrutiny. He was guilty of something. He cleared his throat suspiciously and said, "Dwight isn't thinking clearly if he's trying to cheap-out on the football coach, but telling him he's a cheapskate and should be voted out of office wasn't the way to get him to reconsider the salary budget."

"Uh?" Win said.

"Daddy!" Matt squealed again.

Win gave Amos a push. "Amos, go get Matt before he has a cow."

I arched a brow at Amos. The whole town realized that he belonged with Jayne, that Matt wanted him as a father.

Amos, however, was glaring at Win now. I had a feeling that Win had just stepped in a big pile of trouble.

Hadn't we all?

Amos and the Soccer Mom
Part Two

My favorite part of soccer (besides catching Ida looking at me and my legs way too often for the interest to be accidental) is the late afternoon toast at O'Day's Pub. We won the game. Handily. Even better, I scored the winning goal.

Seemed like the entire city of Mossy Creek was in attendance, screaming their lungs out.

About halfway through the game, my calves had started screaming right along with the crowd. Getting old sucked. Not that I gave a damn how sore I'd be tomorrow. I'd play again in a heartbeat if they asked. I'm sure my expression was smug, because it looked like when they asked, not if. Win was about to stir up some trouble that was sure to keep Dwight off the team for some time. Maybe forever.

"You're serious?" I asked, raising my voice to be heard over the cheering dart throwers.

"As a heart attack. Don't know why I didn't think of it before. I'm a local business owner. I'm as interested in our town as Dwight is."

"What do you know about politics?"

Rob leaned forward. "Win doesn't have to know anything. If he beats Dwight for the city council seat he'll be the personal protégé of Mayor Walker."

I flicked my thumb nail against the label edge on the beer I'd been nursing. "And that doesn't scare you?"

"Better him than me." Rob raised his glass in a toast. Lots of here-here's echoed around the table. I raised and tipped my bottle in Rob's general direction.

Wrapping my brain around Win challenging Dwight for his council seat in the next election was going to take some time. "People don't like change."

"Well, they like revenue, and I've already got some ideas."

"Like what?"

"Like charging a library fee as part of the building permits for all those fancy new homes they're trying to build in the mountains. If they're going to increase our population and tax our resources then we have to gear up. That library is important, especially now that the high school will be here."

That got another round of here-here's. And another round of beers—except for me. I switched to club soda with lime. Pretty soon most of the guys grew tired of Win's new crusade and were driven home by our designated driver—Rob—or they'd drifted off to throw darts. Just Win and I were left at the table. He waved at the waitress and mimed signing his tab.

Time to spring the trap. "If I were you, I'd start spreading your money around. You'd better find a reason to drop into every business in town."

"How so?"

"Because you're not from here. Sure, you feel at home, but you didn't grow up here. People like to vote for the hometown boy. Or failing that, they like to vote for their close personal friend and customer."

"Oh." He nodded. "Not bad advice. Not bad at all. I can do that."

I smiled and attempted to look like a thought had just occurred to me. "Of course, you don't need to drop by The Naked Bean."

"Right. Don't worry. I'm not planning to poach on your fall-back woman."

I choked on my soda. "Excuse me?"

He laughed. "Jayne is your reserve. In case Ida doesn't work out. You can trust me. We all know she's off limits."

The waitress showed up. I couldn't ask him who "we all" was. So, he signed his tab and I fished a twenty out of my wallet and tried not to smile when a thought really did occur to me. You don't move a woman to the "off limits" category unless you've considered her. Win Allen had noticed Jayne Reynolds. That was going to make lying to him so much easier. Poor stupid fool would believe every word I said because he wanted to believe me.

"You need to get your radar checked, Win."

"How so?" He stood up. I walked out with him.

"Jayne is about ready to start dating again, but she wasn't at today's game to watch me."

"Then who?"

I held the door. "You. For whatever reason, Jayne's having a little trouble taking her eyes off you, and we all know what that means."

When he just stood there staring at me, I had to wave him through the door. "If I were you, I'd do something about it before the election. Voters love a man dating a single mom."

"Jayne has a little crush on me? You're serious?"

"As a heart attack. If I were you, I'd think about getting or borrowing a dog. Matt is over the moon about dogs. And I know Jayne takes him to the park most days around 2 p.m. when she closes the Bean for her lunch."

I stopped at my Jeep. He walked on and said, "I'm gonna have to think about this."

"You do that," was what I said. But what I thought was—shooting fish in a barrel.

❦❦❦

Later that night, when I saw that the light was on in the mayor's office, another cliché came to mind. Two birds, one stone. In addition to giving me more time with Ida alone, enlisting her in my mission to help Win get elected to the Mossy Creek city council made good sense. I parked next to her car, but before I could enter the building her light went out. I waited, leaning against the Jeep.

Ida was juggling her purse, keys and empty burp-n-seal food containers. She'd taken to eating at her desk in the last few weeks. All the better to avoid a repeat of the day I'd found her sitting alone at a table in Mama's Cafe. She knew better than to eat at Win's restaurant or at the Bean. So, that just left her desk unless she wanted to risk lunch with me. I had spies. I would know when and where Ida ate lunch.

We both knew all she had to do was tell me to leave her alone, but she never did that. She spent a great deal of time telling me why I was wrong, but she'd never once said, "Go away and stay away."

I made sure she locked the door before I said anything. Locking a door sends a pretty strong message that you're done for the night. "Working hard? Or hardly working?"

She jumped, and—judging from the juggling she did to hang on to her containers—Ida could have hit the road with the circus last month and been guaranteed a job. Once she had everything under control, she said, "Do you creep up on all our citizens or just me?"

"I'm not creeping. I'm standing here big-as-life." I stood up straight and opened up my arms. I will admit that my pose looked a little bit like an invitation for her inspection. And I will admit that after the way she had scoped me out today, I knew she'd do it again.

She did, but instead of the embarrassment I expected,

she finally said, "Fine. You want me to admit it? I will. I looked. So what? I cruise the Godiva counter when I'm in Atlanta, but that doesn't mean I'm taking the raspberry truffles home with me."

"Ouch. I think I've just been insulted. Although you also implied I am Godiva-yummy, so I think it's a wash." I walked over and offered to take the containers. She handed them to me and put on her mayor face. "Is there a reason you're here, Chief?"

"Yes, there is. I need your help."

"Real or manufactured?"

"Real."

With a click she unlocked the driver's door of her classic Corvette and then opened it. "Real?"

"Scout's honor. I need you to talk Violet Martin out of her gun."

Ida whipped around to face me. "Where in God's name did Violet get another gun?"

With an absolutely straight face, I said, "Judging by her age . . . I'd say from Samuel Colt."

My new favorite thing is Ida Walker laughing, with her guard down, leaning slightly against me as her knees buckled the tiniest bit. She sobered up and wiped her eyes. "I feel bad. That's awful of me to laugh, but the woman was older than dirt when I was young."

"Still is. The prevailing wisdom is that God made Violet and then dirt, which would be fine if the Nazi's weren't invading."

Since there really wasn't much of anything one could say after a statement like that, I shut her car door and pulled her toward the Jeep. "Come on. I'll explain on the way."

❦❦❦

I'd called a neighbor of Violet's before I left the station. He wasn't under imminent attack and couldn't see anyone in Violet's yard, which meant that Violet's backyard Germans were 99.9% certain to be fat, bold raccoons dining out of her trash cans. The beggars can make a hellacious racket turning over cans. They can also cast a pretty big shadow if they're standing upright.

Violet, despite her advanced age, did truly, probably, know the Germans weren't invading, but she had a wicked flare for the dramatic. Factor in her bad eye sight and willingness to "pop a cap in those fellas" if I wanted her to, and I had no choice but to extend the earlier ban on her shotgun to her hand gun. I didn't want a tragic accident happening on my watch. My goal was to walk out of Violet's house with her gun for safe keeping.

As usual, Ida had other ideas. She didn't think we needed to take the guns. Just the bullets. Violet was a shut-in. We could get the word out that no one was to replenish her supply. That left Violet with a gun she could brandish if come upon by marauders in the night and I could sleep the sleep of the righteous because I didn't have to worry about her ventilating some poor unsuspecting soul who only wanted to borrow a cup of sugar.

Neither of us said a word once we got back in the Jeep. Violet's shoebox full of bullets were stowed in back. I saw Ida bite her lip and look hard out the window. We made it almost back to Ida's car before I couldn't stand it any more. "I'll need a promise."

Ida kept staring out the window, but she hmmmed in a suspiciously high-pitched way, like she was on the verge of losing control.

I didn't trust her as far as I could throw her. "I'll need better than that."

Then she did lose it. She put her head on her knees and her shoulders shook soundlessly.

I whacked the steering wheel with the flat of my hand a few times. "She handed me the shoebox! How was I supposed to know she wrapped her bullet boxes in granny panties to keep the bullets from 'exploding?' "

Ida sighed and straightened up. She was enjoying this. "Red granny panties. Really big red granny panties."

"And that is the last time those words will ever pass your lips." I parked the Jeep, and swiveled to face her. "What happens at Violet's, stays at Violet's. Or there will be consequences."

She put her hand on the door handle and grinned. "No there won't. Problem with you, Amos, is that you always fight fair."

"No. I don't." I didn't plan to kiss her. That would have been a different kiss, softer. With my left hand I reached out to circle her arm and pull her closer. My right hand slipped over her shoulder to cup her neck and bring her to me. I leaned in to whisper, "But I do fight. You aren't hearing me, Ida. I want you. It's not a game."

Maybe this wasn't the right time or the right place, but it was the right kiss. In front of God and everybody wandering the town square that evening, I laid claim to Ida. I knew it. She knew it, and I was fairly certain a few other folks would know it by morning.

When I pulled back, I warned her. "That's going to happen again. Just you come to grips with it."

My newest favorite thing is the look in Ida Hamilton Walker's eyes when she realizes she has made a serious miscalculation.

The Rabbit Stops Running

Part Three:
How Ida Viewed that Night

I love being mayor, even though it's rarely a glamorous job. I spend a lot of my time in work boots and baseball caps, going out with our crews to look at broken water lines, leaking sewer pipes, zoning violations, to name a few. I don't mind the long hours or the dirty jobs, the boring meetings and the occasional mud-slinging from an unhappy citizen. We've won civic awards under my leadership; more importantly, we've made people's lives safer, friendlier and more hopeful.

But I admit I hide behind my office a lot of times. My cluttered, homey space at town hall feels like a warm hug, a good, secure fit. After the unnerving soccer game—had everyone in Mossy Creek seen me shrivel as little Matthew Reynolds called Amos 'Daddy?'—I headed to my office in a hurry, shut the door and threw myself into the exciting job of reading the state's latest bulletins about everything from crop dusting to art grants for puppet shows.

Hours passed. Darkness fell. I dined grimly on leftover hop n' johns salad from my office fridge. Cold black-eyed peas and chopped onions with vinegar dressing suited my mood perfectly.

I was intent on not leaving my hiding hole before every street was deserted and every Creekite soul had gone indoors for the night. No one, but no one, was going to get the last snicker of the day at my expense.

And Amos was not going to get another chance to kiss me. Hiding from him was nothing new. I'd even given up eating lunch at Mama's, Win's or the Bean because Amos had developed a knack for showing up wherever I was.

Smiling rakishly, he'd settle himself at my table. People always stared and smiled. Yes, I could have told him to bug off, to give me my space, to stop making me choke on my sandwiches and blush like a teenager sitting across from the hot guy in the school cafeteria.

But I didn't. My willpower was fading.

But not tonight.

Finally I snuck out a little after eight. Earlier than I should have. There were people strolling Mossy Creek's picturesque square, but in the spring darkness I could scoot to my Corvette before they caught me.

I locked the building's front door, juggled my growing collection of empty food containers, and right-handed my keys like a shank I could stick in the other inmates' necks if anyone tried to stop me from crossing the prison yard.

Then Amos spoke from the shadows beside his Jeep. Which was parked next to my Corvette.

"Working hard? Or hardly working?"

I nearly dropped my Tupperware in the azaleas. "Do you creep up on all our citizens or just me?"

"I'm not creeping. I'm standing here big-as-life."

He held out his arms.

I took a deep breath and hugged my containers to my chest like a shield. We traded a few more zingers until finally he coaxed the stack of plastic ware out of my grip and admitted he was there on official business.

I eyed him suspiciously as I unlocked the Corvette.

When he said, "I need you to talk Violet Martin out of her gun," I perked up and paid attention. Like many of our older citizens, ancient Violet Martin can still cause quite a ruckus when she's in the mood. I asked Amos where she got a gun.

He deadpanned, "Judging by her age . . . I'd say from Samuel Colt."

Okay, Amos's droll sense of humor is yet another hard-to-resist part of him. Call it nerves, relief, or an excuse to make friends with him again, but I laughed like a drunken sailor, guffawing so hard my legs wavered and I leaned against him. Just as he started to cradle me with his arms I came back to my senses and stepped away.

He said something. It sounded like, "Violet thinks the Nazis are invading." While my brain was trying to imagine that concept he took me by one hand and the next thing I knew, we were in his Jeep together, heading off for an adventure.

🐾🐾🐾

Violet can't see well, hear well or move fast, but she is very capable of analyzing complex current events, like the fact that it's about sixty years too late for Nazis to be a credible threat in her backyard. Still, she enjoys upping the ante on her 911 reports, knowing that Amos and his officers hustle when she calls, because they're never quite certain that this time she's not just crying wolf.

Or, in this case, raccoon.

"I'm gonna pop a cap in the furry Nazi behinds of those fellers," she warned as we examined her trash-strewn backyard. "They've scattered my garbage from here to yon one time too many."

I tried not to patronize her, but it was hard. "Miz Martin, you can't shoot at the raccoons."

"Why not?"

I glanced at Amos for help. He looked at Violet solemnly. "Because even Nazis are protected by the Geneva Convention."

She was unconvinced. "Then you should send 'em to Gitmo with the rest of the terrorists!"

I pulled Amos aside and we conferred out of Violet's earshot. In other words, we stepped two feet away and started picking up her spilled trash.

"I already banned her shotgun," Amos said, stuffing empty soup cans in a plastic bag. "I hate to take her handgun, too. But she's going to hurt herself or somebody else."

Shoving a bacon wrapper into a bag, I looked at him from under my brows. "A woman needs a gun to wave. Even if it's just for show."

"Why, Mayor, are you letting me know you'll only threaten to shoot me?"

"Well, Chief, that's a risk you'll have to take."

He smiled. "Deal."

What was I saying? I was flirting with him. Over garbage. While a woman who looked like Yoda in a shawl now waved a loaded pistol at the birdbath.

"Back to the subject. Violet needs her gun. It's the principle of the thing. But I can talk her out of her bullets. And we'll tell everyone in town not to sell her any new ones."

Amos picked up a raccoon-gnawed stalk of celery. He presented it to me with a slight bow. "Brilliant. I award you the Exalted Celery of Diplomacy."

I took the award solemnly. "I'll share this with Wampa. He'll either eat it or rip it to shreds in a psychotic frenzy."

🌿🌿🌿

We drove back to my car with Violet's treasure trove of bullets in our possession. There had been a little surprise with the bullets. Neither of us could wrap enough breath around the words to discuss it.

Finally, Amos said in a tight voice, "I'll need a promise."

I went "Huh" or "Hmmm" or "Hush," I'm not sure which, because I was struggling not to explode.

"I'll need better than that."

Innocent words. But he sputtered as he said them, and the failing control in his deep voice completely unhinged me.

I bent double, once again hooting like a sailor on a tequila bender watching Wile E. Coyote cartoons.

Amos pounded the steering wheel and growled something about, 'How was I supposed to know about the granny panties,' and 'What was I supposed to do, scream and throw them on the floor when I realized that's what she'd wrapped the bullet boxes in?'

As he swung the Jeep into a space beside my Corvette I suddenly became busy noticing how many late-night diners had just stepped out of Win Allen's restaurant. All of them swiveled their heads toward Amos's well-known vehicle. All of them did a double-take when they realized I was sitting in his passenger seat.

Amos was saying something about swearing me to silence.

I mumbled an answer. Refusing to promise. Told him his problem was that he always fights fair. I tried to change the subject. "We have an audience . . ."

"No, I don't always play fair," he interrupted. The suddenly serious, graveled need in his voice alerted me that we'd just stepped out of the comedy club and onto a dark, sultry dance floor. He slipped one hand around my arm and cupped the back of my neck with the other. Then he leaned in close to my lips and said, "But I do fight. You aren't hearing me, Ida. I want you. It's not a game."

What happened next was inevitable, wonderful, a big

step forward . . . and a clear warning that Amos was closing in on me, and that I was letting him.

On the street, the crowd broke into applause.

❦❦❦

I drove home under a dark, twinkling universe of spring stars, with the Corvette's window rolled down to catch the cool wind on my hot face. The first of the spring frogs sang in the marshy spots of the forests and fields. The lights of town disappeared behind me.

I had wobbled out of the Jeep, glowered at the applauding Creekites, then swiftly ducked inside my car—Jeb's favorite car, a classic silver model. I'd kept it running, in mint condition, for twenty years. My life was filled with reminders of Jeb, of us, of the past.

Yet I drove home thinking about Amos, and only Amos.

I certainly knew where another step forward would take him and me, and I still wasn't sure I was ready for it.

You better get ready, get ready, get ready, get ready for mating season, the frogs sang.

At the farm I parked near one of the barns, saw a light there and found my farm managers inside, doting over the Boggs' miniature goats, pig and burro. My managers are a hard-working husband/wife team who live in a small house on a hill behind my big Victorian. They're very pragmatic about most of our livestock, which includes several horses and a large herd of dairy cattle. They don't usually get sentimental about cute critters.

But there they were, scratching the newcomers' heads, feeding them slices of apple. They suggested we add a petting zoo to the new winery, which was well under construction on a ridge nearby.

I told them that was a good idea. I hoped, for the sake of Mr. Boggs and his little boy, these pets would go back to their home one day. Until then, yes, we'd have a petting zoo.

Walking back up the farm road to my house, where an automatic timer had turned on the veranda lights, I glanced at the patterns of the vineyards that now crisscrossed a distant pasture. They made shadowy lines in the starlight. The grape vines were sprouting leaves. I expected we'd get our first harvest in the fall. Jeb's winery. His dream.

How would Amos feel about all this? Would he be happy dealing with my heritage, all the pompous Hamilton baggage, the eccentricities, the battles with Ardaleen and her son, the Governor? Sure, he'd dealt with my public feuds many times as a police chief, arresting me so often that some people said we'd been dating for years if you counted all the trips I'd made in the back of his patrol car.

I took a deep breath. "What next?" I said aloud to the budding azaleas along the fieldstone path to my front steps.

As if in answer, I heard the rumble of a car on the long, graveled lane to the public road. I squinted into the darkness as headlights came through the trees. My veranda lights glimmered on Rob's silver-gray Prius. He'd gone hybrid. Was even talking about opening a Prius dealership in addition to running Hamilton's Department Store in town. My son was intent on becoming a very rich man. Richer than all the Hamiltons combined and certainly richer than his father's Walker heritage. My people make money and buy property; they live long and prosper, like Vulcans. Jeb's people race cars, fly stunt planes and die young—but leave unforgettable memories.

And Amos? Royden men are somewhere in between, tall, stalwart, sure of themselves. They are lovers and fighters, law men and rebels.

Maybe he was exactly what I needed here. A strong link between my two worlds.

But for now, I had an unhappy son frowning out his open Prius window at me. Rob stopped the car by my walkway gate. He called out, "Mother, how about hosting a sleepover for your granddaughter and her insane rabbit?" Rob held his right hand out for me to get a good look. He had Band-aids on two fingers and a thumb.

I suppressed a smile. "Sure. The evil bunny and his assistant are always welcome here."

Little Ida climbed out of the passenger side, grinning, dressed in a coat over her pajamas, carrying her Miley Cyrus overnight bag and Wampa's personal plaid tote. Wampa looked over the edge with calm pink eyes, though he did glance back at Rob and gnash his teeth.

Rob's eyes narrowed. "I'm going to win that rabbit over."

"Better buy some steel-mesh gloves," I called.

He looked heavenward as if his father might advise him, shook his head, blew me and Little Ida a kiss and drove away.

I went down the steps to meet her. As I hoisted her overnight bag to my shoulder she looked up at me with mischievous eyes. "Nana, do 'just friends' swap smooches in the front seat of Chief Royden's Jeep?"

I sighed. All over greater Mossy Creek, the spring gossip was about to burst into bloom.

Mossy Creek Gazette

VOLUME VII, NO. TWO   MOSSY CREEK, GEORGIA

The Bell Ringer

The New Bell Ringer BLOG!

Subscribe now for 24/7 gossip at
www.bellebooks.com/MossyBlog
on Mossy Creek Gazette's On-line Edition!

by Katie Bell

True-love showdown on the soccer field . . .

Everyone in Mossy Creek is whispering about the heated confab today between Mayor Ida Walker and Police Chief Amos Royden RIGHT IN FRONT OF GOD AND THE SOCCER BALL at the future home of the Mossy Creek Rams High School Sports Stadium.

Chef Bubba Rice, aka Win Allen, was eaves-dropping so hard he got hit in the head by a soccer ball. And THERE'S MORE. Tonight, as of 9 p.m. EST, reports are that a certain mayor and a certain police chief were seen in a certain police chief's Jeep parked outside town hall, locking lips.

Somebody please buy a supply of mentholated lip balm. SOME public officials around here may NEED it.

The Mice that Roared

Part Three

Win Allen

"Good grief," I muttered. "Winfield Jefferson Allen, you're 40 years old, not 14."

"Pardon?"

I turned my head to see that my under-the-breath mutterings had captured the attention of elderly Eleanor and Zeke Abercrombie, who were strolling down the street arm-in-arm.

I shrugged. "Just talking to myself."

"Great game Saturday," Zeke said as we shook hands.

"Thanks," I'd been vindicated for asking Amos Royden to substitute for Dwight at the game on Saturday. He'd made the winning goal.

"That's the first sign of senility, you know," Eleanor said.

"Soccer?"

"Talking to yourself."

"I didn't know. How do you?" I shot back. I knew from a catering job I'd done for them last year that the former mayor's wife's brain was still as sharp as my best knife.

She knew I was teasing her. "Because my seventy-five-year-old husband does it all the time."

I chuckled. It had been twenty years since Zeke Abercrombie had handed his mayor's crown to Ida Hamilton

Walker, but he'd relinquished it because of a heart condition. There was nothing wrong with his mind. "Then I'd say it's a sign of intelligence, not senility."

She waved a dismissive hand at my compliment. "Oh, go on with you."

We chatted for a moment longer about the subject on everyone's mind—the hiring of the new Mossy Creek Rams football coach—then my gaze lingered after them as they moved on. The town had helped them celebrate their golden wedding anniversary last fall, and they were still as close as any couple I'd ever known. Gently teasing, best friends, lovers.

It was probably too late for me to have a fifty-year relationship, but it was possible . . . but not if I couldn't screw up my courage.

I zeroed my gaze back to The Naked Bean across the square. I served good coffee at my own diner, so the only time I went in was when Amos dragged me in for his afternoon fix. I liked Jayne's quaint little business. We weren't competitors, so there was absolutely no reason I shouldn't go in and several reasons I should.

My interest had latched on to Jayne Reynolds when I first came to town. When I heard about the gumption she showed naming her coffee house The Naked Bean and facing down the prudes in the town who wanted her to change it, I'd *definitely* been interested.

But she'd been a new widow expecting a baby, and I'd put my attraction on a back burner. I'd moved it off the stove entirely when I heard rumors about her and Amos.

Since he'd cleared the way, making it plain that his only interests in Jayne were friendship and coffee, my attraction to her had resurfaced. As a matter of fact, to my surprise, I thought of little else all weekend.

Like a lovesick teenager.

I cussed under my breath and crossed the town square.

It wasn't as if I didn't know women. I'd dated plenty in the forty years I'd had on this Earth. I'd even—as weird as it sounds—had groupies when I had my cable TV cooking show. Women would show up at the door to the studio and ask me out. One of them told me that there was something very sexy about a man who cooks. During the first year or two it'd been rather heady, having women chase me instead of the other way around, and I took advantage. Toward the end there, it was just tiresome.

There'd been women.

So where were these nerves coming from?

As I opened the door to The Naked Bean and saw Jayne talking to Josie Rutherford, I suddenly knew that the reason I was nervous was because this was important. I wanted Jayne to be just as interested in me as I was in her.

That threw me for minute. Even the word "important" threw me. I liked women, sure. Enjoyed them immensely, in fact. But I'd lived forty years blissfully single. No woman had ever been more important than another.

I wasn't sure I liked the fact that Jayne had suddenly become important, and I nearly turned around and walked out the door.

However, the bell attached to her door had captured her attention and her hazel gaze caught mine. The sight of me in her shop was so rare, she blinked in surprise. "Win! Oh. How nice to see you."

I could practically feel fate slapping me up the side of my head, and I moved on into the shop. "Thanks."

"Great game Saturday," Josie said.

"Yes, indeed it was," Jayne echoed. "Exciting. Matt has been asking when he can play soccer."

She indicated her young son, who played in a corner of the shop Jayne had set up for children. He was intent on some sort of structure made with primary-colored Legos.

"Matt's three?" I asked.

"He will be in a few months."

"He's got a few years left. I think the summer teams start at five."

Jayne chuckled. "Yes, I've already had to check into it, to shut him up."

"How'd the fund-raising go?" I asked.

"Great. The crowd cleaned us out of both cookies and coffee. We didn't break the bank, but I think we raised enough for a row of bleachers," she said.

"Stadiums are built row by row," Josie said. "Now if we could just get a decent coach . . ."

"The rumor is that Dwight's trying to sabotage the selection process," Jayne said directly to me. "Is that true? Have you heard anything?"

"Afraid that's true," I told them. "Hank said that at the last town council meeting, Dwight ordered the selection committee to only consider the candidates who are willing to work for the lower end of the salary range."

"Dwight," Josie snorted. "How short-sighted can he be? Oh, Harry's going to hit the roof when I tell him this."

"Something should be done," Jayne said. "Why doesn't someone run against Dwight?" She brightened. "Why don't you run against him, Win?"

I was stunned—not only that she thought of the same thing Rob and Amos had said to me, but that she thought enough of me to suggest it. It made me feel . . .

Good grief. Was I about to say 'warm and fuzzy?'

"You'd be perfect!" Josie said. "You've been here long enough for everyone to know you. You're a respected businessman. You've got clout at the state level since you're a celebrity—"

"Hardly a celebrity," I quickly corrected.

"Maybe not nationally, but you're well-known as a chef."

"Oh, Win, please consider running," Jayne said. "You'd be great. And the council definitely needs some new blood."

"Well, to tell you the truth . . ." I stopped to clear my throat. "I've been thinking about it."

There. I'd put it out there to someone besides my closest friends. Soon the whole town would know. I guess that meant I'd made a firm decision.

"That's wonderful!" Jayne said.

Josie was just as excited. "I can't wait to tell Harry. He'll be behind you one hundred percent, Win. It takes something to earn Harry Rutherford's respect, but you've done it."

That meant a lot. I didn't know him or Josie all that well, but I knew that Dr. Harry Rutherford was a respected scientist and ecologist. "Thanks."

"In fact, I'm going to go call him right now. I need to run, anyway. I've got an appointment at Goldlilock's. Rainey's hired a new manicurist and I just have to try her out."

"I heard she doesn't speak a word of English," Jayne said.

"Well, I'm about to find out for certain! We'll talk later about the new arrangement of your café tables, but for now, move that table over there away from the door. It's blocking the positive chi. I'll be by tomorrow. We'll discuss what you're going to wear Wednesday night. I have a little skirt that Dan will love."

"Dan?" I asked because I couldn't help myself. "You're going out with Dan McNeil?"

Jayne's smile was rueful. "Yes, he asked me to dinner. My first date since . . . well, you know."

Since her husband died. And it was with Dan. I didn't like that one little bit. Was I too late?

She moved toward the offending table, but I beat her to it. "Where do you want it?"

She pointed to the opposite wall. "There for now, I guess. Until Josie tells me that's the wrong spot, too."

When the table was moved, she smiled at me. "Thank you. Can I get you anything, Future Councilman Allen?"

"Don't jinx it. But yes, I'd like a mocha latte, if it's not too much trouble."

Her laugh was like a Chopin sonata. "If it were, I'd be out of business before you could say 'espresso.' "

She moved behind the counter and got to work.

"Your place looks great," I said, pointing to the new doorway leading into Beechum's Bakery. Now that place I'd visited. I'd been trying to figure out Ingrid's coconut icing recipe ever since I'd moved to town. Her coconut cake was the best I'd ever tasted. Hands down.

"Thanks. We're not done yet. Still a little more painting to do, and Josie's not done decorating yet, obviously, but we'll get there. Grand opening's in a couple of weeks. I will—" Suddenly she bit off a tiny shriek and jumped back.

Alarmed, I started around the counter. "What is it?"

"It's okay. It's okay," she said, stopping me. She shuddered slightly, as if trying not to, then scooted my coffee across the counter.

"What happened?" I pressed.

Her expression was forlorn. "I can't tell you. I'm horribly embarrassed, plus it's a major health code violation."

"What is?"

She bit her lip, then leaned halfway across the counter to whisper, "I have . . . mice."

She said it in a squeak reminiscent of Minnie Mouse.

As an owner of a restaurant, I could feel her horror. "Oh. Can't you get rid of them?"

"It's not that easy," she said. "Ever since they opened the wall, we've seen at least ten a day. Not just here, but upstairs in my apartment, too. Mainly there, now that I've completed construction down here. It's as if the little critters are taking revenge on me for disturbing them."

"Old buildings are notorious for that. I had a little trouble myself, when I renovated my diner. I had a good mouser, though, who took care of the problem. Isn't your cat helping?"

"For all the good she does. Emma turns up her nose at them."

"That's the trouble with cats, you don't know if they're finicky until the situation arises."

Jayne reached across the counter and placed her hand over mine. "Please don't tell anyone, Win. I'll get rid of them by the grand opening if I have to close down the shop and get the entire two buildings fumigated."

I assured her that her secret was safe, though I knew no secret was safe for long in this town.

Then customers arrived from the busload of tourists parked across the square. They were the first I'd seen this year, there to enjoy the rhododendrons that were just barely starting to bloom. The full panoply wouldn't burst forth for a few more weeks, but some folks liked to get a jump on things.

Jayne turned away to help them, and I meandered over to the children's play area. Matt hadn't even raised his head from his project. I'd never seen such a young child so focused.

"Hi there." I turned a chair around at the table close by and sat. "I'm Win."

"I know," he said without looking up.

"What are you building?"

"I build house," he said proudly.

"That's cool. I—"

"Lookee! Mou—"

I saw it at the same time he did and cleared my throat

loudly to cover the word. "Shhhh. Your Mom doesn't want people to know. Okay?"

He placed a hand over his mostly contrite grin. "Oh yeah. I forgets."

I changed the subject. "I hear you like dogs."

"Yeah!" He practically beamed. "Do you?"

"I sure do. I've got one at home."

"A Bob dog?"

"A Chihuahua?" I frowned that he would even think I'd own such a yapper. I shared most men's aversion to dogs who couldn't bark without bouncing. "No. I have a real dog, an Irish setter. I named her Cherry because she's red. Would you like to come and see her some time?"

"OhBoyOhBoyOhBoy! Yeah!"

I couldn't help but laugh at his enthusiasm. "Well, we'll just have to talk your mom into it, won't we?"

"Yeah. Oh, look! Anudder mou—" He clamped his hand over his mouth before he could say it, then grinned at me.

I grinned back.

Amos was right. Dogs seemed a surefire way to Matt's heart.

I glanced back at Jayne, who was about halfway through her customers.

"Need any help?" I called.

She didn't even glance my way. "Thanks, but I've got it under control."

And a de-micer might just be the way to Jayne's.

Seems as if I'd heard somewhere along the line that some of the smaller dogs were bred to hunt rodents. A way to kill all the mice with one dog, as it were.

I'd say that called for a conversation with Hank Blackshear.

*"If a dog jumps in your lap, it is because he is fond of you;
but if a cat does the same thing, it is because your lap is warmer."*

—*Alfred North Whitehead*

Tale of Two Kitties

Nancy

It was the best of cats, it was the worst of cats. It was the age of Whisker Lickin's, it was the age of feathered toys. My apologies to Mr. Dickens, but the man knew how to sum up a situation. Of course, my youngest son's sacrifice was much less daunting than facing the guillotine.

Charles Finch, whose first word was "doggie" and who asked for one as soon as he could put a sentence together, was now six and hadn't yet received the pet of his dreams. Before you label me as cruel, let me list the reasons why my husband Will and I haven't added a dog to our family.

One, Charles wouldn't be the one taking care of it. Even now, my first grader had to be reminded about his own grooming. If he had the choice, and he doesn't, he probably wouldn't bathe. Reason number two, I have three children ranging from high school to elementary age. I didn't have a fourth child because I'd reached my sanity limit at three. Nobody can say Nancy Abercrombie Finch is a sucker for punishment. A dog would be like a fourth child. Then there's our old tabby, Biscuit, who's been with me longer than my husband. A less frazzling choice than adding a dog to the mix would be to adopt a second cat. Or so I thought.

"Mo-om," Charles crooned as he entered in the back door and left it open to the unseasonably chilly, spring evening air. "I saw Mrs. Blackshear at soccer practice."

"That's nice, dear." I gestured to the door, meaning for him to push it closer to the jamb. He didn't get it, so I added, "Don't heat the entire garage."

He slammed the door on his sister, whose muffled, outraged, "Hey!" followed the slam. "You're such a brat," Mary Alice growled, re-opening the heavy wooden door. Will followed behind her, carrying the duffel bag Mary Alice had left in the car.

Mitts in place, I removed a steaming broccoli-and-chicken casserole from the oven and placed it on a trivet on the table. "Wash your hands and tell Randy to come down for dinner."

"Ran-dy!" she screamed.

Not exactly what I had in mind.

Will and I exchanged a glance of commiseration, then he took hold of Mary Alice's shoulders and re-directed her toward the stairs. "When your mother said 'tell Randy,' she meant to go tell him. He can't hear you."

"I can yell louder," she offered, as Charles tugged on my pants leg.

"Let's not," I said. "Scoot."

My fifth-grader rolled her eyes (yes, we're at that lovely stage of adolescence) and did as she was asked.

Charles tugged harder. "Mo-om."

"What?" Not completely successful at keeping the irritation out of my voice, I filled the children's glasses with milk.

"Mrs. Blackshear said someone left a box of puppies at Dr. Blackshear's clinic. Beagle puppies. She said Melvin said they were prolly Bigelowans. The people who left 'em, he means."

"It's probably, not prolly. Did you wash your hands?"

"No, but I was thinking it sure'd be nice to give one of those—"

"We're not getting a dog," Will said. After issuing his

ultimatum, Will sat in his spot at the head of the table.

I heard the water running upstairs, so Mary Alice must have made her brother hear her without yelling, or she decided to wash her hands first. Either way, I knew that was progress.

Charles pouted, slid into his chair next to his father, and sighed. "It's not a dog, it's a puppy."

"Same difference," I pointed out. "I didn't see you wash your hands."

"I used the sanitizer, like Dad." He raised his palms in the air so I could inspect them for dirt. "It's not fair, Mom. Everyone else has a dog."

"No everyone else does not," I reminded him. "Mrs. Clifton told me that the family who moved in across the street, what's the little girl's name, Melanie? She has a cat like us."

"But she's dumb."

It was a toss-up as to whether he was referring to Melanie or our elderly cat. Both were female, and Charles didn't like either of them. I had an inkling he was referring to the little girl across the street, though, since his complaints about her had grown exponentially since the beginning of the school year. He didn't like Melanie much in August. Now that they'd moved in across the street, he liked her far, far less.

Darn it, I realized with a pang. They'd moved in at least a month ago. Had I invited them to dinner or at least welcomed them with a loaf of banana bread? No, but I'd . . . waved.

Muttering something under his breath, Charles focused on his empty plate.

Things had a way of coming to a head with this boy. I'd find out probably more than I wanted to know about why he thought Melanie was "dumb," soon enough. Pick your arguments, my mother told me, because otherwise, interacting with Charles would be one long fight until the day he went off to college, if he went, which since I wanted him to, he probably wouldn't.

He looked up at me, blue eyes round with false innocence. "Oh, and I guess I shoulda told you Smelanie's mom called."

"We do not call our neighbor 'Smelanie.' "

Eyes downcast, he tried to smother his budding smirk.

"I'm serious, young man. Why did Melanie's mother call?"

He trotted out the fake innocent look again and shrugged.

Lips whitening in exasperation, Will leaned toward our youngest and, yes, most mischievous child. "Punishment's going to be worse, the longer you drag this out."

Charles mumbled something only a Who could hear.

"Louder," Will said, checking the time on his wristwatch.

"I pulled her hair at school!" He pouted. "She was asking for it, being all goody-two-shoes."

Great. My son was about to start World War Three with our new neighbors, who I hadn't yet introduced myself to, and all because Melanie behaved. This part of Charles's personality had to come from Will's Finch clan; it certainly wasn't one of my Abercrombie genes. "That's no reason to pull the child's hair, young man. Where's your folder? What color slip did you get today?"

"Orange."

Uh oh. The Mossy Creek Elementary security alert system: Orange was only one color away from red, the worst color, the color that earned a note home and a trip to the vice principal's office. "I thought our goal was green all week."

"If I stay green all next week, can I 'dopt one of those

beagle puppies at the Blackshears'?"

"No!" Will and I shouted at the same time.

"Can we at least get a dog when Biscuit dies?"

"Charles Albert Finch!"

"But, Mom, Biscuit isn't even a nice cat. All she does is hiss at me."

"Because you bother her," Will said. He looked from the cooling casserole to me. "Where are Randy and Mary Alice?"

I heard the water run for a second time and one set of feet tromping down the stairs. "They're coming."

"I don't bother Biscuit," Charles said. He slipped out of his chair and walked over to the sink, where Biscuit was lying next to her food and water trough. She likes to lie down to lap her water.

I thought Charles had decided to wash his hands with soap and water. But then he looked down at our peaceful, plump tabby.

I warned quickly, "Don't pick her . . . up."

Too late. As Charles scooped the cat into his arms, she yelped. Still held despite the warning, she hissed, exposing her tiny, sharp teeth.

"See," he said, "she doesn't like me."

Will stood up. "Put her down. You know she doesn't like to be picked up. She's old."

Charles placed the cat back on the floor. She promptly swatted at his ankle. She gave his leg a nip as well.

"Hands," I said.

Charles mumbled something about hating cats and goodie-two-shoes girls who like cats as he lathered up.

"Mom, guess what Randy has in his room," Mary Alice said in her best sing-song, tattle-tale mode as she ran to the table.

Our oldest, Randy, slid into his usual spot with a scowl. "Just shut up."

"A Victoria's Secret catalog," Mary Alice said before I could even venture a guess.

Somehow this wasn't the way I pictured family dinners proceeding when Will and I talked about getting married and having children.

And Charles wanted to add a poor, unsuspecting dog to the mix? No way.

❦❦❦

Eileen

"I hate boys," my six year old said, letting her backpack slide with a thud to the floor. For added emphasis, Melanie slammed what sounded like her Hannah Montana lunchbox on something hard, probably the kitchen countertop.

I checked the time in the bottom corner of my computer screen. My goal for today had been to complete the action plan for a tank yank up in Habersham County, about a half-hour's drive north of Mossy Creek, for the engineering firm I work for, then empty the three moving boxes I'd placed on the kitchen table we hadn't yet used in its official capacity. The unpacking hadn't happened yet thanks to two unscheduled calls—my boss and our client.

I braced myself for another installment of my six-year-old daughter's speech titled, "Why We Should Move Back to downtown Mossy Creek," followed by its spin-off, "Why I Hate Charles Finch."

From what I could tell, Melanie's beef with fellow first-grader Charles was that he existed.

Apparently, she had assumed when I built a brand-spanking new house in this new neighborhood outside town, and let her design her room, pick out new furniture and bed linens, she'd somehow get a made-to-order best friend who lived next door. No such luck. Sure, she had friends at Mossy Creek Elementary, but since we moved to

Yonder—a wide spot in the mountain roads anchored by Yonder Groceries and Gas and the tiny Yonder Community Center (which doubles as the voting station in all elections), the casual, after-school play dates had dried up. The only child Melanie's age on our road, with its scattering of new homes and old farms, was Charles.

From the daily reports Melanie provided, my neighbor's son didn't seem any more pleased about her presence across the road than she was about his. And his mother, although diligent enough to force her son to apologize for pulling my daughter's hair, hadn't shown herself to be best-friend material, not that I expected a neighbor to become a bosom buddy. Out in the country, people live by the old axiom that "fences make good neighbors."

"Where's Fluffy Anne?" Melanie asked. "Fluffy A-a-nne! Where are you?"

I saved what I'd completed on my report, squeezed myself between the stacks of boxes inside my office, and met my baby in the kitchen. I tried to ignore the large cardboard boxes labeled "KITCHEN" in thick, black, Magic Marker letters.

Problem number two: Fluffy Anne had become even more adventurous since our move to the mostly rural environs of Yonder.

"I guess she's off exploring," I said. Fluffy Anne had been gone longer and longer each time she explored. I didn't point that out to Melanie.

"Are you sure?" she asked, her voice now small and worried.

"Sure, I'm sure," I bluffed.

"She might have gone back to—"

"What should we have for dinner tonight?" I interrupted, lifting the menu for Mama's All You Can Eat Cafe to distract her. "Chicken fried steak or pork chops? I already called in our dessert order—chocolate pie." It was quite a trek to pick up a take-out dinner from Mossy Creek, but I knew Melanie was comforted by the familiar connection.

Melanie placed her dimpled hands on her hips and sighed. "She might've gone back to Laurel Street. This house doesn't feel right to her. I don't think she likes it here in the woods, Mommy."

As smart as the cat was, I didn't think Fluffy Anne could make the trek from Yonder to Mossy Creek, a ten-mile drive along a roller coaster of narrow mountain roads. I also didn't think Melanie and I were talking about Fluffy Anne anymore.

I traced the apple of Melanie's cheek, still as downy as it had been as a baby. "Fluffy Anne will settle in just fine in time. Once we get everything unpacked and decorated."

I glanced at the neutral-colored walls. 'Baked Scone' paint had seemed like a good choice when in the midst of building and I had fifty million decisions to make. Now, as I stared at the bland palette of our new house, our new life, I wished I'd been a little more adventurous with the color or with the khaki-and-brown furniture. My house was a sepia-toned photograph.

Melanie's big brown eyes filled with tears. She twisted the front flap of her skirt. "Mommy, what if some truck hit her? What if she's lying in the road somewhere dead? Like a possum or a raccoon or a baby bear?" We'd seen a dead bear cub on the road once. Melanie had never forgotten it.

"Fluffy Anne isn't dead." I used my authoritative tone usually reserved for teeth-brushing. "I'd know it if she was. Someone would stop, pick her up and call the number on her collar. Do you have any homework?" I prayed my question would distract her from her maudlin thoughts.

"Reading," Melanie said. "Charles made fart noises in our reading group today. He had to sit in the thinking chair."

She opened the refrigerator and pulled out a juice box. She ambled over to the back door, which she opened. "Fluf-fy A-anne!"

Frowning, she sipped her juice and scanned the barren backyard for any swish of a cat tail. I'd tackle the yard this summer. Maybe hire Sammie Pritchard to landscape it for me.

Still frowning, Melanie turned to face me. "What if she doesn't come back?"

"She'll come back." I hoped I was right. The sound of the can opener might bring her trotting. Unless someone else was feeding her. The bowl of kibble I set out for her was empty every morning, so she had to be eating it. "If she doesn't come back, and I'm not saying I think she won't, but if she doesn't, I'll get you a kitten."

"I don't want another kitten, I want Fluffy Anne."

I went to the den and lifted the skirt on the reclining sofa. One time, on Laurel Street, Fluffy Anne somehow got herself under it but couldn't find her way out. Never mind that Melanie and I were frantic calling for her inside and out. She sat without a meow even when Melanie cried. The kitty let me know where she was only after her hunger overcame her embarrassment.

Yeah, this was the cat we wanted and loved.

Maybe she was hiding in one of those boxes I hadn't unpacked in the garage. Or maybe she'd been eaten by some critter, a bear or a fox. Only time and hunger would tell.

Nancy

Several afternoons following Charles's orange slip, he arrived home later than usual from the bus stop. It was a wet, no soccer practice (hallelujah) afternoon, and he stumbled inside with something other than his sopping backpack, something wet and furry that meowed. If it hadn't, I would never have known the animal was a cat.

Worried to the point that I had actually picked up the phone to call the school, since I'd heard the bus go by ten minutes prior and my son still hadn't hit the back door, I didn't know whether to kiss him or towel him off. He held out the wet, emaciated cat, whose drips added to the growing puddle on my clean floor.

"Her name is Spot," he said, manipulating the cat so that he could show me the white patch on her matted gray tail. "We need to get her dry," he called out as he dripped up the stairs still toting this cat, who (unlike Biscuit) liked to be handled.

He came back down with several towels and my blow dryer. I plugged it in for him. He never let go of Spot or even took off his raincoat.

"Sweetheart, that cat isn't going to . . ." My words dried up as the blow-dryer whirred and Spot stayed put in my son's arms. She actually enjoyed the warm air fluffing out her gray fur.

Biscuit, on the other hand, meowed her displeasure from her seat on the sofa in the den. She ran, belly swaying, up the stairs to escape from the offending noise and the prospect of Charles sending some of that loud, warm air her way.

"Please, pu-lease, can I keep her?" he asked once Spot was dry.

Spot purred and looked at me with the sweetest green eyes. A second cat would be less of a problem than a puppy. And the poor thing obviously hadn't been fed in a good while. No! What was I thinking? I had my hands full with one cat and three children. No more pets. We could take Spot to the new Bigelow County Humane Society. She'd get a good home.

"I'll take care of her," Charles offered. "I think she really likes me." He grinned, revealing his half-grown-in front teeth.

Spot rubbed her pretty gray head against Charles.

"What if she belongs to someone else?" I didn't really think so because, first of all, she was skin and bones. And secondly, who would leave a cat out on a thunder soaker day like today? But she must have belonged to someone at one time, to like people so much. Probably some college student dumped her off in our area since spring break was about to begin. I'd read a story in the *Mossy Creek Gazette* about certain neighborhoods being targets for that sort of thing. The college kids get pets, but their parents don't let them bring them home for spring break or for the summer, so they find a country road and dump them, assuming the pets will survive in the wild or find a nearby house and someone to feed them.

"Charles? Did you hear me?" I said, "What if she belongs to somebody?"

"She doesn't. I swear."

I swear? An odd response for a six-year-old.

"I think she's hungry, Mom."

Probably was, poor thing. I'd never seen a cat so skinny. "Give her some of Biscuit's food, but put it in a different bowl in case she's got a cold or something. I think I'll make some fliers, just in case."

Charles knelt down on the floor and pulled out Biscuit's food from the pantry. "Mommy, I thought you said this food was for old kitties."

"It's fine for now, sweetheart."

He toted the plastic jug of cat food to his favorite cereal bowl, the one with Spiderman on it. As the kibble pinged against the bowl and Spot plunged into it eagerly, Biscuit strolled into the kitchen and stopped just shy of the island. She looked down her regal beige and pink nose; she brandished her tail like a sword, back and forth in indignation.

She blinked her honey-colored eyes at me. I could almost read her mind. Who is this peasant? Why is it eating my food in my kitchen?

A low growl, one that Biscuit usually reserves for Hank Blackshear and his vaccinations, issued from her throat. Spot stopped eating and cowered. Biscuit advanced.

"Mean old cat," Charles yelled.

Spot darted past Biscuit, who sauntered over to me with a self-satisfied crackle in her old joints. She meowed up at me repeatedly.

"He found her. What was I supposed to do, let her starve?" I said.

Apparently, Biscuit thought starving was just fine for Spot. She turned her hind end to me, swished her tail once and padded away.

By dinnertime, Charles had taught Spot tricks in his room, which he declared a Biscuit-free zone. He debuted Spot's talent for the entire family, including Biscuit, after dinner. The first trick involved chasing a die across the hardwood floor and batting it. Charles called this game "cat soccer." The second trick was "cat fishing." He'd taken one of Biscuit's old toys and tied it to the end of his toy fishing rod. He cast the toy out as bait. Spot grabbed hold of the toy, and he reeled her in.

Biscuit looked down from her perch on the back of the couch, her paws crossed in a queen-like pose, and yawned.

Will and I clapped.

"Are we keeping Spot?" Mary Alice asked.

"I don't know," I said, and I was being truthful. She was cute, adorable, lovable. But could the vacuum cleaner take the additional hair? Could the budget take the additional food and vet bills?

"Please, Mom," Charles begged. "I'll even empty the litter box. Every day. I swear. I'll even clean up her hairballs.

They couldn't be nastier than Biscuit's."

Biscuit narrowed her eyes to slits as she focused on my youngest.

Will clicked his tongue and Spot climbed into his lap, settled herself and purred. He'd melted, too. So there was no one to prod my backbone. What could I do but cave?

I still, however, needed to verify that this fabulous foundling that my family loved didn't belong to anyone else. I made fliers that night, and Charles promised he'd distribute them on the bus and at school. I also notified the Homeowner's Association, and they posted a notice on the website.

When I put Charles to bed, I reminded him about the fliers.

"Yeah, yeah," he said as I kissed his forehead.

I switched his nightlight to on.

"And we need to go to Pet Smart in Bigelow," he added. "Spot needs some toys and a real cat bowl and some catnip."

🐾🐾🐾

Eileen

Missing Cat, Day Four. I hadn't seen Fluffy Anne, but her food bowl had been emptied, so she'd come home, I thought. She just wasn't staying, from what I could see. Or she was hiding in one of the boxes in the garage just to vex me. Or that fat possum I saw nosing around the garage the other night had been eating her food and had lulled me into a false sense of security.

All Melanie's conversations included the theme of lost pets and hating boys, especially boys who get new pets for no good reason. Apparently, Charles had a new cat.

I assumed she was jealous because our neighbor's son got a new pet, which he apparently talked about incessantly at school. A dog, I also assumed, because the animal was named Spot, and I was told Charles was bragging at school about the different tricks he'd taught Spot.

I was actually unpacking today. I had the family room just about complete, only two more boxes of books and knickknacks to go. Melanie was so mopey, she wasn't interested in picking out where we'd eat tonight. The kitchen items were at long last unpacked, but I'd gotten in the habit of eating microwave meals and not having to clean the dishes. It's a nice, if expensive habit.

I'd tried several of those thirty-minute meals Bubba Rice touted on his Saturday morning cable access cooking show, but it always took me more like an hour and a half. Where is the truth in advertising?

"There's nothing to do," Melanie whined.

"Polly Pockets."

"You made me pick them up so you could vacuum."

She had a point. I would like to enjoy the clean, unpacked, perfectly arranged, if boringly neutral, den for twenty-four hours before Polly City returned.

"Draw me a picture."

"We haven't found my easel."

This is why I should have been more organized while packing. "You don't need an easel to draw a picture."

"But it's no fun without one."

"Fine," I said, placing a wrought-iron candelabra I'd forgotten about on the mantel. "So watch TV."

"There's nothing on."

"Why don't you go outside and play?" The words echoed in my head. My mom had often said that to me as a child. It's a weird feeling, almost like deja-vu, only I'd call it a 'deja-don't.' I hate sounding like my mother.

"There's nothing to do out there," Melanie whined, which I hate even more than saying things my mother said.

"Sure there is. Chalk yourself a hopscotch, bounce a ball, ride your bike, but put on your helmet if you ride."

Melanie sighed. "It'd be more fun if Fluffy Anne were here."

I had moved onto the dining room and was unpacking the rarely used fine wedding china by the time Melanie returned. "Mom! Mommy!" she called out.

Salad or dessert plate in hand, I wasn't sure which; I waved at the whirling dervish that was my daughter. "I'm in the dining room. What's wrong?"

"Charles stole my cat."

Stole her cat? No way. "Now why would he do that?"

"I don't know, maybe 'cause he's a boy. I'm calling the police."

I placed the plate atop others of the same size inside the cabinet. In the few seconds it took me to do so and walk into the kitchen, Melanie had already looked up the number from the magnet on the refrigerator and had punched the numbers of the police station into the phone.

"Hang that up," I said.

"But he stole my cat. He needs to be arrested."

The faint sound of Sandy Crane drawling hello came through loud and clear.

"Hey, this is Melanie. I'd like to report—"

I took the phone from my daughter's hand. "Sorry to have bothered you, Sandy. Melanie didn't mean to dial."

She crossed her arms over her chest and scowled. "Yes, I did."

"If there's something I can help you with, Miz Meyerson, I'd be happy to. Things aren't real busy today. A ride out to Yonder might be just the ticket for my mornin' sickness."

Sandy was pregnant, and town rumor was she was having problems, blood-pressure-wise. The last thing she needed to do was drive all the way out here on a bogus missing kitty case. "Don't worry about it, Sandy. It's nothing I can't handle."

Once I convinced Sandy that we were fine (it took about five minutes), I put the cordless receiver back in its cradle. I looked at Melanie. "Start explaining."

She wound a piece of hair around her finger. "Well, I went outside to play like you said. I was chalking a picture of Fluffy Anne on the driveway when I heard Charles telling his friends that he was going to show them Spot's tricks. I didn't care about his stupid dog. But then I heard him casting his fishing rod, and I see this cat chasing the toy on the end of the line. A cat that looks just like Fluffy Anne, except the collar was different."

"So Spot isn't a dog?"

"Nope. Spot is Fluffy Anne. And that Charles Finch stole her and is making her do tricks. Cats aren't supposed to do tricks."

"Are you sure it's Fluffy Anne?"

"Mm-hmmm. I checked. When I called her name, she looked at me. She's the same color as Fluffy Anne, with that one spot on her tail white. And Spot likes her back scratched right above her tail, just like Fluffy Anne. She even does that lip quivering thing when I scratch, just like Fluffy Anne. I scratched her right after I told Charles she was my cat. Spot is Fluffy Anne."

Maybe it was PMS or maybe it was frustration from spending most of Saturday unpacking and having little to no time for anything else, but I got a little hot. Who were these people? What made them think they could take a little girl's pet?

I rummaged in the kitchen desk drawer for the Mossy Creek phone directory I'd received when I moved in. I flipped through the alphabet until I found the Finch's number, underlined from last week, when I called about Charles pulling Melanie's hair. I figured I could be more civil on the phone than I could in person.

"Hello," a teenaged male voice said.

"Hi, this is Ms. Meyerson from across the street. I'd like to speak with your mother."

"Sure." Rustling noises. "Mom! Hey, get Mom, Mary Alice."

I heard Mary Alice call back. "Who is it?"

"I don't know. Some lady named Mrs. Meyerson."

"It's Ms. Not Mrs."

"What?"

"Just . . . get your mother."

At long last, a nearly breathless Mrs. Finch got on the phone. "Yes?"

"Hi. Mrs. Finch, this is your neighbor across the road. We moved in about a month ago. My daughter goes to school with Charles."

"Yes. I've been meaning to invite you over for iced tea and cookies but haven't had the time. And I'd like to apologize again for Charles pulling Melanie's hair. Could you excuse me for just a minute?" She paused and put her hand over the phone. "Mary Alice, where are your cleats? We have to go in five minutes. Randy, get out of the snack cooler. Those aren't for you." A huge sigh. "I'm sorry, you were saying?"

"I think Charles stole our cat."

Silence and not the good kind. "Stole? That's an awfully strong word, Mrs. . . . ."

"Ms., Ms. Meyerson." I wasn't going to offer my first name to the parent of a cat thief.

"Charles wouldn't steal someone's pet. Spot happens to be a stray he very kindly brought home."

"Spot is Fluffy Anne, a cat who has a fine home across the road."

Mary Alice started whining in the background that she had on her cleats and they needed to leave. "The cat that my son found was skinny and had no collar, no tags."

Maybe it wasn't Fluffy Anne. I covered the mouthpiece with my hand. "Are you sure?" I mouthed to Melanie.

Melanie nodded.

"Well, she had a collar last week. Pink velvet with a rhinestone F and A."

"Was she skinny?"

"No, she was normal."

"Then Spot isn't your cat. I can understand that your daughter's distressed what with your pet missing. Maybe you should put up some fliers if you haven't already."

"We haven't, and we don't need to now. We know she's at your house. We just want her back."

"Let me get this straight." Mrs. Finch's overly polite voice raised a notch to full-out irritation. "You'd rather accuse my son of stealing your cat than look for your cat. If you're so concerned, where are the fliers?"

"I beg your pardon?"

"If your cat was lost, why didn't you put out fliers?" She whispered away from the receiver, "Hush. I'm on the phone."

"What's going on?" A man, I'm assuming her husband, asked.

"I'll explain it all later. Take the child to her game for me. And don't forget the snacks."

I thumped the phone. "Mrs. Finch? Are you there? Are you done with your other conversations?"

She drew in her breath sharply as if I was the one being rude.

"As I was saying before you were distracted, our cat Fluffy Anne sometimes goes off."

"There might be a good reason for that," she tossed back, her tone still in the barely polite range.

My skin warmed from my chest up to the top of my scalp. "What exactly are you trying to say, Mrs. Finch?"

"If you let a cat roam around all the time outside, there's

a good chance they'll get lost."

"And if you don't, they get obese, which isn't healthy!" Why was I defending myself to this mother of a delinquent?

"Are you saying my other cat's obese?"

"I've never met your other cat. I've never set foot in your house. You could have a Gila monster for all I know."

"Charles would never take someone else's pet," she said with a sniff.

"Really?"

"Yes, really. You can ask him yourself. Charles?"

"Correct me if I'm wrong, Mrs. Finch, but I haven't seen any Found Cat fliers around the neighborhood either."

"Charles made fliers. He even went door to door."

"Not to my door, he didn't."

"Charles?" she called again.

"He ran out the back door with that cat," the teenager yelled.

Silence. I could almost hear what she was thinking. His actions sure did appear guilty. "My daughter cried herself to sleep last night thinking her cat was dead somewhere, and the whole time the cat's been at your house."

"I'm sorry that she's so distraught, but I really don't think Spot is Fluffy Anne."

"Melanie's so sure that she rang the police station. I told Sandy Crane I'd handle it myself. I don't think we need to bring Amos or Mutt out here." Yeah, I was milking it.

"Mrs. Meyerson, would you and your daughter like to come over when Charles returns from walking the cat? I'm sure we can resolve everything."

"'Resolve' meaning you're giving Fluffy Anne back," I said. I wished I'd gotten one of those microchips that Hank Blackshear could read and prove that Fluffy Anne was ours. "And it's Ms."

When Mrs. Finch called about an hour later, Melanie

grabbed Fluffy Anne's favorite brush from the basket where we keep her cat paraphernalia. It used to house my needlework, but I hadn't had much time to needlepoint nor had I found the rest of my sewing stuff.

If I ever move again, and I hope I won't, I will hire a professional organizer to pack and create a color-coded system and spreadsheet, so I can locate items easily. I'll hire someone to unpack me, too.

Melanie shook the fine-needled brush, then shoved it in her pocket. "If we need it, this'll prove it's Fluffy Anne."

Odd? Yes, but our cat likes the scent of her own dander.

We crossed the street, and I was about to knock when Mrs. Finch opened the door.

She smoothed her blue sweater set and ushered us in. Her guarded eyes quickly gravitated to my bare ring finger. "I haven't met Melanie's father."

"Divorced."

"I'm sorry," she said a little too stiffly.

"Don't be. It was a long time ago." I kept glaring at her but she wouldn't stop.

"I haven't seen him around."

"That's because he isn't. He lives in Florida." And about all Bruce did when it came to parenting was send the child support check, and not always in a timely manner.

Sympathy washed over her face. With that look, I knew she'd filled in the rest, that I was basically raising my child on my own, that Melanie was probably so attached to Fluffy Anne because her father barely acknowledged her existence, that I would do anything to get that cat back including writing her a check if that's what it took. And I would.

I brushed past her, and her cute, sleek, not a hair out of place short hairdo. I did note with a considerable bit of relish that her roots needed touching up and her house was far from immaculate. Her eyes widened as she noticed a pile of Legos on the coffee table stacked next to two glasses, one half-full of chocolate milk.

The fact that she wasn't perfect pleased me. Her den looked like kids and, apparently, a very large cat lived here.

Whoa. I focused on the obese beige tabby straddling the top of the overstuffed couch in their den. The cat glanced up at us briefly and resumed licking the skin between its toe pads.

Smile fixed, Mrs. Finch leaned over one of the seat cushions to remove a striped tube sock from the corner of the couch. She tried to hide the sock behind her back. "That's Biscuit."

"She sure looks like she's eaten a few," I quipped. "I guess I know why you thought Fluffy Anne was emaciated."

"Biscuit is an indoor cat," Mrs. Finch said by way of explanation. She gestured coolly toward the matching loveseat opposite the couch. "Won't you sit down?"

Melanie sunk into the soft cushion. "Where's Charles?"

"He's on his way home." She handed me a flier. "See? Charles did try to find Spot's owners."

The teenage son who was on the computer at a desk in the den snorted. "Yeah, Mom. He dumped them in the recycling."

Her mouth dropped open as she stared at her older son. She recovered pretty rapidly, though. "And why is this the first I'm hearing of it?"

He swung his overly long bangs out of his eyes, then shrugged. "I dunno. I figured if it was a problem, I'd mention it, which I just did, and if it wasn't, there was no need to rat on him."

Mrs. Finch shook her head. "This is why you were smart to stop at one."

The back door banged open. About two seconds later, it slammed closed.

"You're toast," Randy called out, earning a glare from his mother.

The sound of the door knob turning reached us.

"You leave this house, young man, and you'll lose gaming privileges for an entire month."

She sounded like she meant business, and that pleased me.

Charles dragged his feet into the den where we were sitting. He had the audacity to glare at my child. "What're you doing here?"

"I came to get my cat, the one you stole."

His mouth twitched as he fought off an impish smile. "Is it really stealing if the cat likes me better?"

Melanie blinked rapidly, her face turned red and, try as she might to hold it in, the sobs shook her little body. I wanted to spank that little boy. I wanted to tell Mrs. Finch what I thought of her mothering skills or lack thereof. But I couldn't find the words. All I could do is hold my crying daughter.

"Sweetheart," Mrs. Finch said, hands fluttering. "Honey, don't cry."

Melanie looked up, focused her tear-filled eyes on Charles, and screamed, "Just 'cause you can't have a dog doesn't mean you can take my cat!"

I was proud she'd slung something back at the brat until she caught her second wind and launched into the loudest crying jag I'd heard since Bruce announced he was moving to Ft. Meyers.

"Charles didn't mean to say something so cruel, did you, Charles?" Mrs. Finch prompted, waving her hand to encourage an apology.

Charles pouted. "Spot likes me. She wants to live here.

If she liked it fine at Smelanie's house, she'd have stayed there."

With the way she was clenching her fists, I could tell Mrs. Finch was ready to swat his backside. If only she would, we could get our cat and never grace their doorstep again.

"Melanie, don't listen to him," I said, hoping my voice was registering with her. "Fluffy Anne likes you. You raised her from a kitten. You even saved her when she got stuck under the porch at the house on Laurel Street when you called Chief Royden to help get her out."

Randy leaned back in his chair. "Can't you shut her up? She's, like, worse than Mary Alice."

Great. The Finch boys don't improve with age.

"Yeah," Charles said. "You're hurting my ears. And you look worse than usual with your face all crumpled and splotchy."

Melanie made an effort to control herself, but the sniffling continued between her words. "It's not like he doesn't already have a cat, Mommy. Why doesn't Fluffy Anne love me anymore? Why won't she come in here to be with me?"

Talk about an arrow to the heart. Now I was choking up. We'd had a similar conversation about her father not so long ago, when he'd canceled a visit she'd been looking forward to. "She does love you."

"But why is she staying away?"

Charles looked down at his feet. He mumbled something that only Randy could distinguish.

"Oh, no, you didn't." Randy snorted. "I thought I was bad when I was your age."

"I guess I can try to train her to like you again," Charles offered. "If I can get a puppy."

"Excuse me," Mrs. Finch said, fists still clenched. She barreled into her kitchen as if her bread was burning.

"What'd you do with her collar?" Melanie asked.

"Spot don't like sissy collars."

"Doesn't!" Mrs. Finch called from the other room. "I think I know why Fluffy Anne is keeping her distance, Melanie. And it has nothing to do with you."

The sound of a chair scraping the floor reached us. Seconds later Fluffy Anne bounded into the den and rubbed up against Melanie. The cat, I kid you not, was wearing a black leather collar with silver studs, a far cry from the cute pink velvet bling Melanie preferred. Fluffy Anne purred. She rolled onto her back, a sign of submission that little Charles would do well to learn.

Mrs. Finch gestured as she spoke. "He had her leash tied to the chair. Where's the Meyerson's collar, Charles?"

"I threw it away," he admitted, then had the audacity to sneer at my child. "Spot must feel sorry for you 'cause you're crying. Here, Spot. Here." He made clicking noises to draw the cat away from Melanie.

Mrs. Finch grabbed her son by the scruff of the neck. He flinched as she whispered something in his ear.

"Come back here, Fluffy Anne!" Melanie called.

The confused cat stopped midway between the children.

Charles frowned. "You can have her back, but only if I can come with you to walk her sometimes."

"No way," Melanie said, the sniffling vanishing for good. "Everyone will think you're my boyfriend."

"No they won't. I'll tell everyone at school I hate you, and I can even hit you on the playground if you want."

The skin on Melanie's forehead wrinkled. "If you hit me, I'm gonna hit you back."

That's my girl.

126

Nancy

"You need to apologize, young man," I said to my youngest, who seemed bent on becoming a delinquent, despite my best efforts to keep him on the right side of the law. I wondered if I could convince Amos, Mutt and Sandy to do a modified Scared Straight, involving a spend-the-night at the Police Station.

"I'm sorry," he said at long last.

"Say it like you mean it." My voice cracked under the strain of wanting to yell at my son, but not being able to do so in front of the neighbors. I'm sure Ms. Meyerson already had a running list of my faults as a mother. I didn't want to add to it.

"Oh, all right." He scowled. "I'm sorry I took your cat, Melanie."

I felt the need to reassure Ms. Meyerson, who had yet to offer her first name or a smile, that I wasn't a laissez-faire parent. "And Charles, your punishment will be to take care of Biscuit for every day you kept Fluffy Anne away from Melanie. You'll feed her, fill her water bowl, brush her, scoop her litterbox—"

"Aww, Mom!"

"I'm not finished. And you'll clean up her hairballs."

That earned a smile on par with the Mona Lisa. Ms. Meyerson leaned over and whispered something in her daughter's ear.

Melanie nodded.

"Could part of the punishment include Charles showing Melanie how to do those tricks he taught Fluffy Anne?" Ms. Meyerson asked.

"I don't see why not." I hoped doing something fun together might help ease the tensions between the kids. But I'd better supervise to keep him in line. "Would you be willing to show Melanie Spot's—I mean Fluffy Anne's—tricks?"

"If I hafta." Suddenly, his eyes brightened. "Hey, I have an idea. Maybe Fluffy Anne can spend the night with me every once in a while."

Jackpot. I now had my son right where I wanted him. I could see Mrs. Meyerson was ready to say no, so I raised my hand to stop her. "That's a fine idea if the Meyersons agree and if . . ."

He looked at me with such hope in his eyes. "If what?"

"If you get green slips every day for two weeks straight." Something he hadn't achieved all year. And I knew, like Dickens, that one day my Charles would look back on his sacrifice and know it was a far, far better thing that he did, than he'd ever done before.

Even Melanie, however, looked stunned at my stipulation.

Her mother tapped her finger against her jaw. "And if you're nice to Melanie at school, on the bus, and in the neighborhood," she added.

Charles groaned. "That's not fair."

"Was it fair to take her cat?" I asked.

"No." He kicked the corner of the couch, disturbing Biscuit, who jumped down and sauntered over to our neighbors for a sniff.

"All right," Charles said, lower lip distended in a pout. "But I get first dibs on any of Fluffy Anne's kittens."

Melanie rolled her eyes not quite with the expertise of Mary Alice, but she had a few more years to perfect it. "Fluffy Anne's been fixed. Don't you know anything? Besides, I thought you wanted a dog."

Charles slid a pitiful glance over to me, his eyes as big, sad, and round as a puppy. He was going for the kill. No mother can resist that look, not even me.

Then, I kid you not, ornery old Biscuit purred so loudly even Randy could hear her in the computer nook. The cat rubbed herself against little Melanie, even though the child had Fluffy Anne in her arms.

Charles looked from Biscuit to Fluffy Anne, then back to me. "Maybe we could trade."

"No!" Both Ms. Meyerson and I shouted at the same time, our voices resonating with an identical inflection.

We looked at each other and smiled. I think we might actually become friends.

Mossy Creek Gazette

VOLUME VII, No. THREE   MOSSY CREEK, GEORGIA

The Bell Ringer

Mossy Creek Rams Say "Bah" to Bigelow Schedule

Biggest Estate Sale Of The New Year This Saturday

by Katie Bell

After twenty years without a high school in Mossy Creek, owing to the dastardly destruction by (suspicious, elephant-related) fire of Mossy Creek High two decades ago, our beloved Mossy Creek Rams football team is gearing up for a historic ground-breaking ceremony at the new Mossy Creek High School complex this fall.

The Rams don't have a head coach yet, but the assistant coaches say the Rams' upcoming team promises an exciting new era for the Mossy Creek football legacy against rival Bigelow County High.

"We're not too durned thrilled to be playing our first season on Thursday nights in the Bigelow stadium until our digs are finished," said Mossy Creek star linebacker Tad "Slam" Abercrombie. "But we'll kick butt in Bigelow 'cause that's what Creekites always do."

The Mice that Roared

Part Four

Jayne

"You're home early," Ingrid said as I walked through the door to my upstairs apartment. She was my chief baby-sitter. Was insulted, in fact, if I used someone else.

"I know. Matt in bed?" I placed my purse on its customary spot, a small chest just inside the door.

"Just," Ingrid replied. "I checked on him about ten minutes ago, and he was sound asleep, the little lamb."

I dropped onto the overstuffed chair across from the sofa. "Good."

"So . . .?" Ingrid said. "How was your date?"

I shrugged. "It was okay."

"Just okay?"

I nodded. "We weren't halfway through the meal when I knew there's no spark between me and Dan McNeil."

"That's too bad." Ingrid idly stroked Bob's head.

The Chihuahua was stretched out beside her leg, his large head resting between his tiny paws, his bulbous eyes sleepily watching me. The little dog had never cottoned to me, although he'd learned to tolerate me. Bob didn't cotton to anyone much, except Ingrid. And Matt, now, too. Probably because his mistress loved my son so much.

"Yes, it is too bad," I agreed after a sigh. "He has such a nice rear en—"

"No need to get graphic."

I chuckled. I never knew when Ingrid was going to go all prudish on me. She was a dichotomy, opposing my use of the word "Naked" then showing up at the closing night party for *Sex and the City* I'd thrown at The Naked Bean. I didn't have a liquor license, of course, but since I'd made it a private party, I was able to serve Cosmopolitans instead of coffee. "You know that episode of *Sex and the City* where Miranda was told that guys don't call women back because they're just not that into them?"

"Of course I do," Ingrid said. "I'm not senile, you know."

"Believe me, I know that. It's just that that phrase kept ringing in my head all evening. And it went both ways. Dan gave every woman there the once over, and I spent more time thinking about you and Matt than I did talking with him. I brought it up over dessert and he agreed. We even laughed about it. There's a physical attraction and we could've taken it further. But what's the point?"

"Well, I'm still sorry," Ingrid said sincerely. "But you'll find someone, now that you've got it in your head to look. You're young and pretty and successful. Who wouldn't want you?"

I beamed at her across the coffee table. She was as loyal as my own mother. "I love you, Ingrid."

She smiled back. "I know you do, Jayne, and I love you, too. And Matt."

I nodded. "That's enough for me for now. I'll find someone eventually. Or not. I just know I won't settle for anyone who isn't totally *'into'* me."

"You shouldn't."

I decided to change the subject. "Any mouse sightings while I was gone?"

"Four," Ingrid said, placing her bookmark in the library book she'd been reading. Ingrid loved romance novels. The more raw sex in them, the better. "No, make that five. Two came out at the same time."

I groaned. "What am I going to do? Dan seems to think they'll disappear once all the work's done. But it's going to be several months before the apartment is finished, and that's if everything goes right, which I've been told over and over, it never does."

"There *have* been fewer mice in the shops since he finished there. Maybe he's right." Ingrid stood, tucked Bob into the crook of her left arm, then picked up her purse.

"Maybe so." I got up to let her out.

"If we have to tent the place, you and Matt can stay with me."

"I know. Thanks. It's looking more and more like that's what we'll have to do."

"Why are you hesitating, then?"

"It's bad publicity. Everyone would know that we have mice. Might keep our customers away. Plus, the poison gets all over everything. We'd be scrubbing for weeks. And what if a mouse died inside the wall? The stink!"

Ingrid paused at the door. "Why not get another cat? One that *will* kill the mice." She glared across the room at Emma, who was curled up in the lap of the largest clown in my husband Matt's clown collection. Ingrid must've taken it down from the shelf above Matt's bed for him to play with.

"Trouble is, you never know what kind of cat you're going to get. If I adopt one, it might take after Emma. Then I'd be stuck with two useless cats."

Ingrid brightened. "Borrow one. The Ramseys have a good mouser. I think her name is Scarlet."

"Well, now, that's a possibility. I could pay them. Cat rent." I grinned.

Ingrid turned to leave. "They wouldn't take a dime, I'm sure, but their boy, Keith, sure loves my chocolate chunk cookies. I'd say that would be a good trade."

"Indeed. 'Cats Who Work for Cookies.' I can see the sign now."

"You go ahead and make jokes. I'll call Emma Ramsey in the morning."

I gave her a hug. "That'd be great. Thanks."

"Water which is too pure holds no fish."

—Ts'ai Ken T'an

Sam's Pond

"Why is it every time I talk to you lately we end up in an argument?"

"Because you don't listen, Dad!"

I watched my seventeen-year-old son stand, the quick angry move sending the ladderback chair crashing to the kitchen floor.

I stared at him, stunned on several levels. First and foremost was the sudden realization that Joseph Buchanan Greene, or Buck as he's known in our family, was no longer a little boy. He stood even with my own six-foot-one height and was broad-shouldered. He'd have no trouble sailing through the physical requirements for a West Point appointment. He had the same brown hair color as I did, something I might not have noticed months earlier, before I retired from the Army and grew mine out a little. He had his mother's lush green eyes.

The second realization was how differently Buck talked to me than how I did to my father. I cowered in fear before my father and his fists, to be honest. There was a world of difference between my reaction to my son's defiance and the way my father would have responded. Though I was proud I had a son who wasn't afraid to voice his opinion, Buck's outspoken anger and disrespect were pushing all my authority buttons.

"In case you haven't noticed, Dad," Buck continued, his voice still loud as he lifted his backpack. "I learned to manage without you for a lot of years. Now you've retired from the Army and you treat me like a kid you can order around. I agreed to apply to West Point. I'm doing what you want me to do. But I'm not a raw recruit quaking in my boots." He walked out of the kitchen.

"All I did is ask if you'd completed your Candidate Questionnaire," I said, following him out onto the deck. "Don't walk away from me, mister. I didn't say you're dismissed." A movement caught my attention and I glanced across the yard to see my wife Meredith and our daughter Grace talking with our new neighbor, Erma. Great. An audience.

Meredith and Grace, of course, were aware of the way Buck and I seemed to constantly knock heads lately. We'd only been residents here in Mossy Creek for a few short weeks, and I didn't want to give Erma any fuel for a potential gossip fire. I held up a hand to prevent Meredith from coming over and running interference.

"Buck," I said, trying to sound more like a father than a commanding officer. Buck had an opportunity that I wasn't prepared to let him toss aside. If I had to, I'd fill out the damn questionnaire myself. "Can't you see that I just want to help you with your future?"

"I don't need your help."

That declaration stopped me short. What parent wants to hear their child no longer needs them?

Buck slammed behind the wheel of the truck, gunned the engine and backed up. I thought his temper was going to carry him all the way to school but he stopped by the break in the hedges between the yards and barked, "Let's go, Grace."

I let out a breath when he drove down the driveway more carefully. Not sure what else to do, I walked over to my wife, Meredith, who slipped her hand into mine and squeezed. I looked at our neighbor.

"Morning, Miz Erma."

"Sam. Having a rough morning?"

"Not one of my better ones, that's for sure."

"I've always thought parenting had a lot in common with gardening."

I took a long look around, at the bright flowers and green bushes. I knew the names of a few plants. Most I didn't. From Meredith I knew Miz Erma was a member of the Mossy Creek Garden Club and known throughout the county for her spring garden. Whatever that meant. I did know that Miz Erma's shirts tended to have enough colorful blooms to rival those in her garden.

"Then I'd say you're an expert at both."

She laughed. "I don't know of any parent who claims to be an expert. Mostly they love and tend what they have." She brushed a hand over a lanky bush filled with bright yellow blooms. "Take this forsythia for instance," she said and then moved over to another plant, one I recognized as the pink bloom of an azalea. "Any good gardener can clip and trim this bush into a form that's to their liking. Or. . ." She eyed me. "They can let it grow the way it wants."

"How do you know which way is best?"

"Depends on the plant. And how strong the root is."

I took another long look around the garden. "It's hard to argue with your wisdom." Then I looked over my shoulder and winced at the barren landscape of our backyard. "The shape of our yard doesn't say much for either my gardening or my parenting."

"I imagine you've been busy getting things set to rights inside. You've got time yet to get to the outside."

"I've been asking Erma for some pointers for our garden," Meredith said.

"Oh?" I look at her with a smile. "We have one?"

"I can only wish."

I'd been responsible for hundreds of soldiers going into battle. I planned strategy with other Army officers and briefed the President. I faced the grief of families of soldiers who made the ultimate sacrifice. I survived my early years with the pain of both fists and words from my own father.

Hearing the envy now in my wife's voice presented me with a dilemma I had no earthly idea how to handle.

I'd be the first to admit I had no skill with dirt and flowers, but this was something Meredith so obviously wanted. The more I thought about it after we returned to our home, the more I knew it would be nice to have something to show off, something that would stand as a visible sign that we'd planted roots here in Mossy Creek. So I did what every person does when faced with the unknown—I searched the Internet. And I found something I thought might work.

"A garden pond?" Meredith asked when I told her my idea later that afternoon.

I heard the pleasure in her voice, saw the excitement sparkling in her green eyes. That's all it took for me. Whatever the odds, whatever the cost, I'd do it for her.

"Oh, Sam. Are you sure?" she asked.

"Well, I admit I ran it by Miz Erma, and she seemed to think we have a good yard for it. She said she'd asked some of the other ladies in the Garden Club if they had any advice. And I found all this information on the web."

"It looks like an awful lot of work."

"What else do I have to do?"

"Sam? Are you sorry you retired and moved here?"

"No, it was the right thing to do, the right time. I'm just feeling a little lost with too much time on my hands."

"Is that all it is?" Meredith pressed. "Are you sure it's because you don't know what to do or is it because Buck won't do what you think he should?"

"He says I don't listen."

"You don't. You expect him to want what you think he should want." She laid a hand over mine. "Exactly the way you expected the troops under you to follow your orders.

Sam, explain to him why it's important to you for him to go to West Point."

I knew she was right, but the discipline and pride the Army had given me made it difficult to do as she asked. Officers didn't explain orders. The men under me had always delivered a crisp salute, then did as they were told. And since I'd been a General, nearly all the men I came into contact with on a daily basis were under me.

Until a few years ago, my son had done the same. Then he'd turned into a *teenager*.

What was so wrong with my wanting him to apply to West Point? For my wanting the very best in life for him?

If he only knew what my life had been like before I'd joined the Army. I shuddered to think of what it might have been like if I hadn't been given that chance.

The next day I went into town. While I'd collected a good deal of information from the Internet and could no doubt find more, I decided to do some local reconnaissance. Along the way I hoped to meet and get to know some of my new neighbors. My first stop was Lloyd Pritchard's Landscaping on the northeast side of town, along the road to Yonder.

"Been expecting you," he said when I entered. "Miz Erma told me I should look over that stuff you got from the Internet about the machinery you're going to need to run the pump for the waterfall and filter. Make sure it's not heading you in the wrong direction."

It had been years since anyone questioned my decisions, and I bristled at Lloyd's interference. Still, I supposed I'd opened that door when I asked for Miz Erma's advice about the pond in the first place. And wasn't that sense of community, the comfort of knowing you had friends and neighbors who cared enough to be aware of your business, one reason why Meredith and I wanted to live in a small town like Mossy Creek?

"I appreciate you taking the time to do this."

"No problem," Lloyd assured me. "So, you doing this pond 'cause your wife's got her heart set on one? Or 'cause you're at loose ends?"

"A little of both, I guess."

"I know if I had a wife as pretty as yours, I'd do whatever it took to keep her happy."

I gave him my sharpest do-you-know-who-you're-talking-to glare. "Is that so?"

Lloyd grinned, so amused at my jealousy that I couldn't help but relax.

"Are you married?" I asked him.

"Yup. Don't stop me from appreciating good-lookers, though. 'Sides, it's more fun to talk about other people than be the one talked about, and since Valentine's Day there's been plenty to talk about. We got Sandy Crane and her husband expecting a baby. Her husband, Jess, is a writer just like your wife." Before I could question how Lloyd knew Meredith was a writer, he hurried on. "Then there's the fact that Colonel Del Jackson . . ." Lloyd looked up from his workbench. "Did you know him during your Army days, General?"

"*Sam* will work just fine and no, I didn't know him."

Lloyd nodded. "I thought maybe that's why you picked Mossy Creek to settle down. Anyway, Del and Mayor Ida were seeing one another but Del left to go back to his ex-wife, leaving the path wide open for Chief Royden." He went on, filling me in on more of the local gossip. After paging through several catalogs and his own parts inventory, Lloyd said, "Okay. I can build you a pump that'll do the trick."

"Oh. I was just asking for your opinion on which one to order."

"I'll give you a better pump for the money than anything you can get on the Internet. Then there's the electrical wiring you'll need for lighting and such. I'll get you all set up, don't worry. Now, how about fish?" he asked, already punching numbers on his telephone. "Hank? I've got the new guy, Sam Greene, here. Yeah." Lloyd nodded to whatever Dr. Blackshear, the local veterinarian, asked. "Yeah, he's the one. He and his son are gonna be putting in a garden pond, so I'm sending him over so you can tell him about the fish he'll need."

And like that, over my protests, I found myself standing outside Lloyd's shop with a pond pump, filter and lighting in the works and an appointment with the local veterinarian to talk fish. Still, it was hard to resent Lloyd's bulldozing tactics. I liked the man.

"You look a little shell-shocked, General."

I blinked and turned to see that Police Chief Amos Royden had pulled up right behind me in his squad car. He was younger than I expected. "Call me Sam. And yes, it feels that way. I didn't even know you were there until you said something."

The chief glanced at Lloyd's shop and smiled. "I know what you mean. You and your family settling in?"

"We are. Thanks. Nice town you've got here, Chief."

"We like it. I hear you're putting in a garden pond."

I didn't bother to question how he knew. "Yes, sir. The wife's wanted one for a long time." I considered what Lloyd had told me. "I was just heading over to the mayor's office to see whether or not I needed a building permit."

"Can't see why you would."

"That's what I thought but figure it couldn't hurt to stop by and introduce myself."

"I'm sure the mayor will be happy to talk with you. Well, see you around."

Remembering that Hank Blackshear was waiting, I decided to stop at the mayor's office another day.

When I drove up to the Blackshear Veterinary Clinic I was greeted by a firm handshake from Hank. I was surprised to see his wife, Casey, in a wheelchair. She held their little adopted daughter on her lap. I knelt down to LiLi, who looked at me shyly. The child had some development issues that worried her parents.

"I have a little girl, too," I told her. "Her name is Grace. She was named after a girl I once tutored in math. That's how I met my wife, as a matter of fact. Little Grace was Meredith's neighbor. She'd been adopted by the base chaplin and his wife, an army nurse, though she had a congenital heart condition." I smiled sadly. "She could come up with the most outrageous comments, most of the time aimed at how she felt my and wife's relationship should develop."

"That's a lovely story," Casey said. "Have you kept in touch with her? The first Grace?"

"We did, yes. Unfortunately she succumbed to her condition last year, just a few months after Meredith's father passed away. That's another reason I want to give Meredith this pond. She needs something to bring happiness back into her life."

Hank spoke up. "There's a good koi farm down toward Atlanta. I could drive you down there whenever you want to go."

"Oh, you don't have to go to any trouble. Just give me the address and I'll find it."

"No trouble. In fact, depending on how your pond turns out, Casey and I are thinking of putting in one here at the clinic."

By time I left the Blackshear's, Hank had decided when we'd make the trip to Atlanta, and Casey had extended an invitation for Meredith, the kids and me to come to dinner the following Friday evening.

🐾🐾🐾

"You what?" Buck asked me later that night when I stood in the immaculate doorway of his room. Like the physical fitness requirements, the boy would have no problem keeping up with the Academy's policy on neatness. Buck lay stretched out on the bed, not studying but flipping through a magazine. He'd probably ace whatever test he wasn't studying for, I thought with equal twists of pride and envy. Every decent grade I'd ever gotten was earned with sweat and hours of study.

"I'd like your help digging a garden pond in the back yard," I repeated.

"Why?"

Calling on my tactical training, I went after his weak spot. "This is something your mom's always wanted, but I never could give it to her before. Now I can. Will you help?"

"I guess." His lips twitched. "What makes you think you know how to do this?"

"It's a pond. Dig a hole, fill it with water." I grinned when Buck goggled at me. "Hey, I'm not stupid. I looked up information on the Internet, talked with a few people in town. And I figure since you did that science project on eco-systems a year or so back, you'd know some things."

"Yeah, right, like you'd listen to anything I said."

"Depends on what you have to say. Right now, though, I'm more interested in your back and arm muscles. We start two weeks from Saturday. Early," I tacked on when he groaned. Then I tossed the folder of papers I'd brought along onto his bed. "Read over these, if you don't mind. Let me know what you think."

"Wait!"

I turned back to see he'd sat up.

"You're talking about digging this thing by ourselves? With shovels?"

"Yep."

"Have you seen the dirt out there? It's hard, red clay. The stuff they use to make bricks."

"Would you rather spend the morning filling out your

Candidate Questionnaire?"

He looked me square in the eye, man to man. "I'll work you under the table."

"We'll see."

❦❦❦

The next day I was outside, pounding marking sticks into the ground for the dimensions of the pond when Buck came home from Bigelow County High. I wished Mossy Creek's new high school was already open. It was a long drive down to the south end of Bigelow County. At least Grace would be able to transfer closer to home once the new school opened.

"Hey," he said as he climbed out of his truck.

"Hey. Where's your sister?"

"Tryouts. Track team."

I wanted to ask if he planned to get involved in any sport but wasn't in the mood for another argument. "Is it different this time?" I asked instead. He looked at me. "You know, because this is the last move." And suddenly the thought of him leaving kicked me in the stomach.

"Kinda." He glanced around the yard, shook his head a little. "This isn't where you're planning to dig the pond, is it?"

"What's wrong with it?"

"You want a waterfall, right?"

"Of course."

He nodded, then walked to a spot farther up the yard by a good hundred feet. "Then we need to start it here." He gestured with his hands, and I could practically see the enthusiasm pumping out of him. "It'll look more natural, like it's always been here, coming out of the woods."

"But it's so far from the deck. I was hoping your mom and I could sit out on the deck and listen to the waterfall."

"I get that. But it's wrong."

I stepped forward, ready to get into that argument, after all, when I realized he was caught up in whatever was going on in his head. I was losing command here, but for once I didn't mind.

"You've got to work with what you've got," Buck said. "You can't go against the way nature would have the water flow. This is the best way." He looked at me hard and I got the vague sense he meant something more than where to place a garden pond. "Do you understand, Dad?"

"I'm trying."

"Okay." He walked down to where I stood. "I can't believe I'm going to suggest this 'cause it's going to mean more back-breaking work, but what we can do is enlarge the deck." He took the mallet and a stick from the ground where I'd left them. "Bring it out to here." He pounded the stick in. "Have it a few steps down from the original, like it's another level. Or we could make a stone patio and have a fire pit."

"I like the patio idea."

I watched him smile—my little boy again. The infant who smiled hello as he lifted his arms to be picked up. The toddler who squealed with delight as he rode on my shoulders. The Little Leaguer who grinned as wide as the gap in his front teeth when he spotted me in the stands after he hit his first home run.

"It's going to mean a lot more work," he warned.

And more time together—a definite bonus. "Draw it up," I told Buck. "I'll talk to your mom."

"I still think you should consider hiring a backhoe."

"Now why . . ." I slapped him on the back. ". . . would I spend good money when I've got free slave labor?"

It took Buck two days to finish the drawing. I was stunned by the detail, which included placement of bushes and flowers. I had no idea my son could draw.

After Buck and Grace left for school, and Meredith went

upstairs to her office to write, I stepped onto the deck and compared the drawing to the yard.

Miz Erma reared up from behind a shrub in her yard, where she'd been planting or weeding, wearing another blindingly bright shirt with a pair of jeans which she used to wipe the dirt off her hands.

"Morning, Sam. I hear that boy of yours drew up some plans for your garden pond. Mind if I see them?"

Since she waved me toward her patio table, where a pitcher of what looked like sweet tea sat, I headed over. As I spread out Buck's drawing, I didn't bother to ask how she knew about it. I liked my new neighbors and figured there would come a time when I appreciated the fact that they felt they could be part of my personal business. I wasn't sure right now was one of those times.

"Your boy's got a good eye and seems to have a talent for gardening." A gnarled finger with a thin line of dirt under the nail tapped one section. "Oh, the butterfly bushes will be great here. But I'd reconsider putting the roses in there. That's too close to those back woods and the deer will eat them down to the ground in no time, thorns and all." She went on to compliment the choice and placement of flowers, the names of which my son apparently knew well enough to pick, ending with a comment that had my back going stiff.

"I'd say the boy has the makings of a dandy horticulturalist. He might want to talk with Harry Rutherford. He's a Professor of Environmental Biology studying the effects of acid rain up on Mount Colchik."

"Buck's going to West Point."

"Ahhh." She studied my face. "Like his daddy?"

"His granddaddy. Meredith's father. I never had the honor. I came up through the ranks the hard way."

She poured tea into two glasses, offered me one and drank deeply of hers. "Seems like it worked out well enough for you."

"Yes, ma'am. But I'd like for Buck to have a better start."

"A body would be hard-pressed to have a better start in life than having parents who love you."

Was it enough? I questioned over the course of the next several days. It was, without a doubt, more than I'd had for the first miserable sixteen years of my life. I had vague memories of my mother, memories that were often blurred by the black and blue bruises left on her from my father's fists. At least I'd never hit my children. Or my wife. Even when the kids had been younger and needed—deserved—a spanking, I left that to Meredith. The risk of what one strike might unleash inside of me frightened me more than any enemy or battlefield I'd ever faced.

I never told my kids about that black time in my life, though Meredith often encouraged me to do so. What would it accomplish? Like any parent, I didn't want them to have any reason to think less of me. Instead, I made sure they had every opportunity available. And I had no intention of standing aside and letting Buck turn up his nose at the best opportunity he'd have in his life.

When Saturday morning arrived, I lay in bed waiting for the sun to come up, as excited as a kid on Christmas morning.

"Sam . . ." Meredith sighed and turned to face me in the bed. "If you keep on tossing and turning, you're going to be too worn out to do any digging."

"I'm sorry, I didn't mean to wake you." I squirmed. "I'm looking forward to building this pond, Meredith. More so than anything I've done in quite a while. Part of it's because I know how much you want one and there's the time I'll spend with Buck. But I also want to make this home really ours in a way we've never had the chance to do before. To feel part of a community."

"It's two hours until sunrise." She cupped a hand on my cheek and leaned in to kiss me. "If you're not going to sleep, why don't we make good use of the time?"

Later, when I stood outside Buck's door, nerves had replaced the excitement. I started to knock but something inside my chest urged me to just open the door. Buck slept as he'd done since an infant—head completely buried under the covers. I crossed the room and nudged the lump my best guess said could be a shoulder. "Rise and shine, son. There's a shovel outside with your name on it." There was a groan but the blanket moved and Buck's messy head poked out. "Mom's making us breakfast. You've got five."

I had to give my son credit. He never balked during that first day. He did as I told him, did what I asked of him and worked hard. In fact, he worked with more enthusiasm than I expected. Miz Erma came over to check on our progress and, of course, Meredith stopped us from time to time with cold drinks.

In the late afternoon we paused when a vehicle turned up our driveway.

"Hey, Buck," a teenaged girl called in a flirty voice from her side of the back seat. She was one of five girls inside the car.

"Someone you know?" I teased.

"They're all on Grace's cross-country team." He waved, and Grace shot out of the house carrying a duffle bag.

"Bye Daddy," she called as she piled into the crowded back seat. "See ya tomorrow." She leaned back out the window. "Buck? You coming tonight?"

"Not sure," he called, then explained to me. "The team is making banners for next week's meet, then there's a party followed by a sleep-over."

"What kind of party?"

"Chill out, Dad. I wouldn't let Grace go if the kids were that kind."

"What do you mean you wouldn't?"

He shrugged and bent for the pickaxe. With strong sure strokes he lifted the weighted tool and planted it fork-side down to break the hard-packed red clay into chunks.

"I keep an eye out for her and the kids she hangs with."

"You do?"

He took a few more swings and then stopped to look at me. "When you went on that first tour to Iraq, you told me to keep an eye on Mom and Grace." He plunked down the axe again. "I make sure she doesn't get into any trouble."

"Good God, Buck. That was six years ago."

"Yeah."

"You weren't much more than a kid yourself."

He stopped and looked me in the eye. "You trusted me. I wasn't going to let you down." He shrugged again, obviously dismissing my surprise.

I felt something hard in my chest break into chunks as surely as the red clay at my son's feet.

As clear as a photograph I could see it—the taste of tears on Meredith's lips as I kissed her one last time, the feel of Grace's face buried in my neck, the hard floor under one knee as I squatted in front of Buck. He was trying so hard not to cry as he stood tall and at attention. His eyes had been serious as he listened to me ask him to look out for his mom and sister, as he nodded understanding and acceptance of the request I made of him.

I felt a moment's shame that I'd expected so much of so young a boy—and immense pride that he'd followed those orders even to this day.

"I know you never had a brother," Buck said. I blinked and brought my son back into focus. "I always figured that's why it was so important to you that we all look out for one another. You know, since neither you nor Mom had a brother to look out for you."

I could have corrected him, could have told my son something I'd only told two other people in this world. But wasn't it more important to express faith in his future than to expose a shadow from my past?

"You're going to make a helluva good officer one day, Buck." My son stared at me for a long moment, and I wished I'd said something else.

Then he cocked his hip so he could slide his chirping cell phone out of his pocket.

"Hey, what's up?" he answered while continuing to hold my gaze. "Not sure, let me check with the General." He held the phone away from his ear. "How much longer are we going to dig?"

"This about the party?" He nodded. "Go ahead." I gestured toward the ground. "You deserve a break after all you did today."

Buck completed his call and climbed out of the shallow hole. As he walked away, I again felt frustrated over not ever saying the right thing to my son.

"Buck?" I called on impulse.

He glanced over his shoulder.

"Thanks for your help today."

He nodded and went inside.

I did a little more half-hearted digging until Buck came out and took off in his truck. Meredith came out quick on his heels.

"What happened?"

"Nothing." I rammed the shovel into the clay dirt and avoided my wife's knowing look. "Buck had a party he wanted to go to. I told him I thought we'd done enough for the first day."

"And yet you're out here still digging." When I didn't answer she sighed. "Sam, why don't you take your own advice and stop, too? Come inside, take a shower and I'll treat you to dinner out."

❧❧❧

Over the course of the next few weeks, people felt obligated to stop by and observe, and occasionally question, the progress of the pond.

Harry Rutherford came by. I'd seen a lot of scarred men during my army days, but the burn scars on his face made even me wince. They surprised me even more because no one had mentioned them. Everyone in town spoke of "Dr. Rutherford" with respect and a little bit of awe, but no one mentioned the scars. Were they so accustomed to them, they no longer saw them?

After talking to me, he had a conversation with Buck—one I wasn't able to overhear since they were at the spot where the waterfall would begin. What I did see was the easy camaraderie between the two of them as they talked.

Hank Blackshear stopped by to suggest I visit a piece of land just outside Bigelow, where a builder was clearing a spot to build another new subdivision. "Free rocks," the veterinarian explained. Bigelow kept expanding. One year soon it would become a full-fledged *city* instead of the large, affluent town it was today. I was beginning to understand why Creekites remained wary of every Bigelowan encroachment on their pristine mountain world.

I spent a couple of days while Buck was in school hauling rock from the excavated ground. Hank came along one day and helped. It was after a long day of hauling rocks by myself that I went into the house, tired and dirty, to find an unexpected and unwelcome delivery.

The fish.

Five minutes later, I was on the phone to the fish farm. "What do you suggest I do? We're nowhere close to having a pond ready for fish. I specifically asked you to wait to send them until after I called to say it was ready." I used my thumb and forefinger to massage the throb between my eyes. My knuckles were white where they gripped the cordless receiver.

After a list of suggestions, blissfully short, there was another apology.

"Thanks," I managed when the caller offered to send a peace offering of a bag of feeding pellets. "I just hope they're alive to eat them."

I clicked off the phone. Computer error be damned. How the hell was I suppose to keep four expensive koi fish alive until Buck and I finished digging the pond and had all the filters in place?

I glanced through the stack of mail sitting on the center of the kitchen table, distracted by my frustration until I came across a letter for Buck . . . from the University of Georgia School of Horticulture.

It felt like a kick in the gut, coming face-to-face with the fact that Buck was doing this on his own while ignoring all my pleas for him to fill out his West Point application.

I wanted nothing more than to toss the envelope in the trash. I'd be damned if I let my son throw away the opportunity of a lifetime so he could play in the dirt.

Then I stopped. Had I made the situation worse by getting him involved in creating this garden pond? Would my attempt to get closer to my son end up pushing him further away?

"What did the fish farm say?" Meredith asked.

I glanced over to where she sat on the floor beside the Styrofoam box the fish came in. "Someone ignored the note on the computer to delay the delivery."

Meredith looked down into the box and slowly swirled a finger in the water. The fish had come in plastics bags, but we'd opened them to give them more oxygen.

"They're so pretty," she said and all of my temper disappeared. "Like butterflies that swim."

I remembered our honeymoon in Hawaii. She said much

the same thing the first time we saw a koi pond.

"The breeder did tell me how to take care of them until we get the pond finished," I reassured her.

The rest of my day was spent at the *I Got It Store,* yet another of Mossy Creek's quirky local businesses, where citizens could find everything from extra-short extension cords to iron fry pans. I found a container that would give the fish ample swimming room, and then I went over to Lloyd Pritchard's for his help in constructing a system to pump oxygen into the container. I had everything good to go, or so I thought, by the time Buck got home from school.

"You can't just leave it out here in the open like this," he said waving a hand over the child's swimming pool I'd placed in a corner of the deck. "It's unprotected. Didn't you read any of that research I did for you? Animals like raccoons or even plain cats can reach in and have a picnic. By morning the only place your fish will be swimming is in the stomachs of their killers. Good grief, Dad, if the Army is filled with a bunch of morons who can't figure out something as simple as this, I'll have my General star *years* before you got yours."

His teenaged arrogance tripped the trigger inside me. My fear of turning into my own father had made me go too easy on Buck.

Maybe it was the physical exhaustion of digging the pond or the frustration of the day's events. Maybe it was the still-new adjustment to civilian life. Maybe it was the continuing tension between Buck and me and his questioning my ability to solve a problem. Maybe it was that damn envelope sitting on the kitchen table—a physical reminder that Buck didn't respect all I had accomplished and hoped for him in the future.

All I knew was that Buck's words and the tone of his voice jolted me back to my childhood.

Instead of standing in the spring sunshine, I cowered in a corner of a shabby house. Instead of looking at my son who I would die to protect, my vision filled with the image of my father standing over me, swinging his fists and shouting in a drunken voice about what a failure I was. Calling me a moron.

Something broke inside of me.

I lunged for Buck.

He stood close to the house, so instead of sending us over the side of the deck, I pinned his shoulders to the brick wall. I stood toe-to-toe and got in his face the way a drill sergeant or officer had done to me during basic. The way my drunken father had done too many times to count.

"Don't you dare talk to me that way! I'm not stupid. I'm not worthless. *I am not a moron!* I made something of myself, something I'm proud of even if you can't be." I slammed him against the wall again.

"Dad," Buck said. His voice broke. He stared at me as if he'd never seen me before.

As quickly as the haze came, it disappeared. No longer were the past and present confused in my mind. I'd done something I'd lived in fear of doing my entire life. I'd lost control.

Sick shame swam in my stomach as I saw the horror in my son's eyes. With forced slowness I released him and stepped back. In my peripheral vision, I saw Meredith and Grace watching at the screened back door.

"Did I hurt you?"

"No. Just scared me a little." He jammed his hands into the front pockets of his jeans and hunched his shoulders. "Dad," he said as quietly as before. "I *am* proud of you. I've always been proud of you." Tears swam in his eyes, hitting me in the heart as surely as a sniper's bullet might have. "What I said . . . I didn't mean anything. How could you think I think you're a moron? It was just temper talking."

"Son, I've seen soldiers destroyed as much by words as by bombs and bullets. I've held the hands of men dying with their bodies torn up, their blood pouring out of their wounds. Searching for the right thing to say to them was nearly as hard as watching them die. I've fought my temper since I was a kid. Not just to keep myself from using my fists to dominate my loved ones the way my father did, but to keep from saying mean or stupid or outright cruel words. My father could destroy people with either his fists or his mouth. Words *do* matter."

Buck's face went sheet white. "Dad, you've never told us any of that stuff before. I didn't know about your father . . . why didn't you tell us?"

The way I saw it I had two choices—continue to ignore the past and hope I didn't repeat anything close to this behavior. Or I could face my fears and let my kids know how much I love them by finally giving them my trust along with the truth. When faced with an enemy, sometimes the best course of action was face-to-face confrontation.

I thought about suggesting we go inside and sit, as families do, at the kitchen table. But I needed to be outside, in the sunshine, surrounded by the garden I hoped would represent the roots we were planting here. I needed to be in the center of what I'd made of my life.

I waved a hand at Meredith and Grace. "C'mon outside. If I'm going to finally do this, I only want to go through it once." Meredith reached for my hand and squeezed lightly. That one touch, that one show of faith and love gave me the courage I needed.

After taking a deep breath, I started. "My father was a miserable drunk. He worked odd jobs, or pawned stuff he managed to steal. He stole even more when my older brother grew up enough to help him."

"You have a brother?" Grace asked.

"I let you believe I was an only child because I was

ashamed of my family. My brother's nine years older then me and was the spitting image of my father in looks and temper. Most of the money the two of them got from thieving they used to buy booze."

"That's why you never drink," Buck said.

"That's right. When the old man wasn't beating my mom or me, he used words to belittle us, to make us feel worthless. His favorite taunt was that I was too stupid to ever amount to anything."

Grace let out a small gasp and reached for her mother's hand, but I continued to look Buck in the eye. "I believed him, especially the night he knocked me out cold after throwing me against the wall when I tried to get between him and my mom. When I woke the next morning, my mom was gone. He had a field day with that one for the next two years, always saying it was my fault that she left. Who would want me when I was too stupid to do anything right? Then I came home one afternoon and he and my brother were gone, too. I was sixteen."

"They left you alone?" Grace asked.

"I didn't care. For once I didn't have to worry about someone beating me or yelling at me. But I also didn't have food. So I did what I'd seen my old man do. I stole from a convenience store. It didn't take long for me to get caught." I smiled at the memory. "Only instead of being thrown to the cops, the store owner told me he knew about my father and brother taking off. He gave me two choices. I could end up like them or he could pull a few strings to get me enlisted and let the Army make a man of me."

"At sixteen?" Buck asked with something like awe in his voice.

"The Army gave me the chance I would never have had otherwise. I had three squares a day, a bed with clean sheets, money of my own and I didn't have to worry about getting a beating. For the first time in my life I didn't feel stupid or worthless. When I received orders to Fort Benning I met your maternal grandfather and he saw to it that I completed my degree. I got more than I'd ever had then, too." Meredith and I shared a smile before I looked back at Buck.

"That's why I've pushed for you to go to West Point, so it won't be so hard for you. You'll have advantages I never did. Do you understand?"

"Yes sir." He stood. "I'm sorry, sir, if I said anything to make you think I don't respect you, because I do, very much. Now, sir, let's get this fish situation settled so I can get to work on my Candidate Questionnaire."

For the next two weeks Buck and I worked on the pond with none of the previous tension between us. He dutifully completed all the paperwork and additional requirements for his admission application to West Point.

One afternoon Miz Erma brought by members of the Mossy Creek Garden Club, and I watched my son patiently answer questions and discuss plantings. While I couldn't fault my son's diligence while we worked together, I had to admit this was the only time during those two weeks that I saw a spark of enthusiasm for the work.

It was the day we had a backyard party to show off the completed pond and waterfall for all of our new neighbors and friends when I overheard a conversation between my son and Peggy Caldwell, a member of the Mossy Creek Garden Club.

"Did you ever hear back about your application from the School of Horticulture at UGA?" Peggy asked.

"Yes, ma'am. I was accepted."

"Oh, Buck that's wonderful. Your parents must be thrilled."

"I'm going to West Point, Mrs. Caldwell. It's what my Dad wants."

"What about what *you* want, Buck?"

"There are worse things than a career in the Army. I'll be fine. To be honest, it feels like this is the way I've been heading my whole life. Kind of like the water for this pond, everything works best when it goes the way nature meant for it to."

I glanced across the yard, at all the new friends who'd been interested and supportive of this project from the beginning. Just as they'd welcomed my family into theirs. These were the kind of people who stood by a friend, offering support in whatever way was needed. How could I accept that kind of approval when I couldn't give it myself?

The Army gave me my chance at the life I now enjoyed. No matter how it came about, there was nothing I wanted more than for my children to be happy. I'd done everything within my power to try and give them the life I'd not had growing up. Even if it meant giving up my dream for my son.

With my hand in Meredith's, we stood beside the waterfall and I called for everyone's attention. Slowly the chatter died down.

"It's a good day," I began. "Not only have I finally finished the pond but it means there's less yard to mow." The crowd laughed. "I wanted to build this pond as a way to show we've settled here in Mossy Creek. But it's been all of you who have really made us feel at home." I looked over the crowd, spotting Miz Erma, pregnant Sandy Crane and her husband Jess, Hank and Casey Blackshear among so many others. "While it might have been my idea and my money, it was my son's design that made it all come together. He taught me a lot while we worked on the pond." I looked at Buck.

"He taught me that some things are supposed to go a certain way even when we imagine them going another. He was right about the way the water should flow from this waterfall and stream into the pond. And he's right about what he wants out of his own life.

"That's why I'm sure he'll be the best student the School of Horticulture at The University of Georgia has ever seen."

Among shouts of "Go Dawgs!" our new friends applauded and congratulated Buck the way I expected. He stood rooted to the spot, staring at me. It took several minutes before the impromptu celebration settled down and Buck and I had a chance to talk.

"Dad, what about West Point?"

"It's not where you want to go, Buck. I might not always listen, but I've got good eyes. All I have to do is look at what you did here to know this what you want."

"But you want me to go to West Point."

"I did, yes." Surprisingly it was an easy dream to let go. It had, after all, been *my* dream, not Buck's. "The Army was good for me. It gave me what I needed. I'm proud that you don't need something like that." I wrapped an arm around his shoulders and we both looked over the landscape we created. "Besides I don't know squat about this gardening business. I'm going to need your help keeping all these plants alive so I don't have the Mossy Creek Garden Club coming down on my head."

"Are you sure?"

"All I want is for you to be happy."

"Well, you know, I was thinking Mom would get a kick out of a pergola with a writing desk at the back of the yard. She could hang flower baskets and maybe do some container planting. Hostas do great in the shade."

"Why do I feel like I've created a monster?" I asked, but with a smile.

"Dad?" Buck stepped back so he could see my face. "I want you to know that the reason I don't need the Army is because I've had you to show me the kind of man I want to be."

Those simple words make up for all the bitter insults and criticisms of my childhood.

"C'mon." I gave his shoulders a squeeze and felt my chest swell with pride and love. "Let's see what your Mom says about this latest idea of yours."

Mossy Creek Gazette

VOLUME VII, NO. FOUR　　　**MOSSY CREEK, GEORGIA**

Koi Are Our Friends, Not Our Food

by Forestry Ranger Bradley "Smokey" Lincoln

I recently got asked to advise on remedies for protecting people's backyard koi ponds from critters that like to munch on pet fish. As I am primarily trained by the state conservation service to advise on protecting wild mountain trout and big fat lake bass, and thus "koi fish" are to me as unnatural as wiener dogs to a lion tamer, I am hereby asking my fellow Creekites to help me out with suggestions for keeping General Sam Greene's koi fish safe from raccoons.

As for me, my best advice is to sit by your koi pond with a loaded shotgun, but I don't think that tip is in the state regulations handbook. So you didn't hear it here, okay?

I want to hear from y'all, though. So sound off! Topic: how to discourage coons from fishing.

Regards, Forest Ranger Smokey

The Mice that Roared

Part Five

Win

After I closed the diner the next day, I drove out to Hank's veterinary clinic and found him doing his rounds in the kennel. He'd already examined the animals who were there for medical reasons, and invited me to help him feed the five dogs that were boarding. Casey and her beautiful, silent daughter LiLi had already taken them for their evening exercise, so all we had to do was feed them and clean out a couple of cages.

I did more petting than feeding as we went through. I'd had to board Cherry a couple of times, so I knew how lonely dogs get without their families. These dogs were so grateful, I hoped that someone had done the same for her.

Hank had already heard that I was considering running for town council. Since he was a member, he had an opinion about that.

"You're going to make a lot of people very happy," he said to me as he dug his scoop into the dry dog food we were wheeling down the row of cages. "Dwight's overstayed his welcome on the council. That's more than my opinion. That's flat-out fact. I won't be the only one who's happy to see him gone."

"I haven't been elected yet," I reminded him, scratching behind the ears of a spotted Springer spaniel, sending her floppy ears flying.

"Unless you run naked through a service at the First Baptist Church, I think you don't need to worry. You're the first person in years who's had the gumption to oppose Dwight in an election. He fights dirty, but you've been around long enough to know that. Have any skeletons in your closet? If you do, he'll dig 'em up and expose them to the world."

"I don't know of any that would make me unelectable. My life's pretty much an open book. Always has been. There've been some women in my past, but I've never been married, so it's not as if I was cheating on anybody."

"Good to know, although people tend to like steady family men running their town. We can make that not be a problem, though."

"So you'll back me?"

"Heck, yeah."

We shook hands, and when I made no move to leave, he asked, "Something else I can help you with?"

I cleared my throat. "I need your expert advice."

"As a vet or councilman?"

"Vet."

"Shoot."

"What kind of dogs make good mousers?"

Hank regarded me for a long moment, then his brow cleared. "Jayne Reynolds." He grinned. "Going to give Amos a run for his money, are you?"

"Seems Amos isn't interested in Jayne. Not romantically, anyway."

"I guess he hasn't been exactly subtle lately about where his interests do lie, now has he?" Hank slapped me on my back. "You and Jayne, huh? I can see it. Yes, indeedy, I can. Good for you. I approve."

"Well, don't go spreading it around or anything. I haven't exactly . . . well, I haven't . . ."

"Ah, I see. So you're trying to win the lady's heart with

a dog? Well, I hate to break the news to you." He leaned in for a stage whisper. "She's a cat person. I should know. I'm her doctor. Well, her cat's doctor."

I shook my head. "Her cat's not doing its job. Jayne borrowed the Ramsey's cat yesterday, but Emma terrorizied it with sneak attacks, so it didn't catch a single mouse. They fought so much, Jayne had to take it home."

"What makes you think Emma will tolerate a dog any better?"

"She may not, but she tolerates Ingrid's Chihuahua. I've even seen her licking his head."

"True enough. Okay, let me think." Hank rolled the barrel of dog food back into its closet. After making sure it was sealed, he washed his hands. As he dried them with a paper towel, he said, "It'll most likely have to be a terrier. The small terriers were the ones bred to hunt vermin. I'd recommend either a Jack Russell or a Cairn."

I couldn't hide my disgust. "Yappers?"

He shrugged. "They can be. Depends on how well they've been trained. Terriers definitely need good training. They can be independent little cusses, with minds of their own. Like any dog, they need regular exercise. It's better if they have a job to do, but it sounds like this one will. If they don't have an outlet for their natural instincts, they tend to invent new and fun jobs for themselves, which might not be so fun for their families."

"Job?"

"Well, they were bred to hunt vermin, and this one will have that job, so that's a good thing. And, boy, are they smart. You can train terriers to do just about any trick. Normally I wouldn't recommend a terrier for a single woman with a young child. These dogs aren't exactly tolerant of ill-behaved children. But I've seen Matt with Bob. Ingrid's taught him how to love and respect small animals, so that shouldn't be a problem."

We paused at the door to the kennel. "Sounds perfect. Where do I get one?"

Hank thought about that for a moment, then said, "In order for it to be able to do the job immediately, you'll want a full-grown dog. They tend to be calmer, too. I've got contacts. Let me make a few calls."

I extended my hand. "Sounds like a plan. Thanks!"

"To err is human, to purr, feline."

—*Robert Byrne*

Great Cat Heist

They say no good heist goes off without teamwork. You've got the idea man, the technical specialist, the inside man, and the getaway car driver. And then there's the fence, of which, I was an unknowing recruit.

But I'm miles ahead of myself.

I, Hermia Lavender, have been home on school break from the University of Georgia for a day. I arrived home to an empty house. My mother, Anna Rose Lavender, who will return home tomorrow evening, is right now on a luxurious spa vacation down in Atlanta with her lover, Beau Belmont. No, they are not married—yet. That would imply doing things the conventional way. And my mother is as unconventional as white strappy sandals after Labor Day. She gets points for that.

But she lost points when I recently found out my father had not died in a motorcycle accident when I was a baby, as I'd been told. Instead, for over twenty years, my mother hadn't known how to tell me my father was really the handsome movie star who I'd many times paid eight dollars and fifty cents to watch pursue robbers, solve crimes, and flash his pearly whites on the big screen.

That's right, *the* Beau Belmont is my father. Or Beau Belmondo, as he's known by millions of screaming female fans.

If they only knew the man's heart belonged to my mother and Mossy Creek, the furthest holler from Hollywood, photo ops and red carpet designer couture a movie star can see to putting his heart.

You might think I put up a big stink after learning the news. I didn't.

I've accepted that suddenly I have a father. The guy is, well, nice. And he doesn't have a big head like you'd expect of most movie stars. And I think he genuinely cares for my mother. He's good folk. Not that I've spent much time with him to know. Since I've learned about *the father*, I've been in college. It's become a hiding spot of sorts for me. While I'm there, I don't have to deal with a father who may or may not have an interest in a relationship with me.

How does one go about fitting a fully-grown father into their fatherless life? Awkward silences flourish between the two of us. Sheepish smiles and uncertain conversation starts are a given.

Can a man walk into my life and make up for two decades of my believing I had no father? Of pining for a fatherly hug? The jury is still out on that one. I'll let you know as soon as I figure it out.

My mother once told me these are my years to gain wisdom. To make mistakes and learn from them. And to be carefree more often than careful.

I don't do carefree very well. Attribute that to my mother's perfectionism. It wore off on me. Sure, when I'm home from school I love to drive down to Bigelow with my best friend Darva for a few drinks at one of the hot nightclubs— but just a few. I don't like to lose control.

Anyway, I had the house to myself for a whole blessed day. A welcome change from dorm life and my pseudo-anorexic roommate who counts her rice grains before eating them and won't exceed six hundred calories a day. "Pseudo" because of the stash of chocolate she keeps in her top bedside drawer. I figure she gets at least a thousand calories daily from sweets alone, so I haven't started worrying about her yet.

After sweeping the front porch and breathing in the gorgeous spring mountain air, I decided to step around back and inspect mom's garden. Carefree, here I come.

Humming the catchy tune from an old Pink Panther heist movie Darva and I had watched the night before, I did a double-step the cartoon panther always does as he's coolly walking across the screen. Mercy, but I do have the moves.

Well, I try. I'm not sure what, exactly, it is I have or what I'm made of, but probably *the moves* is far down the list. An interest in theater is a given, seeing as how my mother instilled that in me since birth. I can take the stage with grace and have yet to forget a line. I've a bit of fashion sense. I don't mix my plaids with my stripes, and complimentary colors add warmth to my pale complexion. And I can whip up an apricot cobbler so fierce it'll give Rosie down at *Mama's All You Can Eat* reason to cry.

I'm finishing my third year at UGA. I'd like to be an environmentalist. Yes, I want to save the world, one forest or toxic waste dump at a time.

But I'm still uncertain. A twenty-something single girl should be uncertain about some things, right? I mean, I shouldn't have it *all* figured out. And given my knack for orderliness, I like to look at the whole picture, piece small parts together and form the bigger landscape. Clues are always good.

Speaking of clues . . .

The heist started with Colonel Mustard, in the Billiard Room, holding the Candlestick.

Wait one moonlit minute. That's not right.

I had played the board game *Clue* with Darva last night. Regarding the game: one must always suspect Colonel Mustard. He's a wily old fella who stirs up doubt with a sneer and a twist of his handlebar moustache. Mercy, but there are days I feel like the colonel is following *me* around with all that doubt, especially when it comes to brand-new fathers.

Okay, here's how it really began.

Miss Lavender stood in the Garden, holding the Hoe . . .

I picked up the small hand hoe my mother must have forgotten, stuffed in the dirt at the garden's border. The forsythia was in bloom and the egg-yolk-bright flowers lured me to sniff, but the scent was so soft I couldn't be sure it wasn't the catmint frothing along the garden border.

A thicket of raspberry my mother hadn't thinned out last fall resembled a brown mass of razor wire. The shrub shivered. I gave it a double take.

I didn't have time to let out a yelp when the beast charged from behind it.

It was orange. It was stout. It snarled and beat the ground toward me. I turned to make escape when the excruciating pain of vicious talons entered my thigh. I was hit!

More surprised than frightened I was being attacked in my own garden, I wobbled and fell to my knees. Shaking my right leg, I tried to disentangle the creature from my thigh. It clung. And meowed.

The cat wasn't in the mood to disengage its talons— okay, *claws*—from my jeans. The beast now only clung to the fabric, and not my skin, so I was able to lumber back to the porch, where my passenger promptly ejected itself from my leg and proceeded to sniff out the territory.

"Do not pee on my mother's chrysanthemums," I warned. "Who do you belong to? No tags or collar. You look well fed and your coat is shiny. Bet you shed at the mere sight of black velvet, eh?"

The cat *meowred* in reply. I smiled. I've always wanted a pet.

I live in a dorm. No pets allowed. Though I can't be certain my roommate's fuzzy pink slippers aren't considered part of the animal species. They've yet to growl at me, but do tend to trip me up often during middle-of-the-night mini-fridge raids.

"Sorry," I said as I opened the screen door, "you'll have to stay out—"

The creature had gumption. It zipped past my ankles and headed inside, down the hallway, and toward my mother's antique velvet sofa.

🐾🐾🐾

I plucked a few orange hairs from the emerald green velvet. The cat had disappeared, and no amount of whistling or cajoling would bring it out of hiding.

I wandered into the kitchen to look for the milk in the refrigerator. I'm not cruel. A treat would probably lure the critter out. Yes, I know if you feed it you can never get rid of it. But was I responsible after I returned to school?

Heh. *I wonder if Beau Belmont is allergic to cats?*

So I have a wicked bone in my body. Just the one. And it hasn't been scratched lately. I didn't know how to up and have a conversation with the man. *Hey, how's it going? Father any more kids you don't know about lately?* But sending in a pinch-hitter might work. Though I was doubtful a cat could open a line of communication any better than I could muster.

There he was again, Colonel Mustard and his doubt. I wonder if a good ole *thwap* with a candlestick would do the trick?

"Here, kit—"

The closing fridge door revealed a charging orange streak of cat. I cringed and braced myself.

I barely avoided spilling milk as my new fashion accessory attached itself to my thigh. No pain this time. The talons—very well, *claws*—hooked neatly into a denim pant leg without slashing skin.

I gave my leg a shake. "What's with you? If you need human contact, there are better ways. Like sitting on said human's lap, for instance."

But no matter how much I did the hokey-pokey and turned myself about, the critter had no mind to disengage. I poured the milk into a bowl, and as I performed a sliding, stretch/split to place the treat on the floor, the cat ejected itself. While it slurped milk, I petted its silky orange coat.

"You definitely belong to someone who cares. But who?"

Last time I'd been home was Christmas vacation. I have developed a tendency to visit only once a year. Awkward father situation, don't you know. I couldn't recall anyone in the neighborhood with a cat. There was Bob the Chihuahua down the street. Cats could kick that puny dog's—well, you know. But then the cat had better high-tail it out of there before Bob peed on it. That dog was one loose spigot.

"Maybe I should put up posters at The Naked Bean and the library."

The cat *meowed.* I interpreted the slightly peevish tone as, "Is this all you got, lady?"

"Fine. I need to run out for some groceries this morning. I'll see what I can find for you."

🐾🐾🐾

The lot at Mossy Creek's Piggly Wiggly was small, but I am never surprised people can't be bothered to push their carts back into the store. I collected four wobbly-wheeled carts, and shoved them toward the automatic doors, which did not slide open even as I waited patiently.

This day was just filled with unpleasant minor catastrophes.

I narrowed the evil eye on the electric sensor above the door. Okay, the *nuisance* eye. I don't do evil. (Just wicked.) The door opened, and I pushed the carts through.

Hey, it's a talent.

Captain Crunch and milk were first on the list. I turned down an aisle and walked right into a frantic set of limbs and springy blonde curls.

"Darva! I'm still convinced it was Colonel Mustard—"

"Mia!" She gave me an abbreviated hug. "Forget the colonel, we need to talk."

"We talked six hours last night. More talk?"

"Emergency talk."

I don't believe I've ever seen Darva so agitated. Her curls sprang up and down in blonde perpetual motion. Normally subdued and a bit of a follower, Darva worked part-time as assistant stage manager at the theater with my mother, and was up for directing the next staging of *Bye Bye Birdie*. Darva was always the first to suggest we start drinking soda after a few tipples at the bar. Once in second grade, Luke Henry had teased me about not having a daddy. Darva had shot back that his daddy was already on wife number three which shut him up properly. A rare moment in Darva daring. We've been friends ever since.

She tugged me down the Baby Goods aisle, and the sweet smell of powder and baby wipes curled up my nose.

"Can you keep a secret?" Darva asked. Her wide blue eyes shifted down the aisle, then the opposite direction. "Please, Mia?"

Now, normally best friends would do anything for one another. Borrow clothes, take the blame for the cigarette butt forgotten on the porch steps, lie about being sick when really we skipped to watch the matinee horror flick, sneak into the boy's locker room—keep secrets. I've done them all, and Darva has reciprocated.

But my life had changed since the big reveal. *Secret* had become a nasty word to me. I don't like secrets. I don't like knowing them, making them, or keeping them.

For a girl who'd thought her father dead for twenty years, I've come to believe that's a very reasonable reaction.

"Hush your mouth, Darva, you know how I feel about secrets." I walked past the brightly colored plastic packages of diapers and feigned interest in a squat jar of creamed peas. "Ask me anything but that."

"But, Mia." Darva did the big sad eyes so well. Attribute that to her role as Juliet to a string of handsome Romeos three years consecutively at the Mossy Creek theatre. "Oh, lordy, I forgot. I shouldn't ask you. I know the whole thing with your father—"

I turned abruptly. Darva dropped her anxious grimace, and lowered her eyes, nodding. "Sorry. I mean, just . . . sorry."

Silence isn't always golden, sometimes it can be loud, uncomfortable and bright chartreuse. I hate uncomfortable silence. But I wasn't willing to stick my foot any deeper into this bucket of paint.

"We good for a movie tonight?" I asked, hoping to reclaim our easy camaraderie.

"Sure. Right. Maybe. We'll see how things go today. I've an errand to do—" Darva's eyes went wide. She clasped her pink-polished fingers together before her O-shaped mouth.

I knew that pose. Handsome male in the vicinity. I whipped my head around to spy a hunky young store clerk limping down the cereal aisle, wielding a ticket gun, unaware he was being checked out by two single young females.

Jason Cecil? I believe he graduated from Mossy Creek High a year behind Darva and me. His mama was Trisha Peavy Cecil. Last time I saw Jason he was thin and wore his pants loose on his hips like some kind of geeky pocket protector gangster. He wasn't handsome in a conventional way, but he had put on a wallop of good-looking muscle since high school. Since he was obviously injured, I wondered if he'd been hurt playing on one of Mossy Creek's new community league soccer teams.

"So," I began, thinking to wheedle out the dirt on Darva's latest crush, but she had slipped back into the nervous twitter. Blonde curls *boinged*.

"I'll call you later, Mia. Bye."

"Right. Uh . . . bye?"

Huh. That girl was acting strangely.

Was it because of Jason or my refusing to hear her secret?

🐾🐾🐾

Cato greeted me in his usual manner. Claws to denim. Besides cat food, I had also picked up some rubbing alcohol to tend my wounds.

The name fit. Cato. Like in the Pink Panther films. Inspector Clouseau's wily assistant was always jumping out from behind things to surprise him with an attack. Unlike the bumbling Inspector, though, I didn't fight back. Instead I found a few calming strokes under Cato's chin caused him to relax and disengage, and to nuzzle against my ankle.

I fed my desperate lodger, then decided a phone call to Darva was in order. I couldn't let our conversation in the Piggly Wiggly end as it had. She'd seemed worried about something. Best friends didn't let each other down.

But a secret? Mercy. I rubbed my palms up my arms. To consider the secret my mother had kept for so long made me sad, and yes, even angry. Hadn't she trusted that I might like to know about my father?

I've come to understand that she hadn't the courage to tell Beau at the time. My granddaddy had been the one to convince Beau to stay away from my mother. (I suspect a shotgun may also have been involved.)

But why not let me in on the truth instead of manufacturing the motorcycle accident story?

Beau Belmont had learned I was his daughter the same time I learned he was my father. Had Beau not arrived in Mossy Creek to sweep my mother off her feet during production of *A Midsummer's Night Dream*, I might have gone through life never knowing the truth. That was the part that really stung.

It appeared Mom and Beau had picked up where they'd left off over two decades earlier, happy in each other's arms and stealing kisses when they thought no one was looking.

So where did I fit into the picture?

Colonel Mustard in my Brain wielding Doubt.

Certainly whatever secret Darva was dying to tell couldn't be as life altering as a new daddy. I bet it had to do with Jason. That look of utter adoration. And then she'd clammed up right there in the Piggly Wiggly. Was Darva in love? But that was no secret; it was something we always shared with one another. Heaven knows we'd been through crushes, infatuations and dalliances aplenty.

Picking up the phone, I set it down when the doorbell rang.

Darva stood out on the step. Her curls worked double-time. Before I could invite her in, Cato rocketed through the room and landed—*sprong*—wrapped about my thigh.

"Hey, Mia, what the heck is—" Darva's eyes grew wide. "Eek!"

I grimaced through the pain. "Did you just say eek?"

"Yes, Mia, I said *eek*. It means 'oh no!' and is used as an exclamation of shock or bestartlement."

"I know what it means. I just never heard a real person actually use it. I think you have to be a cartoon character to be allowed usage of that exclamation. And *bestartlement* is not a word."

"Duly noted." She pointed at Cato. "Is that the—? Oh, my goodness gracious, it *is* the cat I stole!"

A deduction seeped into my brain, slow yet sure as molasses creeping over a stack of steaming flapjacks. I twisted my leg to better display my catch. "Is *this* the secret you wanted me to keep, Darva?"

She nodded mutely, her eyes comically fearful.

"That's the insane cat!" Darva burst out. "The one that got away. The crazy, wild, snarling creature from the deepest depths."

"The depths—? I do believe I've missed out on something since Colonel Mustard wielded the Candlestick and Miss Lavender found the Hoe in the Garden. Come inside and fill me in, Darva."

"B-but it's a secret."

Again, I twisted my leg to display the furry orange barnacle. Cato purred sweetly, but gave no indication of wanting to detach from his post. "A secret? Not so much anymore, Darva. Not so much anymore."

❦❦❦

Darva relayed her adventures in catnapping, which took place last night *after* I'd left her alone with the Clue game board and a half-empty bowl of honey pecan popcorn.

Seems she'd been planning a particular heist for a couple weeks, but didn't know I'd be home on vacation at the time, else she would have asked for my help.

"You couldn't have done it alone," I guessed as I strode to the kitchen, Darva in tow, to scavenge for another bottle of root beer.

"Well . . ."

Ah. Secrets are always much more complicated than one initially suspects.

As Darva twisted one leg and she screwed up her mouth sweetly and eyed the ceiling, I made another deduction.

This one wasn't so easy as the first, but the grocery store conversation did add another piece to the puzzle.

"Aha!"

"What aha?" Darva protested all innocent. "You can't *aha* me like that after I've been so open with my secret."

"A secret that grows more twisted and intriguing."

"Do tell," Darva challenged.

"You weren't alone on the heist. You had help."

Darva lifted her chin. Impudently.

"And I guess it was one Limping Grocery Store Clerk in the Cereal Aisle with the Ticket Gun." I thrust out my wounded thigh. "Cat got his leg? The way he's limping, Cato must have caught him just right on a major muscle."

Darva nodded mutely. Then she burst out with the confession. "As we were stealing it, it attacked Jason, then took off like the governor running from Mayor Ida's shotgun. Jason was as frantic as the cat. He ran like a chicken with its head cut off. When I finally caught up with him, he wouldn't let me steal a second cat, and insisted we cancel the whole plan."

"You're not making a whole lot of sense at this point. I'm sure you have a good reason for stealing cats. You should have asked me to help."

"Well . . ."

The rising tone of that single word prodded me to make another deduction, but I wasn't up for it. "Well what?"

"You *are* helping, Mia. You're the fence."

"The fence?"

"You know, the one who holds the stolen goods for the crooks? Every heist needs one."

I glanced out to the living room, where Cato snoozed on the velvet sofa before the bouquet of red roses Beau had given Mom last week. "I'm fencing stolen goods. Darva, how did this happen? *Why* did you steal a cat? And why, of all the cats in the world, would you steal a *crazy* cat?"

"I didn't want a crazy cat," Darva explained. "I wanted one of those fancy cats Mrs. Pickle keeps in her garage. Do you know she just brought home *thirteen* show cats?"

"Show cats? She's going to breed them? Or she's starting a cat boarding kennel? So?"

"She keeps them locked in cages! That's cruel, Mia, and you know it is."

I nodded. Couldn't imagine anyone trying to contain Cato. No wonder I couldn't scrape the poor thing from me for any longer than it took to close myself in the bathroom for a few private moments. The cat needed contact. It needed love.

"You think she's abusing them?" I asked. Since the deed was already done I didn't bother pointing out that ditzy Darva could simply have asked the humane society to investigate Mrs. Pickle. I also didn't point out that since everyone in Mossy Creek knows everyone else's business, Mrs. Pickle's caged show cats wouldn't stay unnoticed for long. Besides, people might not like the idea of cats in cages, but caging them wasn't illegal.

"Not sure. But don't you think owning that many cats and keeping them in cages is abuse? That's why I did it. I wanted to bring attention to what she's doing over there. The plan was to borrow one of the show cats, then report I'd found it to the *Mossy Creek Gazette*. Katie Bell would have a field day with that one. Then we'd all march over to Mrs. Pickle's house to return it, and voila! The whole town would see how she treats her animals."

"Borrow, eh?" I sighed at her well-intentioned but idiotic logic. "You haven't been so daring since second grade, Darva."

"I er . . . got the idea from my partner in crime."

"The same partner who abandoned you at the scene of the crime?"

She shrugged, and I do believe she blushed. "Jason was

bleeding, Darva. He took one for the team."

"Isn't he the guy you had a crush on in twelfth grade but he was too busy with the chess club to notice you?"

"The one and only. He's noticed me now."

"I guess like attracts like. Criminals, that is."

"You should talk, Miss I-Fence-Stolen-Goods."

I gaped. Me, an accessory to a crime! "Now wait a minute. I never agreed . . . and by the way, instead of stealing a cat, you and Jason could have easily taken photographs of Mrs. Pickle's cat cages to prove your point."

"Please, Mia, I know we didn't think things through very well, but you can't tell anyone. The heist went wrong. The cat escaped, and we didn't get our evidence. All we did was set a gnarly, psycho cat loose on the world."

"Hey! I happen to like that gnarly thing. Cato is my kind of cat."

"Disturbed and manic?"

"No, desperate for love." I looked away, gripping the root beer bottle.

What in heavens? I suddenly felt a little teary-eyed. And for what reason? I had love in abundance. Maybe. Mom *had* been dividing her time between me and Beau lately. Course, I wasn't around. And she did call me every single day. Beau never called me. I'd probably hang up if he did. Mom said I had to make the first move, give him a signal.

Giving signals was sort of like having the moves. Which I don't. I sighed.

"I can't keep him," I said. "He belongs to Mrs. Pickle. Poor kitty. Even if he is gnarly, he doesn't deserve to be treated poorly and kept in a cage."

"Maybe if we bring it back and talk to Mrs. Pickle? There might be a reason for the cages. Or if we found evidence of mistreatment, we could report her to the police. But Darva, stealing isn't going to save any cats, only see you on a wanted poster in Amos Roydan's office. Although, if your point is to get publicity, it'll take Katie Bell less than a day to spread the news about your arrest. You'll probably be the lead item in her next column."

"I know. Though . . . I've never been gossiped about, Mia. It might be kinda—"

"Darva."

"All right. All right! It was, well . . . Jason thought it was a clever idea. He's an Eagle Scout, you know. Last year he spent two weeks surviving alone up on Colchik Mountain. He's so strong and sexy. And when we were standing in Mrs. Pickle's garage trying to decide which cat to take, he kissed me."

"Oh." I said it on a sigh, because stolen kisses in inappropriate settings are always worth a sigh. "Is he a good kisser?"

"If he were popcorn he'd be extra buttery with caramel coating *and* peanuts."

Now *that* was good.

"But then that crazy cat dashed out and Jason ran after it. Oh, Mia, I want another kiss. But now Jason is freaked because we lost the cat."

"But you didn't. I've been 'fencing' it all along."

Darva's grateful smile made me glad I'd let this secret into my life.

🐾🐾🐾

So this was the plan. Darva and I would return Cato to Mrs. Pickle. We'd nicely explain we'd found the cat. (No, Darva could not be cajoled into confessing to breaking and entering, and okay, that's one secret I felt compelled to keep.) While visiting Mrs. Pickle, we'd try to deduce whether she was a cat abuser.

I served Cato a goodbye meal of milk and Kitty Nibbles. Then I combed his sleek coat with an old brush I'd found in the garage.

Cato purred appreciatively on my lap. "Bet you'd have no idea what to do with a father either, eh, Cato?"

The cat stretched out its legs and settled.

"It's not that I mind so much, but how do I start? I've wanted to have a relationship with him for over twenty years. I shouldn't waste another year wondering. But . . ."

But I was nervous. Unsure. Colonel Mustard's doubt gushed through my veins. Could Beau be as anxious as I about starting a relationship?

The doorbell rang. Darva had the getaway car out front. Rather, the *giveback* car. I hugged Cato's purring muzzle to my cheek. Oh, misery.

🐾🐾🐾

Darva let me drive while she held Cato. She was nervous, and didn't think she could operate heavy machinery just then. Cato took to Darva fairly quickly, considering he was living proof she failed as a cat burglar.

We cruised slowly through town. It was dark and drizzly and the headlights beamed upon the rain like flecks of falling diamonds. It was pretty, but it made Cato nervous.

"Should have brought some Kitty Nibbles along," I said as I pulled to a stop across the street from the Piggly Wiggly. The store was well-lit, and customers were loading their cars from its awning-covered sidewalk to stand out in the rain.

"There he is," Darva said in the dreamiest tone.

I didn't have to wonder who she meant. That tone can only mean one thing. "Jason?"

She nodded and hugged Cato. "I did it for love, Mia. True love."

I tapped the steering wheel and focused on the limping hunk of muscle sliding grocery bags into the back of a young woman's SUV. I could understand the love part. I've been in love more times than I could count. Sometimes all it took was a kiss to fall head over heels, crashing into promises of forever devotion and scribbling his name over and over on the telephone directory.

"Lord, don't do this to me!"

Darva's tone changed so quickly I flicked my gaze from her hyperventilating clutch on Cato to the scene across the street. Jason had closed the back of the SUV, and now he drew his hand along the woman's arm. Suggestively.

I clicked the windshield wipers on and did an evasive right turn down the street away from the grocery store.

"Where are you going?" Darva screamed. "Did you see that? The man I love is—was—aggh!"

Yet another utterance I'd only seen in comic books—but I'd give it to Darva this time.

By the time I found a spot to park far enough from sight of the clandestine liaison occurring in full view of Mossy Creekites and the heartbroken Darva, her tears had reduced to sniffles and she stopped shuddering.

Which was remarkable only because I knew Darva could turn on the waterworks over something so small as a crushed caterpillar.

When I glanced over, I saw why. Cato snuggled his paws on her chest and nuzzled her tear-stained chin with his moist pink nose. His purrs resembled an outboard motor revving on high gear, but softly muted enough to instill precious calm.

My heart went out to Darva, and I reached for her hand.

"He's st-still very h-handsome," Darva murmured through sniffles. "And s-so smart."

"He is. But I think he's a player."

"Miss Scarlet in the Study with a Lead Pipe?"

I smiled at Darva's suggestion. Whenever we were angry or upset with someone we suggested methods for their demise.

"I suggest the imperious Mrs. Peacock."

"In the Library . . ."

"With the Wrench," we said together.

Cato agreed with a *meowr*.

🐾🐾🐾

"Why are we doing this on the sneak?" I asked. "I thought we agreed to talk to Mrs. Pickle as if we'd simply found the cat and are now returning it."

Darva pulled a black facemask over her head. It was crooked and one blonde ringlet popped through the left eyehole. "I'm afraid she'll guess the truth. We can't risk making her suspicious."

"We? Don't you mean you and Jason?"

"The cad." She dismissed the grocery store clerk with a brave *pfft*. "You did admit to fencing the cat, Mia."

"And I won't recant my confession." Cato sat nestled in my arms. "It's all right, Cato."

"You shouldn't call him that, Mia. He probably has a name. Are you sure you can do this?"

"Of course." *Maybe.* "I can't have a cat at the dorm." *But Mother could keep it.* Would she have room for another feisty male in her life? *Oh, Mia, give it up. You know deep down that Mother and Beau belong together.* "Me and Cato? Just acquaintances. Not attached at all."

I hugged Cato closer. Could I really give him back?

🐾🐾🐾

I didn't want to know how Darva was able to jimmy the electric garage door open. "You act like you've done this a time or two, Darva."

She shrugged and offered a forced smile. The things we do for love.

Even more surprising? The empty garage, sans cages or abused show cats.

Darva flashed the beam of her handheld around the space. Neat cardboard boxes lined two walls. A shovel, rake and garden hose hung near the door leading into the house.

"I thought you said Mrs. Pickle had dozens of cats in here?"

"Maybe she moved them inside." Darva flashed the light around as she crept about. "Very sneaky, Mrs. Pickle, hiding the evidence. But I know better. I saw the cages. Let's leave the stolen goods inside the garage."

Cato squirmed in my arms. "We can't leave him alone out here and risk him getting run over by the car when Mrs. Pickle returns. Darva!"

"Oh, Mia, I'm scared now." She pulled off the stupid face mask and stuffed it in her jeans' pocket, then flipped up the flashlight, which hollowed her eyes like a late-night television spook. "I should have never done this in the first place. Sure, it was for love and all—curse you, Jason Cecil! But I was trying to do something good, too."

Cato *meowed*, as if to say, *Lordy, but humans can be stupid sometimes.*

"I see what you mean about secrets," she said. "They can never be good."

I shrugged, feeling the need to lessen Darva's angst. Who was I to claim mastery over a natural human impulse? "I suppose I shouldn't rule out *all* secrets. There are some necessary ones."

"Really? Coming from Miss I-Don't-Do-Secrets?" She crossed her arms. "Name one."

"Sometimes it is wise to fib about weight and shoe size."

"Don't I know it." She posed a hand on a hip that was more ample than slender.

"It's just, you know the really big ones aren't right. But I guess . . ."

Was I going to admit this? Cato nuzzled against my neck, his purring an encouragement that made me stronger, and stand a little straighter.

"I guess some people keep them because they believe the secret is best. And then when they grow wiser and learn otherwise, they speak it."

"Like your momma's secret?" Darva switched the flashlight to beam on me now. I winced and she shut it off.

Standing there in the cool darkness of Mrs. Pickle's garage, with Cato snuggling into my chest, I suddenly felt alone. And yet, not. Darva was my best friend. I'd told her the big awful secret that same morning after my mother had revealed it. I'd blurted it out and forced a smile, then stormed out to become this weird kind of woman who kept a smile on her sleeve, but her inner torments locked away.

So it surprised me when the first teardrop spilled down my cheek.

"Oh, Mia." Darva hugged me, drawing me carefully into her embrace so we formed a kitty sandwich. Cato turned on the outboard motor. He was loving this double-hug, poor little misunderstood fella. "It's going to be fine when you want it to be fine."

Stunningly sensible words from Darva, who only yesterday had decided that stealing a cat was a prudent decision.

"It is fine," I said. And meant it. "But I'll never get back those years without my daddy."

"He's a real nice guy, Mia. I bet he'll make up for the lost time. And if he can't, you'll have a great future to look forward to. If you'll give him a chance."

"You, Darva, are one wise woman."

She shuffled Cato's furry head. "Sometimes."

A set of bright headlights pulled up the driveway. We both turned and made like stunned deer.

❦❦❦

Mrs. Pickle stood in the garage wearing a red feather boa over her spring sundress.

I cringed, wondering how soon it would take Mrs. Pickle to realize her garage door was open. Maybe she thought she'd pressed the opener.

Hey, it could work. I prepared the nuisance eye—just in case.

"You found my Fluffykins!"

I held Cato out and studied his green eyes. "Fluffykins?" Didn't seem to bother him that he'd been shackled with a humiliating name. "Er, right. Fluffykins."

"Mia found him in her mother's garden," Darva quickly provided. "I knew he must belong to you, Mrs. Pickle, because you got all those pretty show cats last week. Er . . . where are they, by the way?"

"Show cats? Oh, I don't have show cats. I did have a mess of them for a couple days. Mr. Brown over in Bigelow had a bit of trouble with termites. Had to evacuate all his champions, so I said I'd keep them for a few days. I didn't want the herd running all over my white carpeting so had to keep them caged, the poor things. But they were no worse for wear. I took them out in shifts and let them scamper about the garage."

She reached for Cato, but I clung to his soft furry body. If I'd had talons—er, *claws*—I'd have been a force.

"I've just been sick to think I'd lost Fluffykins. He must have got out yesterday afternoon. This old garage door has a mind of its own. Opens and closes at will. It's a might creepy."

"Creepy." Darva exchanged glances with me.

I holstered the nuisance eye.

"So you don't harbor large numbers of show cats and keep them caged cruelly?" I asked, still hugging Cato possessively.

"Oh, dear no, girl. Nor does Mr. Brown. He felt real bad about me keeping them in cages, but there wasn't any other option. The man has a mansion, I tell you, and the cats have their own floor! They really do rule the roost. Come to Mommy, Fluffykins."

Cato jumped into Mrs. Pickle's arms and made himself at home in her thin, crossed arms nestled amidst a snake of red feathers—without a glance to me. Traitor.

"Poor thing." Mrs. Pickle kissed Cato's head. "He's a mutt. I have no idea who his daddy is, but his mother was a prize winner."

"Just because he grew up without a father doesn't make him a mutt," I protested. I sniffed back a rogue tear.

"Of course not, dear." Mrs. Pickle stroked Cato's back. "Fluffykins will never win any prizes, but I love him so much. There are lots of things we don't know about people and the world, but we take them as they are. For the joy."

"For the joy," Darva said, sighing. "Hear that, Mia?"

"I do." And I hugged myself and smiled. "Does he like to jump up and cling to your leg?"

"Oh, yes, the feisty fellow. He's young. I'm having him neutered soon. The world is so cruel to unwanted kittens. No irresponsible fatherhood for you, Fluffykins. Dr. Blackshear says neutering will calm his wild streak a bit. And my drapes will be thankful for it, believe you me. Will you ladies come inside for some lemonade?"

Darva took a step forward, but I offered an excuse for getting back home to greet my parents when they returned from the spa. Yes, my parents. *Both* of them. For the rest of my life.

Ladies and gentleman, Colonel Mustard has left the building.

𝕸𝖔𝖘𝖘𝖞 𝕮𝖗𝖊𝖊𝖐 𝕲𝖆𝖟𝖊𝖙𝖙𝖊

VOLUME VII, NO. FIVE   **MOSSY CREEK, GEORGIA**

Cat Burglars Steal Cats

by Gazette Correspondent Jess Crane

The recent disappearance of Mrs. Pickles' cat, Fluffykins, sparked local rumors that a cat napper was at work in Mossy Creek. We can now report that Fluffykins was merely lost. Mia Lavender, home from UGA to visit her parents, found and returned Fluffykins to a very happy Mrs. Pickle. So Creekites can rest easy that no mysterious feline felonies are fully festering in full sight of full-time fluffy friends. Nor has Chief Royden received reports of any possible puppy purloiners, rabbit rustlers, snake snatchers, parakeet pluckers, hamster hoisters, weasel wranglers, mouse movers or fish filchers. If *Gazette* readers suspect otherwise please contact Ace Ventura, Pet Detective, care of this newspaper.

The Mice that Roared

Part Six

Jayne

"Now that the painting's done, we can concentrate on furniture placement," Josie said. "It's a good thing that the counters were on opposite sides of the same wall. That'll make the new layout more coherent. I'm glad we decided to close off the front door into the bakery so customers have to use this one entrance."

"That was a practical decision," I told her. "It has nothing to do with feng . . . sh . . ." I trailed off as she turned an odd shade of green, then raced for the bathroom.

This was the third day in a . . .

Oh!

I quickly followed her to the bathroom and banged on the closed stall. "Josie McClure Rutherford, you're pregnant!"

"I know," she called miserably.

"Does Harry know?"

"You think I could fool Harry about something like this?"

I smiled. Harry was a fine man. He loved Josie so intently he noticed if she wore a slightly different shade of lipstick. I believed he watched her so closely because he was afraid of losing her. He'd been in a car accident years ago which had left him horribly scarred. He'd hidden himself on Colchik Mountain, ostensibly to do research, but more to hide away from the world because of his physical and emotional scars . . . until Josie had found him.

He knew how fragile life could be and now that he'd found someone who loved him not in spite of his scars but because of them, he wanted to hold onto her with everything he had.

Now they were having a baby. I can't say that I hadn't been expecting it. Josie and Harry were so in love, it was bound to overflow into a baby.

Babies were your own small piece of immortality. My own son, Matt, was evidence of that. I saw my husband in Matt every day.

Josie emerged from the stall and gave me a rueful smile. "Okay, yes, I'm pregnant."

I wanted to drag her into a hug, but I couldn't resist messing with her first. I crossed my arms across my chest. "And just *when* were you planning on telling me?"

"Harry and I wanted to keep it to ourselves for a few weeks," she said as she splashed water on her face.

"So LuLynn doesn't even know?"

"No, and don't you dare tell her." She reached for the paper towel I'd pulled from the roll. "Mama'd kill me if someone else knows before she does. Don't tell anyone!"

"Like you can keep secrets in this town."

"Jayne . . ."

"All right, Swami, I'll keep my mouth shut." I used the nickname I'd given her because of her love for astrology and feng shui. "What's the little tyke going to be?"

"An ox baby, I'm hoping. Either Capricorn or Aquarius. Either will do. I didn't want to wait another year and have a little rabbit. Oxen fit much better with mine and Harry's charts."

She was so serious, I had to laugh. "That's good to hear."

She stuck her tongue out at me and reached for the bathroom door. "Remember, don't tell— Eeee!"

A mouse ran across the bathroom floor and disappeared behind the toilet.

Josie leaned against the sink, her hand over her heart. "When are you going to do something about those critters?!"

"I'm importing another cat this afternoon. Argie Rodriguez's Rudy." I pushed the door open. "If that doesn't work, I'll call the fumigators tomorrow. Everyone in town knows about the little rodents, anyway. Might as well suck it up and hire a crew to clean up the poison afterward."

"I'll hel—"

"Oh, no, you won't. You, little mother, will not come near this place for a week after they're done."

"SSssshhh!"

I rolled my eyes and we stepped back into the shop.

I immediately spotted Win Allen at the counter, ordering a mocha latte from Ashley Winthrop, who I'd stolen away from Poppy's Ice Cream Parlor. She worked for me after school and on weekends. I knew it was a mocha latte because that's all he ever ordered.

"Hi, Win," Josie said. "What's up?"

He glanced over at us and smiled. "Josie, Jayne. I just closed the diner for the day and thought I'd come let y'all know that I've definitely decided to run against Dwight for town council."

"That's great," Josie said with as much enthusiasm as her still-queasy stomach would allow. "Harry was so excited about the possibility when I told him."

"I know," Win said. "He ate lunch at the diner today, hoping to persuade me to run, but I'd already made up my mind."

"Well, that stinker!" she said. "He didn't even invite me to eat with him."

"You ate lunch with me," I reminded her. "Remember the tuna salad we ate upstairs? Oh dear, do you think that's what made you—"

"Win!" Josie said a little too quickly. "Have you thought about the colors for your campaign?"

He blinked. "Well, no. To tell you the truth, I haven't gotten that far. What do you think? Red, white and blue?"

"Gracious, no! Too much of a cliché. We need to plan this carefully. Good luck follows us when we align with our true selves, so using the colors that are best for your sun sign will help enormously."

Poor Win looked nonplused. "Sun sign?"

"Your astrological sign," I said. Sometimes Josie needed an interpreter. "As in 'What's your sign?'"

His brow cleared. "So what colors go with Cancer?"

"Cancer? Really? Cancer. Hmmm." Josie glanced from Win to me, and I knew the path her mind was taking. "Interesting."

"Josie . . ." I said with menace in my voice. Her matchmaking acumen hadn't been successful enough with Dan that I wanted to try it again. At least, not so soon.

"I'll have to study on it," she told Win. "We'll get you going, don't worry. Jayne and I are 100% behind you. Do you have a campaign manager? Jayne would be terrific."

"Josie!"

"Well, you would!"

"Don't pay her any mind, Win. Sometimes she gets a little too enthusiastic."

"Actually, Jayne, I came by to ask if you'd consider letting me launch my campaign with a party here in The Naked Bean. When's your Grand Opening?"

"A week from Saturday. Ingrid's talked me into renaming it Naked Beans & Buns."

Win grinned wickedly. "I like it."

"You don't want to launch your campaign at your diner?"

He shook his head. "No, I'll have enough details to worry about without having to cook. People might expect more food than I want to do, if we have it at the diner. No, the Bean is perfect. It's on the square and we can limit the refreshments to coffee and cinnamon rolls and such."

I was flattered. Win Allen was a famous cook around these parts. He'd had a cooking show until a couple of years ago when a fire he blamed on a clown destroyed his set. Since then he mostly did catering jobs, some as far away as Atlanta from what I heard. His diner was only open for lunch, and that only two days a week. But on those two days, people were lined up before it opened.

I'd only eaten there once, when Josie made me get away from the shop during my last month of pregnancy. I enjoyed it, but hadn't been back since.

"I'd love to help you, Win. Why don't we go upstairs and make plans? You want to come up with us, Josie? You're always full of ideas."

Again, Josie glanced between me and Win with piqued interest. "I'd love to, but I can't right now. I . . . have to meet Harry."

"Tell him I said hello," said an unsuspecting Win.

"Oh, I will," Josie called on her way out. "Bye now!"

WMOS RADIO

"The Voice Of The Creek"

Hello again, fellow Creekites! This is Bert Lyman, as always, of WMOS-FM and its sister station, WMOS-TV, local cable access channel 22, bringing you breaking news and tattered gossip. News flash! Jayne Austen Reynolds announces that her Naked Bean coffee shop has now re-opened as the new-and-improved Naked Bean & Buns Shop.

Excuse me while I ask my worldly-wise wife, Honey, if that's one of those double entendres. Otherwise known as a naughty play on words. Anyway, Jayne's taken over what used to be Beechum's Bakery, so the Bean is now a full-service coffee shop. But don't worry, folks. Ingrid's still at the oven-helm. We won't miss any of her cookies, pies and cakes. Y'all run by there and tickle your sweet tooth!

*"The bird of paradise alights only upon
the hand that does not grasp."*

—*John Berry*

Me and Mr. Tibbs

I didn't start the day looking for adventure. Living in Mossy Creek, however, you don't always have to look too far for adventure or, as my mamma likes to call it, trouble. It can find you whether you want it to or not.

I'm Ida Walker. No. Not *that* Ida Walker. She's my grandmother and mayor of Mossy Creek. I'm just Lil Ida to almost anyone who calls me by name.

As it turns out, that's part of my problem. Being "lil" anything is just plain annoying. Being a grown-up is easy. You do what you want, when you want and there's no one to tell you otherwise. I understand grown-ups still have rules. Mamma is a lawyer so I know all about rules.

I wish I could be more like my Nana. She usually has no problem handling her adventures, like with the police chief, but I'm not supposed to know about those.

Yeah, right.

My day started off kind of rocky. I was supposed to be learning next week's vocabulary words (which I already knew) but Mamma said . . . and once Mamma says anything you should pretty much stop right there. I wish I had.

Mamma fixed me and Daddy a good breakfast every day, no matter what. She says breakfast is important brain food. Guess I should have studied more and talked less because I ended up ridin' my new Schwinn Ranger bike over to the library on a Saturday to find out why getting more pets is so much work and why I wasn't old enough for that responsibility yet. Geez. I've already proved I can take care of a pony, two cats, three dogs, a lizard, two parakeets, my hermit crabs and Mickey and Minnie, my ferrets. Not to mention my new rabbit, Wampa. Well, okay, Mamma, Daddy and our housekeeper have to help me feed and tend all my critters, but I'm not a baby. I'm ten years old. Not that anyone has noticed.

I turned my bike down Trailhead towards South Bigelow Road and stopped on the bridge over Mossy Creek, which is where the town got its name. It runs right behind Hamilton's Department store where Daddy works. When me and Mamma bring him lunch during the summer, we take our picnic out by the creek and watch the minnows swim up to catch imaginary flies. Daddy says they're trying to catch the sunshine that glints off the water because Mossy Creek sunshine is all the nourishment a body needs. That and Mamma's cinnamon banana crumb cake.

Spring is a good time in Mossy Creek. It has to be the prettiest place on Earth and I've even been to Disney and Atlanta at Christmas time. It's an explosion (one of my vocabulary words) of color with pink and white dogwoods hiding under the great oak trees older than even my grandma's grandma. Out at Hamilton Farm where they grew my daddy, there are roses of every color you can imagine and wisteria even older than me! Not much leaves Mossy Creek. As Nana says, 'Ain't going nowhere and don't want to.' It was written on the silo at her farm, so it had to be true.

But all of this was part of my problem, I realized that as I started back towards Bigelow Road. Things in Mossy Creek didn't really change although they were pretty weird to start. I'd been asking for another pet since Mamma and Daddy said I couldn't have a brother or sister for Christmas. Because Mamma is a lawyer Daddy said that meant she would always win the arguments in our family. I wasn't giving up yet, however.

I didn't want another dog or cat. I wanted to be different. That's pretty hard in a town like Mossy Creek, especially when you share a name with the women who invented 'different.' The Ida Walkers before me had done great things. They'd settled towns and fought for suffrage (another vocabulary word for this week), run farms, raised families and made fortunes. Nana had even gotten arrested (more than once) for standing up to the governor! I couldn't let them down, could I? What was I going to shout about, as Nana liked to say. Mamma said it was natural for a young girl like myself to want to break out of her shell. I just better be sure that shell doesn't end up all over her living room carpet.

I guess you could say I was feeling sorry for myself as I peddled into town. I'd just turned the corner at South Bigelow Road when I heard a voice that would change my life.

"Look out belooooowwwww!"

I had time to squeal to a stop, plant my feet on each side of the bike and look over my shoulder when a wind-storm of green and red feathers swooped down from the poplar tree hanging over the road and landed itself on my handlebars. I had to blink twice to believe it, but there it was.

A parrot! A *talking* parrot!

It was so beautiful! The bird fluffed and settled his bright feathers, stretching his wings and tail to display spots of red and yellow underneath the green. He wasn't as big as some of the parrots they had down at the zoo in Atlanta. Those were called Macaws. I wondered what kind of parrot this could be? Luckily I was headed towards the library. I'll bet I could figure it out there. Mamma wanted me to learn about taking care of another pet. Maybe the answer had landed right in my lap. Or at least on my handlebars.

He then lifted one claw and cupped his face, scratching the light blue patch of feathers above his beak, as if he were thinking about what to do next. He turned his head left, then right and I followed his gaze, wondering what a parrot would be looking for in Mossy Creek. More importantly, who would be looking for him? Surely something this beautiful had to belong to someone. Secretly, though, I was already beginning to hope he didn't belong to anyone.

With a shake of his head, his crown of yellow and blue feathers ruffled and he nodded twice. "It's a beautiful day in the neighborhood."

"Excuse me?" I couldn't believe it was actually talking to me, but sometimes you just have to go with things. Especially in Mossy Creek.

Squawk. "Toto, we're not in Kansas anymore."

Too funny! "You're in Mossy Creek." I wondered what else he could say. "Polly wanna cracker?" Not that I had a cracker, but couldn't all parrots say that?

He laughed instead with this full, wonderful chuckle that made me smile even more. "Hah. Hah. Hah. Dat's jes so ree-deek-u-lous!"

Could he really understand me? I wanted to reach out and touch him but his beak looked really sharp and Daddy always said not to pet strange dogs. Surely parrots had the same rule. "Do you have a name, pretty boy?"

He squawked really loud and stretched out his body, his feathers standing on end until he looked like he'd been blown dry at the Goldilock's Salon. "They call me *Mister* Tibbs . . . *squawk.*"

Wow. Maybe he did understand. At least he answered politely. That's better than some boys in my class at Mossy Creek Elementary.

"Okay, Mr. Tibbs. I wonder if you live around here. I've never seen you before or heard of anyone talking about a parrot like you so maybe you're just out for an adventure today. Is that it?"

Mr. Tibbs didn't answer, and I was already expecting

him to do just that. Instead he broke into a cowboy song I'd heard on the TV while at Nana's house. "Rollin', rollin', rollin'. Keep them doggies rollin'. Rawhide!"

Before I could go "huh" I heard Casey Blackshear's scooter whirring towards me. I looked over as she rounded the corner from Hamilton Street in her scooter, her daughter LiLi sitting on her lap in the baby carrier the coach wore whenever they were out.

As they approached, LiLi pointed one chubby finger at Mr. Tibbs.

"What in the world do you have there, Rabbit?" Mrs. Blackshear asked as they rolled to a stop next to my bike. She adjusted the safety harness that held LiLi.

Casey Blackshear was my softball coach during her first summer in town. She'd been paralyzed in a car accident, but ever since coming to Mossy Creek she'd been burning up the sidewalks with her neat, motorized scooter. Her husband was the town veterinarian and had a practice over on Trailhead.

Coach Casey was the one that gave me my nickname. I was Rabbit because I ran so fast in my first softball game when we beat our arch enemy, the Sky Ravens, in the battle to beat all battles. They're still talking about that defeat down in Bigelow. I remind them every chance I get, just in case they forget. Bigelowans are big on forgetting stuff like that.

"This is Mr. Tibbs." I moved my bike so Mr. Tibbs was more or less facing Coach Casey. "I was riding down South Bigelow and he just landed right here. Can you believe it?"

"Seeing is believing," Mr. Tibbs added.

"This is Mossy Creek, Rabbit." Coach laughed. "I'd believe almost anything. How do you know his name?"

"Elementary, my dear Watson," Mr. Tibbs squawked, and we both laughed.

Coach Casey smiled. "He's quite the talker."

Mr. Tibbs started nodding and turning his head while LiLi somberly held out her hands in a "gimme" gesture towards the bird. Her mother, however, pulled her hands back, eyeing the beak. Couldn't say I blamed her.

As I told the coach about breakfast and why I was going to the library on a Saturday and more about the parrot, Mr. Tibbs spread his wings and hopped from my bike onto her scooter as easy as frog from a rock.

"I'm an excellent driver," he informed us, then let loose the perfect imitation of a wolf whistle.

LiLi fell backwards against her mom, looking startled. Lili was way too quiet, people said. There might be something wrong with her.

Mr. Tibbs laughed. "Ha! Ha! Ha!" he roared, puffing out his feathers, which delighted LiLi.

LiLi struggled against Coach Casey's hands.

"No, LiLi." Coach Casey said gently, and LiLi stopped wriggling. I was just as scared of Mr. Tibbs's beak as the coach. I'd seen parrots at the zoo crack walnuts. Imagine what they could do to a baby's little fingers.

Suddenly Mr. Tibbs started to whistle the tune to *Rock-A-Bye Baby* and lowered his head towards LiLi, who quieted at the familiar song. Mr. Tibbs presented the back of his head to Coach Casey, rocking back and forth in a slow, to-and-fro motion. We were both a little surprised. He had to be the smartest bird on the planet!

Still unsure, she held LiLi's hands in one of hers but reached out and helped LiLi pet Mr. Tibbs' head. "Gentle, sweetie."

The bird stopped moving but never stopped the lullaby. He held perfectly still, his song still as soft and steady as the spring breezes that circled us on South Bigelow Road. LiLi and Coach Casey stroked his head a few times, the little girl's eyes and mouth forming a perfect "O."

When the coach and LiLi withdrew their hands, Mr. Tibbs bobbed his head in excitement and did a little dance on the scooter's handle. He clicked his tongue loudly in what had to be approval of the attention. The kids at school were going to love him! I'd have the coolest pet ever.

"Think I can pet him, Coach?" It was everything I could do to keep my own hands on my bike's handlebars.

"He seems tame enough, Rabbit."

Like he knew what I wanted, Mr. Tibbs ducked his head and cackled, "Go ahead . . . *squawk* . . . make my day."

I tentatively touched his crown feathers with my fingertips, but his tune changed. As I stroked his head, his eyes closed and he leaned into the palm of my hand.

"I don't believe it!" Coach Casey shook her head. Even LiLi had relaxed at the start of the new tune.

"What song is that?"

"*Love Me Tender* by Elvis Presley. That's got to be the smartest bird in the world."

Since I agreed, I just continued to pet Mr. Tibbs and listen to him sing to us.

"Do you know who he belongs to?" Coach settled LiLi on one side and reached into the backpack she had strapped to her scooter and removed a worn Teddy. LiLi grabbed the animal and immediately put its ear in her mouth. Kids.

"No. Maybe I'll just keep him. I was going to library to find out about owning more pets." Not exactly a lie, I told myself but guilt nibbled at my insides.

Mr. Tibbs woke from his little nap and shook out his feathers like a dog emerging from the creek.

"Having a pet is a lot of responsibility, especially one like this. They can live a really long time." Coach Casey put her hand beneath Mr. Tibbs's belly by his feet and he gently stepped onto her fingers. "We don't see a lot of birds at Hank's practice. This one's well trained." She brought him closer, still careful of LiLi's reach although she was more interested in the Teddy at this point. "Smart as a whip, too. Someone spent a lot of time for him to be so friendly. I'll bet he just got away from his home."

I was a little disappointed to tell the truth. I'd already started picturing Mr. Tibbs in my room at home, taking him to school to show off. No one had a pet that could talk, much less sing.

"What should I do?" I knew the answer to the question already. Mr. Tibbs was just the one that said it out loud.

Squawk. "Take me to your leader."

Both Coach and I laughed. LiLi watched her mother's face but didn't smile.

Our laughter energized Mr. Tibbs, who bobbed and danced back and forth from one foot to another. "E.T. Phone home."

"He sounds just like the little alien in that movie. Amazing!" Coach set Mr. Tibbs back on my handlebars and moved her scooter back a few inches. "I guess you have your answer, Rabbit. Might as well head over to see if anyone's put out word about a missing parrot with Chief Royden. Or maybe with your grandmother. They'll be able to help you."

"I guess you're right, Coach." I replied, low at the prospect of turning over Mr. Tibbs to someone else. Only I didn't want her to be right.

"I think Hank is over at the theater working on the sets. Why don't you stop there, too." Coach Blackshear backed up her scooter with a quick flick of her wrist, circling her free arm around LiLi's belly.

"Thanks, Coach Casey."

"Be sure and let your parents know where you are, okay?" she added, then revved her scooter back down Trailhead.

"Okay."

This was going to be one of those life lessons grownups liked to talk about. I didn't want a life lesson. I wanted Mr. Tibbs.

❦❦❦

I wasn't sure if Mr. Tibbs would stay put on my handlebars once I started riding, but I didn't know what to do about it. It wasn't like I had a leash for a parrot in my back pocket. He seemed settled enough, grooming the big red spots on his wings like he had all the time in the world.

Since there was only one way to find out, I pushed the bike slowly forward and watched as Mr. Tibbs adjusted to the tilt. "Ready to go, Mr. Tibbs?"

With one wing out he squawked loudly, "Hi-Yo Silver," and off we went towards town.

South Bigelow Road took us towards the town square. The roads aren't generally busy on a Saturday, so you can ride your bike in the street without much worry. Most Creekites aren't in a big hurry, either. We'll get where we're going eventually, so we enjoyed the ride along the way.

I liked coming into town this way, because sometimes you get a peek at the actors outside of the Mossy Creek Theater in their costumes. Their next play was going to be *The King and I,* and as we passed you could hear the music from the song, *Getting to Know You,* coming from the open doors. Mr. Tibbs must have liked it because off he flew in the direction of the theater.

"Mr. Tibbs!" I shouted, pushing the bike faster in pursuit. Panic tumbled in my stomach like Jujubes after a ride on the Tilt-o-Whirl. What kind of pet owner would I be if I lost him on the first day? I couldn't lose him. I'd just found him!

The parrot sailed on a burst of wind onto the stair railing outside the theater, bobbing his head to the rhythm of the music escaping from inside. I dumped my bike in a jump-and-roll maneuver but he glided inside before I reached the stairs. Taking the stairs two at a time, I burst through the open door to find him perched on Mrs. Lavender's head, whistling along with the music blaring from the boom box in the corner of the stage. Everyone inside was sitting in a circle, sheet music in hand, but their eyes were glued to the parrot.

"Getting to knoooowwww you," Mr. Tibbs crooned off-key, and he started his little dance. Everyone laughed. Well, everyone but Mrs. Lavender.

Someone cut off the music, and Mr. Tibbs yelled at the boom box. "Play it again, Sam . . . *squawk* . . . play it again."

Everyone laughed so hard Mr. Tibbs did his little dance then stretched out and fluffed his feathers.

"Uhh, Lil Ida? Is this your bird?" Anna Rose Lavender kept very still. She didn't look scared, exactly, but having a strange parrot on your head can't be very comfortable.

Mr. Tibbs glided off Mrs. Lavender's head to the boom box. "Say hello to my little friend." He pecked at the shiny silver knobs. "Hello. Hello. *Squawk*."

"Yes. I mean, No . . . not really. Sort of?" I eased forward, and the circle of actors opened for me. They laughed in the way that grownups do when they think you're being a silly kid. I felt my face go red. "I found him this morning on my way into town. I was taking him to the police station to see if there's an APB out or something."

Using official language should prove to them I'm not a silly kid. I followed Coach Casey's lead and put my hand beneath Mr. Tibbs' belly. He came right to me.

"APB?" Mr. Beau Belmont repeated, as sly a grin on his face as I'd ever seen. "All Parrot Bulletin?" He was Mrs. Lavender's boyfriend, and his teasing even got her to smile. I wasn't impressed at the moment however.

Everyone laughed even harder, which of course started Mr. Tibbs to laughing in his deep chuckle.

"Hey, Hank!" Mr. Belmont shouted. "We need you to make a house call out here."

Hank Blackshear poked his head out from behind the stage curtain. "Sure thing, give me a second."

Squawk. "Who's on first? What? Second base."

Laughter rolled around the circle like the wave at an Atlanta Braves baseball game. Dr. Blackshear came out from behind the curtain with a paintbrush and paint can in his hands looking a little puzzled by the laughter. He shielded his eyes for a second to see what the ruckus was about, then put the paint supplies down and hopped off the stage.

"What's up, everyone? Hi, Lil Ida."

Mr. Tibbs whipped his head sideways as Dr. Blackshear came closer. "Well, hello big boy," he drawled in a sexy Southern accent that sounded a lot like Jessica Rabbit. The whole room burst into laughter. I mean Dr. Blackshear was cute in a geeky sort of way. Not as cute as Orlando Bloom but then again, who is?

He put his hands on his hips and adjusted his ball cap, two bright spots of red on his cheeks. "Well, hello back," Dr. Blackshear greeted Mr. Tibbs. "Who do we have here, Lil Ida?"

"Bond. *Squawk.* James Bond." Mr. Tibbs announced in a proper British accent that would've impressed our snooty neighbors in Bigelow.

"Think he wants a martini?" Mia, Mrs. Lavender's daughter, joked.

Squawk. "Shaken, not stirred."

Once the laughter quieted, I introduced everyone to Mr. Tibbs and explained how we'd met.

Dr. Blackshear moved towards us and squatted down until he was eye level with me and Mr. Tibbs. He had a big smear of blue paint between his eyes and looked like Mr. Tibbs. "I'm not all that familiar with parrots, but I think he's

211

an Amazon. They're supposed to be good talkers."

"Oh he is!" I petted Mr. Tibbs' head to show everyone how friendly he was and how much liked me. "And he can sing, too." I told them about meeting Coach Casey and LiLi and how Mr. Tibbs sang to us.

"Maybe we can give him a part in the play, Anna Rose," Mr. Joe Biddly said. "The bird can't sing any worse than Del."

"Looks like he remembers lines better than you do, Joe," Lt. Col. Jackson added. The lieutenant colonel had been Nana's sweetheart for a while but things were different now. I heard Daddy tell Mamma it had been just a matter of time before Chief Royden won that war, but they caught me eavesdropping outside the kitchen and sent me back to bed. Still, I knew plenty about Nana and the chief.

"Think I could keep him?" Dr. Blackshear was sure to be on my side after seeing how much me and Mr. Tibbs liked each other.

Dr. Blackshear stood to his full height and thought about things for a bit. "I think Casey was right. You need to head over to see Chief Royden or your grandmother. He's valuable. Birds like these can live more than fifty years."

Squawk. "I'm older and I have more insurance."

He smiled at Mr. Tibbs. "Judging by his vocabulary, I'd say someone has taken a lot of time with him." Then he ruffled my hair like I was a kid. Geez. "I'm sure they miss him," he added.

"Maybe somebody didn't want him and let him go," I added helpfully and hopefully. I brought Mr. Tibbs closer to me, feeling him slipping away. "It could happen, right?"

"Anything is possible, Lil Ida." Dr. Blackshear scratched Mr. Tibbs' neck, but the look he gave me said he didn't believe it. "I'm sure your grandmother and the chief can help you out."

We said our farewells (vocabulary word from last week)

and let everyone get back to practice.

Even Mr. Tibbs said good-bye in his own way. "May the Force be with you."

Mr. Tibbs took up his place on the handlebars after I righted the bike.

"Wagons ho!" he squawked as we rode away from the theater.

I could have gone straight to the police station or maybe towards town hall, where Nana sometimes worked on Saturday morning, but I wasn't really in a hurry. Instead, I decided to head on by The Naked Bean and see if Ms. Reynolds was there with her son, Matt. I knew he'd get a kick out of Mr. Tibbs as much as LiLi.

The Naked Bean was a coffee shop next to the bakery. People in town had problems with the word "naked" when Ms. Reynolds first opened up her business. The *really* old people wouldn't even whisper the name when she hung up the sign. I asked someone what the big deal was and all they would tell me was it was a "grown-up thing." I didn't have to be a grown up to read the sign. I don't know why I had to be a grown up to understand what it meant. Heck, naked was a vocabulary word back in third grade!

Anyway, I had a dollar from my allowance in my pocket and the closer we got to Ms. Beechum's bakery, the easier it was to smell the fresh pies and cakes she made for Sunday dinners and church socials. Ms. Reynolds also had cookies in her store, but they weren't the regular kinds of cookies. I tried one once when Daddy ordered coffee and thought she must have left out a few ingredients. I wouldn't tell her that, however. Daddy would've shot me dead. A slice of pie wouldn't hurt while I figured out how to talk Mamma and Daddy into letting me keep Mr. Tibbs.

This is really where the trouble started, but it wasn't entirely my fault. Even Mr. Melvin, who worked over at the vet clinic with Dr. Blackshear, said he couldn't have predicted (another vocab word) the circuits would blow like that. It was just one of those things, you know?

I parked my bike in front of the Bean and took Mr. Tibbs in with me. Everyone else had enjoyed him so much I couldn't imagine that Mrs. Beechum or Ms. Reynolds wouldn't like him. Not to mention Matt.

But I forgot about Bob.

Bob is Mrs. Beechum's Chihuahua, a nervous little dog if ever there was one. He can't weigh three pounds soaking wet and if he *is* wet, it's usually because he's peed on something. Nana told Mamma that Mrs. Beechum should take Bob to a therapist if she could find one that specialized in Chihuahuas. I wasn't supposed to hear that either, by the way.

Anyway, Bob hasn't had the best of luck with people other than Mrs. Beechum. Not too long ago my friend John Wesley McCready bit Bob to teach him a lesson after Bob nipped John Wesley. It worked, too, until Nana and Bob got into trouble over in Bigelow at the governor's mansion down in Atlanta. Bob took after a champion dog in the governor's office and gave him a good chomping, proving again it wasn't always about size but about attitude. Me and Bob were alike in that way.

Bob's luck with birds, however, had been even worse. Like with the hawk that nearly had him for lunch. It even picked him up and flew him around town for a few minutes. He has been kind of leery about things with feathers since that.

Because Mrs. Reynolds from the coffee shop had bought the bakery (I remember Nana telling me about that), I had to go in her door. As soon as I walked in I smelled pure heaven, like spring and Christmas wrapped up in a graham cracker crust. Mrs. Beechum was famous in all of Bigelow County for her Italian Cream Cake. What I loved, however, was her lemon meringue pie, and wouldn't you know there were three of them lined up on the counter just waiting for a customer like me!

I guess it kind of put me in a trance, and that's why I didn't see Mr. Melvin working on the side of the counter. I opened the door and peeked around the new opening between the shops so Mr. Tibbs and I could wait until Mrs. Beechum came out from the kitchen. I wanted to make sure it was okay to bring Mr. Tibbs over to her side.

As I hovered, another customer came in and the bell over the door rang.

Mr. Tibbs shouted, "Every time a bell rings . . . Ha Ha Ha . . . an angel gets its wings."

And that's when things started to go downhill.

Mrs. Beechum called out from the back, "Hello?" and she appeared behind the counter with Bob in her arms. Bob took one look at Mr. Tibbs and yelped at the same Mrs. Beechum and I said, "Oh, no."

It all happened kind of fast from there.

"You dirty rat!" Mr. Tibbs yelled as Bob leaped from Mrs. Beechum's arms straight into the first lemon meringue pie. Bob sank up to his ears in meringue, yelping like someone had stepped on his tail with baseball cleats.

Mr. Tibbs flew from my hand onto the cash register behind the counter, knocking over the sign advertising the daily specials, which clattered to the floor. "Houston, we have a problem," he squawked loudly and puffed up his feathers, stretching his neck and wings outward.

Bob scrambled to get out of the pie. Lemon filling sprayed onto Mrs. Beechum and showered down onto Mr. Melvin.

"What's going on in there?" Mrs. Reynolds called from the other side of the shop.

"There's a bird—Bob, no!"

The Chihuahua dived into the second pie and Mr. Melvin stood up, a collection of wires on his shoulder falling to the ground as he blinked through the pie filling. The meringue formed a perfect white mohawk on his bald, dark head.

Bob must have thought Mr. Tibbs was coming after him like that hawk did a few years back, because Bob looked over his shoulder and stepped right off the top of the counter, sliding down the glass pane that covered the cookie and pastry display on his back. He somehow managed to land on his feet as Mr. Melvin finished wiping lemon pie filling from his eyes.

Then Bob did what Bob did best.

I don't know much about electricity but I do know that water, or *any* liquid and electricity shouldn't mix. There was a loud *zzzt* and the lights went out.

Bob jumped about two feet into the air then took off running like the devil himself was on his tail. Mrs. Beechum chased him into the Bean side, calling his name, her lemon pie footprints fading across the floor.

Customers scattered from their places, then Judge Campbell opened the door. Bob shot out onto the sidewalk.

Mrs. Beechum cried, "Stop him! Somebody please!" then took off after him.

Frozen in place, I could hear Bob yipping in-between Mrs. Beechum's cries. A weird smell filled the two shops, like someone had baked a fur coat.

Mr. Tibbs sat quietly for a second, surveying the damage. "*Squawk*. What a dump." Then he followed Bob and Mrs. Beechum out the door Judge Campbell still held open. I heard Mr. Tibbs shout, "Come back, Shane. Come back!"

Stunned by the ruckus, Mr. Melvin and I stood there watching the lemon-filling slide down the glass display window to plop on to the floor. Voices started to gather outside the bakery and then I heard Mrs. Reynolds ask, "What happened to the lights?"

❦ ❦ ❦

Dr. Blackshear checked out Bob while I sat on the front steps of the police station with Nana. He said the nervous twitch from the electric shock should stop in a day or so. He gave Mrs. Beechum some liniment for Bob's . . . um-mmm . . . burns and told her there wasn't any permanent damage. I wasn't allowed back in the bakery without adult supervision.

Daddy, Mamma and Chief Royden were standing near Dr. Blackshear. Mr. Tibbs was sitting on edge of a planter eating some sesame seeds Mrs. Reynolds had given him. Mr. Melvin was working to restore the power to the bakery and coffee shop. I was staying out of the way and away from Mamma's and Mrs. Beechum's stares.

"Are they going to put Mr. Tibbs to sleep?" My voice kind of choked and I tried to fight the tears but they filled my eyes at the thought of Mr. Tibbs being in trouble.

Nana squeezed my shoulders then wiped some lemon pie filling off my nose. "Heavens, no, sweetheart."

"What's going to happen to him then? I want to keep him."

Nana thought about that a bit. "I heard the chief tell your Daddy that he'd called around and heard of a lady over in Chinaberry that had lost a bird like Mr. Tibbs. Her bird's name was 'Simon Says' because he could repeat famous lines from movies and TV shows. They'd been together for 55 years. A new housekeeper started this morning and Simon got out accidentally."

"What should I do, Nana?" Something hurt deep inside me at the thought of Mr. Tibbs going away. I'd only known him a day but I already loved him. He didn't see me as a little kid.

"You know, Ida. I think you're old enough to make this decision on your own."

Nana gave me another squeeze and a kiss then went and joined the police chief and my daddy.

I thought about Mr. Tibbs and me and a lady I didn't know over in Chinaberry, then watched Mrs. Beechum hug Bob and talk to him like he was her baby. She'd had Bob a long time and they'd been through a lot together. I loved Mr. Tibbs after just one day.

I put my head on my knees and looked over at Mr. Tibbs. Matt and Mrs. Reynolds were talking to him and feeding him more sesame seeds. When Mr. Tibbs looked my way, however, he spread his wings and glided over, landing on the railing of the stairs where I was sitting.

"We'll always have Paris," he squawked and lowered his head like he wanted petting.

I stood up and scratched his head, sniffing back the tears. "I'm going to miss you, Mr. Tibbs."

"Hasta la vista, baby." Then he leaned over and kissed me.

Maybe mamma was right. Being grown up is tough.

Mossy Creek Gazette

VOLUME VII, NO. SIX   **MOSSY CREEK, GEORGIA**

The Bell Ringer

The New Bell Ringer BLOG!

Subscribe now for 24/7 gossip at
www.bellebooks.com/MossyBlog
on Mossy Creek Gazette's On-line Edition!

by Katie Bell

Howdy, fellow Creekites, I have a big ol' scoop of double-dip dish for you: Win Allen, aka Chef Bubba Rice, is stepping up to the gossip plate with a chef-sized appetite for public brawling. He's thrown his chef's hat into the political ring against Mossy Creek Chamber President and City Councilman Dwight (Native American name: "Sits On A Fist") Truman, for the Chairman's position. Folks, this is bound to be a delicious food fight. Dwight wasn't expecting any opposition whatsoever.

The Mice that Roared

Part Seven

Win

"This dog is perfect," Hank said before he even said hello.

I closed the door to his office and sat in the chair on the other side of his desk. "Glad you're so pleased with yourself."

"I picked her up last night at the new humane shelter in Bigelow."

"Her?"

"Yes, a Cairn female, wheaten. Very small, even for a Cairn. Only 9 pounds, full-grown. I think she's around three years old. Must've not have been fed too well as a pup. Might be why she was in the humane shelter."

"Good mouser?"

"Boy howdy. She's already killed two mice and one rat in my barn, where I let her go to see what she could do."

"Wow."

"Yeah. Best thing is, she's the friendliest little Cairn I've ever seen. I've known Cairns that are a lot like cats—can take you or leave you, love to hang out in high places, love to kill mice. Well, our little gal has two of those three. So she's probably enough like a cat that Jayne should like her, but she seems starved for affection. Which also makes her eager to please. Always a good trait. She gets along well

221

with other cats and dogs. I've tried that, too."

"Wow."

Hank leaned back in his squeaky office chair. "I can't say enough good things about her. If Jayne doesn't want her, I sure as heck can place her somewhere else. Easy. I might even keep her myself."

"Oh, no, you won't. Sounds like a perfect match for Jayne . . . not that she knows that yet. Well, don't keep me in suspense! Where is she?"

I followed Hank out to the kennel. A tiny blond dog in the very first cage snapped to attention as soon as we entered. She let out one plaintive yelp, then stood at the door to her cage, her whole stocky little body shaking with delight.

She was less than a foot high with a thick, shaggy platinum-blond coat. She had a strong stand-up tail, wagging furiously now, small pointed ears and stubby little legs. She practically vibrated with the words, "Pick me up!"

When Hank let her out, she bounded straight up into my arms and licked as much of my face as she could reach.

I couldn't help but laugh. I couldn't help but fall in love that instant.

"Obviously, I told her you were coming," Hank said dryly.

I laughed again. "Heck, if Jayne doesn't want her, I do! Little lady, one way or another, you've got a home."

"Don't accept your dog's admiration as conclusive evidence that you are wonderful."

—Ann Landers

Louise and the Marauders

If we hadn't fenced the back yard and put in the dog door, we might have had a chance. If Charlie had not been the ultimate kind-hearted do-gooder, we still might have been saved.

I like dogs. Truly. The fence and dog door allowed us to keep my daughter's Labrador when they went out of town, but we had no dog of our own.

Having an animal ties you down. We'd both reached the age where we wanted freedom to go and come without considering the needs of another critter.

It started innocently enough. My husband Charlie—a semi-retired enginner who works on various projects only when he wants to—called me late Friday afternoon and said, "Hey, honey, how would you like company for the weekend?"

Back when the circus was stranded in Mossy Creek, I had the most delightful houseguest. We still email one another. She helped me through a very rough patch and still keeps me on track in my relations with Charlie.

I was not, however, interested in taking in someone else.

"I'd have to vacuum the guest room," I said at my most curmudgeonly, "and put on fresh sheets. And go to the grocery. I can't stretch dinner. We're just having soup and sandwiches."

Charlie chuckled. That should have warned me, but it

didn't. Charlie is not a chuckler. "No, you wouldn't have to do one single thing. They bring all their own things."

"Bedding and towels? They eat a weird diet? Who are these people? Oh, Lord, more than one? How many?" I could hear my voice rising.

"Calm down, Louise. Only two, and only from this evening through Monday morning. They won't be a minute's trouble."

"Do I have to entertain them? Take them for a tour of Mossy Creek? That should take up half an hour if I drive slowly."

"They entertain themselves. I'll introduce you when I get there. I'm headed home." He hung up.

Hung up! Would you believe?

I stuffed the lunch dishes into the dishwasher and turned it on, ran upstairs to hang clean towels in the guest bathroom, grabbed a fresh roll of toilet paper out of the big cupboard where we keep the extra TP and paper towels we buy in bulk at the outlet store, and unwrapped and set the fresh roll on the back of the toilet to supplement the partial one already in place.

I set a fancy box of tissues on the counter, fluffed up the bath mat and that rug thingie that goes around the bottom of the toilet, then hit the guest room.

The sheets on the guest room twin beds were clean, but hadn't been changed in a couple of months. They'd definitely be musty. I stripped both beds, remade them with the Paisley sheets that matched the Paisley comforters, stuffed the old sheets in the hamper to wash later and rushed downstairs to straighten the magazines, books and morning paper that were strewn around the den.

Of course, all that activity brought on a hot flash. I could feel the sweat rolling down my back between my shoulder blades. Maybe Southern ladies are supposed to 'glow,' but I sweat like a field hand. The hair on the nape of my neck was soaking wet, and I knew if I looked in a mirror, my face would be the magenta of an autumn dogwood. I poured myself a glass of iced tea and steeped another batch, then put the coffee pot on. Who knew what these people drank?

We live in an old Queen Anne cottage that we restored and have added onto again and again. Our latest project was a big double garage, so I knew Charlie would drive our guests around and usher them not through the front door, but via the mudroom, where we drop jackets and Wellington boots and winter hats. I was putting Charlie's golf clubs into the cupboard that we had designed specifically to hold them and which he never uses, when his SUV drove into the garage.

Should I wait at the mudroom door like the madam of a brothel to invite these unknown strangers in? Or should I sit in the den with a magazine on my lap? Actually, I'd probably use the magazine to fan myself with. That made my choice for me. The den it was.

"Louise? Louise, honey, come meet our company."

I stood with as much aplomb as I could manage, pasted a hostessy smile on my red face and turned with hand outstretched.

A moment later I was flat out in the wing chair with my legs stuck out in front of me and a hundred pound furry weight trying to climb into my lap as it drooled on my shirt.

"Benjamin, down!" Charlie yelled.

A second weight hurled itself on top of the first.

"Mirabel! Get off her! Louise, shove them off!"

"Arrghhh! I can't feel my legs!" I gasped. I could, of course, but I wasn't about to tell Charlie that. "You get them off! You let them get on!"

Past the shoulder of the one called Benjamin, I saw Charlie yanking on a pair of heavy leather leashes. I gave a concerted shove. Eight sets of claws fought to embed themselves in my clothes and/or my flesh as they were dragged backwards. I felt as though I'd been mauled by bears attempting to flay me to get to the good stuff.

"Sit!" Charlie yelled. He doesn't usually yell unless he's upset or frightened. I had no idea which at this point. All I knew was that his command had no effect whatsoever on the two gray behemoths milling around and trying to figure out how to get back into my lap.

I shoved myself to my feet and put the couch between me and them.

"What," I choked, "Are those? And why are they in my den?"

Charlie dropped to his haunches and began to play with the one called Benjamin, who seemed uncertain whether to enjoy the fun or bite Charlie's head off. At the moment, I would have backed him in the latter option. "These are our weekend guests. Aren't they gorgeous? Louise, say hello to Mirabel and Benjamin."

"They are dogs. Large dogs."

"Yep. Grand champions, both of them."

"Grand champion whats? Dinosaurs?"

Mirabel decided that Benjamin shouldn't have all the fun. She loped around the end of the couch and skidded on the wood floor to crash into my thigh. I managed to keep my feet, but it was a near thing.

"Come on, Louise. They're Bouviers des Flandres. Aren't they beautiful?"

I shoved Mirabel's nose away from the crotch of my jeans. "I might enjoy looking at them through bars at the zoo, but I don't want to share a cage with tigers, either. Why are they here?"

Charlie sat back on his haunches. Benjamin responded by crawling into his lap and knocking him back on his butt. Charlie giggled like a crazed hyena, closed his eyes and actually hugged the thing close to his breast, which it then drooled on.

"We're looking after them for the weekend."

"I'm going to a motel."

"Louise, be serious. They won't be a bit of trouble. They can go and come through the dog door. They're housebroken, and they've got the whole backyard to play in. I've got their beds, their dishes, their food and their toys in the car. We can take them with us on our morning walk and add an evening walk, which we've been saying we were going to start. Do us both good."

"Charles, you have bursitis in your shoulder. Can you imagine how you'll feel with those two giants yanking you all over the neighborhood?"

"They won't yank, will you, boy?" Charlie rubbed Benjamin's small, gray, floppy ears that looked as though they belonged on a Jack Russell rather than on this beast. "I told you, they're both champions. They're show dogs. They know how to walk on a leash."

"As I recall, show dogs actually trot when they're being shown. Their handlers sprint to keep up with them while stuffing raw liver down their gullets. I refuse to carry raw liver."

"Now you're just being obstinate. Look at Mirabel, there. She already adores you."

Mirabel, obviously the quieter of the two, sat at my feet and stared up at me. Her eyes did look adoring, but whether I was looking at love or at meal assessment, I had no way of knowing. She ooched closer, so that she was actually sitting *on* my feet. I managed to yank them out from under her. She whimpered.

"Charles, dear, please explain this—this—invasion." I was trying to sound rational, but it wasn't easy.

"It's Millie at the office. Her mother had a stroke last night. She lives in Athens, and she's in intensive care. There wasn't any room at Millie's usual kennel for Benjamin and

Mirabel over the weekend, so I said we'd take them. She'll pick them up either Sunday afternoon or Monday morning. I knew you'd want to help out."

What do you say to that? Take your two monsters into intensive care to climb onto your mother's hospital bed? Obviously not. "I didn't know Millie had a mother," I said lamely. "Or dogs." As though I could solve the problem by denying knowledge of it. "Lord help us, Charlie, Millie can't weigh more than ninety pounds! How does she handle them?"

Charlie still sat on the den floor. Both Benjamin and Mirabel collapsed in front of him with their heads in his lap. "She seems to manage, but she did say they can be a little hyper. Shoot, Louise, Benjamin is only a puppy. He's barely eighteen months old."

"He's not full grown? He's already the size of a pony."

"He won't get much taller, Millie says, but he'll probably put on another ten pounds or so." He chuckled again and scratched both sets of tiny ears. "What good dogs," he simpered. "Yes, you are. Come on, Louise, help me get their toys and bedding in. Once we show them the dog door, they won't bother us." Famous last words that must rank right up there with the cowboy's epitaph, "That ole horse won't do nothin'."

"They are your responsibility," I said. "I am not cleaning up dog doo."

Trying to fix dinner with those two roaming the kitchen was like trying to create a soufflé in the elephant pen at the zoo. Ben could reach the kitchen counter without lifting his feet off the ground. We no longer eat a big dinner, but even after I moved the soup to the back burner of the stove, Ben put his paws up and almost grasped the handle of the Dutch oven to pull the whole boiling pot over on his paws.

Then I discovered that Bel could open the refrigerator.

Obviously Ben was the brawn of the operation, while Bel was the brains. Charlie kept himself out of the way until I screamed so loud he was afraid I'd either killed or been killed.

"Problem, Louise?" he asked. He was holding the morning newspaper, which he never reads until he comes home from the office.

"Get them out of here. Put them outside and lock the dog door if you want any dinner." I thought I sounded reasonable.

"About that. I just tried the dog door. Ben doesn't fit through unless he scrunches down. I don't think he's figured out how to manage that yet." He held up his hands. "I'm sure I can teach him after dinner." He tried a smile. It didn't work. "Millie sent along one of those child gates. She said she didn't think we'd need it, but it's in the car. We could put it across the door to the back hall. They'd be able to see us, but not get into the kitchen."

"And you did not think of this until now?"

"I thought they'd settle down."

I pointed my ladle at him like a weapon, which, under the circumstances, it was destined to become if he didn't get that precious pair out of my kitchen.

Of course they didn't want to go. It took Charlie on the front pulling and me on the back shoving to get first one dog, then the other, in the hall, then snap the gate into place before they could get out.

They voiced their displeasure at once in a series of hair-raising ululations that would have done Lawrence of Arabia proud. I hardened my heart and served the scrappy supper on the breakfast bar under the doleful eyes of the grief-stricken canines.

I had taken two whole bites of my sandwich when Ben vaulted the gate, followed at once by Bel. She didn't quite make it and fell splat onto the kitchen floor.

Before I had time to put my sandwich down, Ben had snatched it out of my hand. I grabbed my glass of tea and the other half of my sandwich, stood up and said, "I'm going to lock myself in the bedroom and not come out until Monday. Have fun."

I have no idea when Charlie came to bed, although I heard male cusswords and dog toenails for quite a while. I stayed in the bedroom. The dogs apparently had not figured out how to turn a round doorknob yet.

Although we don't sleep late on Saturday and Sunday, we do sleep later than on weekdays, so when the alarm in the kitchen went off at 5 a.m. we both sat bolt upright.

Charlie had locked the dogs in the kitchen and back hall before he came to bed after first securing the refrigerator door with a heavy-duty bungee cord and crawling back and forth through the dog door. Finally, he had hauled Ben in and out until he figured out how to crawl through on his belly. According to Charlie, Bel regarded her brother as a mental defective and ignored his impassioned pleas from outside until he mustered the courage to come in on his own.

"For Pete's sake," Charlie grumbled, when the alarm went off. It's in the kitchen. If we leave it in the bedroom, one or the other of us turns it off and goes back to sleep without waking the other. Charlie went to shut it off.

I put a pillow over my head and waited for it to stop. It didn't.

Five minutes later, Charlie stormed into the bedroom, climbed back into bed and put a pillow over *his* head.

"Why is that thing still ringing?" I asked.

"You just had to have that darned state-of-the-art sound system," he grumbled. "'Look, honey,'" he imitated me. Badly. "'No knobs at all on the tuner. Just this simple little clicker.'" He raised up on his elbows. "That simple little clicker is in nano-pieces on the kitchen floor. Until I get another FEDEX-ed from the manufacturer, I cannot cut off that alarm. I unplugged it, but I have no idea how long the batteries last. Are you happy, now?" He rolled over and stuffed the pillow over his ears.

I considered holding mine over his face until either his breathing or the alarm stopped, whichever came first.

The alarm gave up and turned itself off in thirty minutes, by which time the dogs had decided it was past time we got up, fed them and took them for a walk. I knew dogs barked and whined. The song these dogs sang sounded like an alien language. Loud, expressive and totally incomprehensible for those of us from planet earth.

"We're supposed to walk them before we feed them," Charlie said. "You can handle Bel. I'll take Ben. Just say 'heel.'"

Having watched those dog training shows on TV, I know that a tired dog is theoretically a calm dog. I also know that at least one of those trainers is an expert on in-line skates. I haven't skated since I was twelve when skates had four small wheels, so that was out. I didn't dare try to handle a leash while riding my bicycle. One good sideways yank and I'd be lying in the road with a broken hip or under the wheels of a semi.

Without Charlie straining on his end of the leash, I think Ben could have outrun the Batmobile. At the end of twenty minutes, I was wondering how fast the EMTs could get to us with their defibrillators.

We did have a few moments of peace while they gobbled their breakfasts. I, for one, spent them in the recliner in the den fanning with a magazine.

"Just one more day," Charlie gasped from the sofa. "They go back to Millie on Monday morning, thank God."

Only of course they didn't, although Charlie went back to work and left me with both of them.

Sunday night Millie called. Charlie talked to her a

long time, and I heard words like 'really sweet' and 'no trouble.'

Liar. They were really sweet, I had to admit. When Bel climbed onto the sofa on Sunday afternoon, laid her head on my thigh and looked up at me with those shoe-button eyes, I must admit I melted and spent the rest of the afternoon half paralyzed from the weight of her while I scratched her ears and read my book.

Charlie eventually stretched out on the floor cushions in front of the football game and went to sleep with Ben tucked close beside him.

Very sweet.

But no trouble? As if.

"Well? How's Millie's mother?" I asked after Charlie hung up the phone.

"Still in a coma. She's showing some signs of coming out of it, but Millie can't possibly leave her. She's an only child. There's no one else."

"So you're taking the dogs to the kennel tomorrow morning, right?"

"Actually, I said we'd keep them. Just a few more days. She'll have to come back to work sooner or later."

Charlie escaped to his consulting job—he's semi-retired now—after our race on Monday morning and left me alone with the terrible two. He was supposed to come home with a taller, stronger gate that Ben couldn't jump and every book available on Bouviers from the bookstore or the library.

In the meantime, I tried to ignore them, while I got at least a modicum of house tidying done. I quickly realized that they were like toddlers. If they were quiet, they were doing something bad.

I found both of them asleep on our unmade bed, wrapped in the duvet, gray ears peaking out from under the covers. I would haul one of them onto the floor, then when

I started pulling the other, the first would crawl back under the covers. I am not generally a screamer, but I'm afraid I gave vent to some alien language of my own before I got them locked out of the bedroom long enough to make the bed and pick up Charlie's socks. Make that one sock. The other had disappeared. I still haven't found it.

I expected them to be sitting outside the bedroom door waiting to pounce, but they weren't in evidence. The house was quiet. At that point I hadn't realized that quiet equaled disaster. I walked into the den and sank onto the modern recliner. Designed to ease back problems, it is the world's ugliest but most comfortable chair. It flipped directly from upright all the way to nearly flat when you pulled on the lever.

I sat and promptly went over backwards. I lay teetering back and forth and completely unable to control the mechanism that sat me upright.

Past my knees I saw Benjamin happily tearing a hunk of dark green leather that should have been tacked onto the bottom of the chair. The mechanism that tilted it lay in pieces around his feet.

Then the doorbell rang. The dogs dropped what they were doing and raced to the front hall barking like foghorns.

It was my daughter, who already thinks Charlie and I are one step from senility and should be earnestly searching for The Home in which to spend our declining years.

I shoved the pair out of the way, opened the door a crack, grabbed her arm, yanked her inside and shut the door behind her. She cowered against the door, both hands protecting her crotch. "Good Lord, Mother, what on earth have you done now?"

You can certainly see why I immediately rose to their defense. It was fine for me to criticize them, but they were my guests, after all.

I told her about Millie and their short-term visit.

"Huh," she said. "Get rid of them as fast as you can. They'll knock you over and break your hip, then where will you be?"

"In bed with a broken hip, I assume. Are you here for any specific reason, or merely to see whether or not I am still alive?" I had a right to be grumpy, didn't I?

"I came to invite you for lunch. Can you leave them?"

"Of course. They are perfectly well-behaved," said I as I steered Margaret to the kitchen so she wouldn't see the recliner. They padded cheerfully behind me. Benjamin, having been baulked of sniffing her crotch, shoved her in the ass instead. Her midriff connected with the edge of the breakfast bar with an audible thud.

I agreed to lunch and got her out of the way before she could spot the disaster in the den.

I had time to take the clean dishes out of the dishwasher and put them away before I had to fix myself up and drive downtown for lunch. Since this is an old house, the new cabinets go high. I keep wine glasses and little-used casseroles and such on the top shelves and out of the way. Since Charlie and I had hosted a small dinner party Thursday night before the Monsters showed up on Friday, I had set the dishwasher to run during last night when it was full.

I set all the glasses on the counter, brought over the step stool, took off my shoes and climbed onto the counter in my stocking feet so I could reach the top shelves.

Benjamin decided I had invented a new dog game. He barked once, nearly scaring me off my perch, put his front feet on the counter beside me and cheerfully rolled six wineglasses onto the quarry tile floor where they exploded.

He jumped straight up, yelped once, knocked my step stool halfway across the kitchen and decamped, leaving a snail trail of blood drops behind him.

Oh, Lord, I'd wounded Millie's dog. I had to get the

mess cleaned up before Bel decided to investigate and cut herself as well.

She hesitated at the kitchen door. I screamed at her. She disappeared into the den. I could no longer reach the overturned step stool. I sat on the edge of the counter and carefully slipped over the edge to stand in the midst of the disaster, preferably avoiding the broken glass.

I felt at least one shard pierce my sock and the big toe of my left foot. I checked my shoes for stray bits of glass, shoved my bleeding left foot into my shoe, put the other on my apparently intact right foot, took a flying leap across to the broom closet, then swept up the broken glass and dumped it into the compactor.

My left foot hurt like hell. I could feel the stickiness of blood when I took a step.

But Benjamin was hurt as well. He took priority. Thank God he left a trail of droplets, because he lay flat on his belly under the recliner and regarded me balefully.

"Come on, sweetie," I crooned. "You dear little nitwitted, idiotic, ridiculous throwback to a tyrannosaurus rex. Yes, sweetie, come to Mommy so I can cut your benighted throat and make the world a better place for all mankind."

His ears drooped while his nearly invisible stub of a tail wagged gently.

He scooted out on his belly and laid his head on my lap. I expected to be bitten or at least snarled at when I inspected his paw, but he let me look at it. The blood had already stopped. It was a tiny puncture with no shards embedded in his flesh so far as I could tell. My foot, on the other hand, had obviously been impaled and was pumping my life's blood into my shoe.

I heel-walked to the master bath with both dogs padding after me. They were very subdued. I sat on the edge of the tub and disinfected Ben's foot. He bore the pain manfully. Or dogfully.

When I took off my sock, I discovered a good-sized shard of wine stem in my big toe. The sock was scarlet, but the blood had already clotted. The dogs eddied around me sympathetically. I could almost believe they were concerned about me. I tweezed the shard out, cleaned, disinfected and bound up my toe, sponged the blood out of my shoe, put on a clean sock and eased my foot back inside. It hurt.

I had to walk normally at lunch or my daughter would know something was wrong. I also had to find someplace to put the dogs where they wouldn't destroy the house while I was gone. If I left them outdoors, they would howl or bark, and Amos would show up at my front door with a citation about noise pollution.

The safest place for them was the upstairs guest bath. It was small; they could lie on the bathmat in comfort, play with their toys and wait until I came home.

I managed to get through lunch without my daughter's catching on, but by the time I got home, I was gray with pain.

The house was blissfully quiet. No doubt the dogs were asleep upstairs in the bathroom. "Good doggies," I called. "Mommy's home. Time to go out."

I heard toenails click on the tiles and panting as I twisted the knob to open the door.

It refused to turn. I continued to try as they began whimpering and scratching inside. "Dammit, I can't get the door open."

They refused to understand.

Since I have boys for grandchildren, Charlie and I put in real locks on the bathroom doors, not those stick-a-hairpin-in locks. Somehow Benjamin and Bel had managed to lock the door from the inside. Where they were.

I worked, sweated, cussed and screamed at them to shut up for a good hour. I knew I'd have dog doo to clean up when and if I got inside. No dog could hold it that long.

Finally, I called Charlie.

"Louise, what do you expect me to do about it? Call a locksmith, for Pete's sake."

Triple A lock arrived an hour later to find me sitting on the floor in front of the upstairs bathroom door. The dogs were quiet, either because they trusted I would get them out, or in despair.

He spent five minutes getting the door unlocked, presented me with a bill for eighty dollars and his business card and left, asserting that he didn't want to meet a pair of gigantic dogs that had been locked up in a small space for hours.

"It's all right, doggies." I said as I heard him shut the front door. I twisted the knob and opened the door before they could lock it again.

They sat neatly on their haunches in the middle of the bathroom floor with beatific smiles on their faces and festoons of toilet paper hanging from their jaws and ears.

Around them lay a foot deep cloud of torn toilet paper and paper towels. The storage cupboard behind them gaped open. Not one roll remained on the shelves.

I started to yell, but found myself laughing so hard the tears rolled down my cheeks. The proud pooches ooched across and laid their toilet-paper draped heads in my lap. I'm sure they thought I had gone insane and needed cosseting.

I shut the door behind them, limped downstairs and lay down on my bed. I didn't say a word when both dogs slipped up to lie beside me, one great head on my stomach, the other against my shoulder. That's the way Charlie found me when he came home.

"Everything Okay?" he asked. I merely pointed upstairs. "*You* clean it up."

The new gate was tall enough to contain even Benjamin

at his most agile, so they sat in the hall and glumly watched us eat the cheeseburgers that Charlie had brought home. He unwrapped my foot, checked it carefully for bits of glass and rewrapped it. "I'm sorry, baby," he said. We left the dogs, went into the den and cuddled on the sofa. With his chin propped on the top of my head, he said, "Millie's mother is no better. They're moving her to a step-down unit. Millie doesn't know when she'll be home."

I closed my eyes. "I can't keep them," I said. "I don't have the strength."

"Millie knows that. She's quit her job here and doesn't know when she can come back, if ever. She's going to try to find a home for them. Poor things. They're littermates. They've never been apart, but nobody's going to be willing to take two of them. They've both been neutered, so no breeder will want them."

That's when I broke into tears. I felt sorry for them, but sorrier for me.

"I told Millie I'd get on the Net and find some breeders who might know of homes. There may even be a Bouvier rescue site."

The next morning I called Dr. Blackshear and told him about the dogs. "They are so sweet, but I'm afraid they'll knock one of us down, and we'll break something. Frankly, they're driving me nuts. And they're not happy. They need more exercise, but I simply haven't the strength to give them any more."

"They need a job," he said. "They're working dogs. Left on their own they can destroy the world."

"They're definitely destroying mine." I hesitated. "What sort of job?"

"In Belgium they used to pull milk carts."

"Of course they did. Riiiiighht. Sorry. Fresh out of harness, cart, or cows to make the milk."

"They also herded sheep."

"You are a great help. I happen to be fresh out of sheep as well."

"Mr. Boyd has plenty of sheep."

"I am not bringing sheep into my back yard for those two to herd."

"He teaches sheep dogs to herd. He could probably teach yours."

"And maybe find us a sheep man to take both of them! Yes!"

I hung up feeling better. I called Mr. Boyd, made an appointment for him to assess Ben and Bel, took them out into the back yard and began my daily trolling for loot. They both had the souls of magpies. They regularly stole anything shiny they could get into their mouths. This morning I found my second-best wristwatch, two silver teaspoons, a bunched up piece of aluminum foil and a part of the clicker for the sound system that Charlie hadn't noticed.

The new clicker lived in the topmost cabinet. Having the alarm go off for thirty minutes at 5 am for a week had nearly broken up our marriage.

Both dogs did understand getting into their crates for travel, although they positively refused to go near them the night we brought them in the house to try to crate them while we ate and slept. We drove the thirty minutes out to Boyd's farm and found him waiting for the three of us. He looked both dogs over while they were still in their crates.

"Need to try them one at a time, see what kind of sheep sense they got."

"What's that?"

"Dog's born and bred to herd sheep looks on 'em the way a wolf does. Dog hates sheep like the good cutting horses hate cows. The instinct to kill has been bred out of 'em. Or most of 'em. You get a dog that wants to kill a sheep, you got a problem."

"They're both sweet," I protested.

"You got two legs. Ma'am. Sheep's got four. Come on. Let's take the big 'un first."

Bel began to call when she realized Benjamin was being led away on his twenty-four foot telescoping leash. I gave her a treat, and she settled down with a sigh and went to sleep.

Mr. Boyd had a fenced pasture of about three acres where he kept what he called his herdin' herd. Twenty or so big white sheep with black faces grazed contentedly all over the pasture. I looked down at Ben to see him straining at his leash so hard he was cutting off his air.

"What we're gonna do is put this long leather leash on him so we can grab him if he tries to attack," Boyd said. "I'll walk him in and let him look around a little, then we'll let him go and see what he does."

What he did was go straight for the four sheep at the far end of the pasture at a dead run. Took him perhaps five minutes to begin to organize the herd and bring it all into one group. Then he moved it around the pasture.

"Don't sheepdogs nip at the sheep's heels?" I whispered.

Not taking his eyes off Ben, Boyd said, "Some nip, some don't. Some just bark and run. Corgis nip at the heels of cows. That's why they're so low to the ground. Kick goes right over their heads."

"So what do Bouviers normally do?"

"They're the linebackers. Watch him flat run into that ewe and shove her back into the group. See? Now, in New Zealand I've watched Huntaways run across the backs of the sheep." Ben launched himself at another ewe and barked in sheer joy.

One big ram took off and when Ben tried to turn him, he rounded on the dog with his head down. His horns were immense.

I gasped.

Ben narrowly avoided those horns and that forehead, ran around behind the ram and chased him all the way back to his ewes, barking in triumph the whole way.

After about twenty minutes, Boyd walked out, grabbed Ben's leash and brought him trotting back to me, proud as your average peacock. Ben collapsed at my feet with his tongue hanging out and his sides heaving.

He'd be much too tired to cause havoc this evening at home.

We discovered Bel was slower, sneakier and less apt to bark. She was smaller, but used her weight more efficiently and moved the sheep with greater purpose than Ben. Each was effective, but in different ways.

When she also collapsed at my feet with a grin on her face, Boyd turned to me with a smile on his. "You got the makings of a champion pair there, Ma'am. How much you want for 'em?"

I froze. Boyd would give them the training and the life both deserved. They could stay together with land to run and sheep to herd. I knelt to scratch Bel's woolly head and smiled at Benjamin in his crate.

My heart thudded. I felt as though I was going to faint. No more chairs or clickers torn to pieces. No more searching for the good spoons in the back yard. No more splinters of glass in my feet. Charlie and I could get back to our quiet lives.

The perfect solution.

I took a deep breath. "They are not for sale." And they weren't. Not now, not ever. They were ours, Charlie's and mine, whether we liked it or not.

He nodded.

"But would you be willing to train them?" I asked. "And me?"

"Can you whistle?"

"Certainly." I puckered and blew.

He shook his head. "Naw, not like that. Like this." He pulled his lips tight against his teeth and let out a screech that brought both dogs to instant alert.

I shook my head. "My teeth aren't built right for that. Does that mean you can't train us?"

"Naw. Just means we got to get you two whistles. And you need a crook to point with. See, each dog responds to his calls and his only." He narrowed his eyes. "I charge twenty bucks a lesson, five minutes or two hours, my choice. You need a couple of lessons a week. You afford that?"

I'd have been willing to mortgage the house to pay him if that's what it took, but forty dollars a week was doable. We'd just have to eat a bit more mystery meat and not go out to dinner so often. Not that we could anyway with Bel and Ben at home alone. I nodded.

He glared at me. "Take a fair amount of walking. You ain't no spring chicken."

"Neither are you. What are you, a hundred?"

He glared at me. "First rule. Don't make fun of the teacher."

"Yes sir. Can we start now?"

"Hell's bells, woman, ain't you run them two into the ground already today? Come back two days from now at nine o'clock in the morning. I'll get you your whistles. Ought to carve your own, but I don't guess you can do that either, can you?" He sounded disgusted.

On the drive home I wrestled with whether I should tell Charlie about Boyd's offer. I pulled into a fast food place to get an order of chicken nuggets for the dogs. I know they shouldn't have them, but they deserved a treat. I called Charlie from the parking lot. "Sweetie," I said, "Call Millie and tell her not to bother trying to place the dogs. We're keeping them."

"She was planning to sell them, Louise, not give them away."

"Ask her what she wants for them and write her a check. Don't quibble."

"You sure about this? You said you couldn't . . ."

"Charles, we are keeping them, period. Mr. Boyd is going to train them for sheep-herding. I wasn't aware, but apparently there are sheep-herding contests all over this area. He thinks they're going to be champions at that, too."

"You sure you don't want Millie to sell them?"

"I'm sure. Mr. Boyd offered to buy them, but I just couldn't. You don't sell family."

The Mice that Roared

Part Eight

Jayne

I've always closed the coffee shop at six p.m. every night except Friday and Saturday. Figured not enough people needed coffee and its inherent caffeine after that to warrant the cost of staying open.

At six-thirty sharp, Win Allen knocked on the back door, which was, at least in theory, the front door to my apartment.

"You're right on . . ." My words faded as I took in the wiggling bundle in his arms. "Oh. Is that . . . a dog?"

It looked more like a blond hamster with a pink bow on top of its head.

Win held up the furry creature, looking proud and pleased with himself. "This, Ms. Reynolds, is your new mouser."

It took a moment for me to process that. "Mouser? That's a cat?"

"No, Glinda's a dog. A Cairn Terrier."

"Glinda? Karn? What are you talking about?!"

"No, Cairn. C-A-I-R-N. I looked it up on the internet. It's an ancient Scottish dog, bred to kill vermin for farm—"

The little dog who'd stopped wiggling to sniff the air alertly, suddenly jumped from Win's arms, leapt past me, hit the landing next to me so close I could feel a whoosh of air and fur, then bolted up the stairs.

I gaped at Win in surprise. He gaped back. "What is she . . ." Then I remembered my son, "Matt!"

I raced up the stairs, Win right behind me. I burst into the apartment only to see Matt just getting up from where he'd been playing with Lincoln Logs on the living room floor.

"Dog, Mommy! Dog!"

I took a deep breath. "I know, little darlin'. Where did it go?"

Matt pointed at the bedroom. "Dere!" He took off toward it.

Win caught him after two steps. "Whoa, there, Matt. Let's see what she's up to first."

"What *would* she be up to?" I demanded.

"Mice," he said firmly.

"Mice?" I repeated. "*Cats* chase mice. Dogs chase cats. *That's* the natural order of things."

"Wanna bet?"

His smile was so smug, I stared at him. He was acting very oddly. Not that I knew Win all that well, but this was odd for *anyone*.

To bring an animal into someone's home was a . . . well, it was a *familiar* thing to do. Familiar in the sense that it's only done by people who know the person they're bringing it to intimately. People don't bring pets to other people unless they're absolutely certain the animals would be welcome.

The hand that wasn't holding Matt settled on my shoulder and turned me toward the bedroom. "Let's go see, shall we?"

"What did you say her name is? Glinda?"

"If you like it. I call her that because that's the name of a character in the Wizard of Oz. The good witch of the North. Toto is a Cairn."

"Oh," I stopped. "Oh!"

Glinda pranced—I swear, she *pranced* around the end of the bed with a mouse clamped between her jaws. The loathsome gray critter was hanging limply, so Glinda had already dispatched it.

"Doggie!" Matt cried in delight.

Win handed Matt to me, then went to kneel down in front of Glinda. "Drop."

Glinda looked as if she wanted to argue, then gave a tiny whine and dropped the mouse on the floor. It didn't move, so it really was dead, not just playing possum.

Matt clapped his hands. "Good doggie!"

Obviously my child had no qualms about the violent death of mouse. All he cared about was the dog.

I shivered as I envisioned bird dogs and shotguns in my future.

Win gave a crisp snap above Glinda's head. "Sit."

Glinda sat promptly, looking up at him and wagging her tail furiously.

He smiled over his shoulder. "I taught her that last night. She's *incredibly* smart."

Matt clapped again as he giggled loudly.

I didn't know what to say. I was too dumbfounded by everything that had happened in the last three minutes.

"If you'll take Matt out of the room, I'll dispose of the body," Win said.

Without a word, I turned.

Matt twisted in my arms. "Here doggie!"

I heard the pitter patter of tiny feet following us. I plopped Matt down on the sofa then sat beside him.

Without breaking stride, Glinda popped up between us. She gave Matt a quick tongue up the side of his face, then turned soulful eyes to me. She placed a paw on my leg, as if asking permission to stay.

Hesitantly, I extended a hand and gingerly stroked her

head. "I don't know what to say, little dog. I don't know what's going on."

Gracious. Had I really answered her?

But it was as if she'd really asked the question.

I heard the toilet flush. So much for a mouse funeral.

Matt stroked her back. "Ginda stay. Right, Mommy?"

"I don't know, Matt . . ." I glanced up as Win appeared in the doorway. "What's going on? Whose is this dog? Where did you find her?"

He stepped into the room. "Hank found her."

"Just like that, Hank found her? Sit down, please."

He settled into the overstuffed chair, then squarely met my eyes. "Hank found her because I asked him to."

I remembered the words that had passed through my head earlier. *To bring an animal into someone's home was a familiar thing to do. Familiar in the sense that it's only done by people who know the person they're bringing it to intimately.*

Or who *want* to know the person intimately.

My breath caught. Was Josie right? Was Win interested in me?

"You asked him to . . ." I still couldn't wrap my mind around the fact that Win had not only recognized a need that I had—most of the town knew about my predicament—he'd acted on it. Had gone to quite a bit of trouble to act on it. For me.

Win nodded. "Specifically, I asked him to find a canine mouser for you. And I have to tell you, he's very proud of finding this little lady. She's perfect for you."

"But I—"

He held up one hand, as if holding off her objections. "I know you're a cat person, but Matt is so crazy about dogs, and I think that if you give her a chance, Glinda might just grow on you."

To hide my confusion, I looked back down at the dog.

She'd curled up in Matt's lap, the perfect size for such a small person. He gently stroked her from her head to her tail, like Ingrid had showed him.

"Glinda?" I said.

The little dog twisted so she could see me. *Yes, Mama?*

I would've sworn on a Bible she said it.

"Look there," Win said proudly. "She already knows her name. Smart as a whip."

"Where did Hank find her?"

"At the Humane Shelter in Bigelow. You'd be rescuing her."

Glinda settled back down in Matt's lap.

I liked that idea, and I liked the way she was bonding with Matt. Smart indeed. She'd probably already sensed that there wasn't much I would deny my son. "She's so small. Is she a puppy?"

"No. Hank said she's around three years old. Perfectly healthy, though small even for the breed. He thinks she wasn't fed very well, and that's why she was in the Humane shelter."

"Well, we can certainly take care of that," I said.

"I have food in the car," Win said. "I took her and Cherry down to PetSmart in Bigelow last night. Went a little crazy. But you've already got some food, a leash and a crate."

"Crate?"

"Dogs like having their own 'den.' A place of their own to go and sleep or get away from it all. And you can lock them in it if you need them out of the way for awhile. Cherry has one. She sleeps in it, though I rarely lock it. Did when she was a puppy though. Helped with house training."

"Oh. Will I have to . . ."

"Shouldn't. Glinda seems to be housebroken already. I didn't have any problem last night."

Emma suddenly jumped on the coffee table and hissed

at Glinda. Glinda popped up and for a minute, I thought we were about to see a chase scene worse than The French Connection.

"Sit," I said. snapping my fingers over Glinda's head.

She sat immediately, though she kept her attention on Emma.

"I don't know about this," I said, ready to grab Glinda if she lunged for my beloved cat.

"Just wait," Win said.

For a long moment, the natural enemies stared each other down. Then as if they'd reached some agreement they weren't sharing with the humans, Glinda laid down and Emma turned her back and began licking her paws.

"'Plays well with others' is on her resume," Win said. His smile was so proud, you would've thought Glinda was his own offspring.

Glinda's ears perked up, then she was off the couch in a flash.

"Anudder mouse!" Matt scrambled off the sofa.

Win and I followed. Sure enough, Glinda produced another kill.

"I didn't realize there were so many in the bed . . ." I turned to find Win's horrified attention directed toward the shelves in the corner of the bedroom over Matt's single bed. I followed his gaze to the clown collection.

"You . . ." His voice was squeaky, and he cleared it. "You collect clowns?"

I shook my head. "Not anymore. Matthew, my husband, loved clowns. We never missed a circus. He and I both collected them. Though the fact that I haven't bought any since he died tells me that my interest in them was all for him. Why? Is it a deal breaker?"

His gaze dropped to mine and held.

In that single question was a wealth of information, and I watched as he processed it. First he realized that I'd seen through his gift, knew that it was his version of a bouquet of roses brought by a courting swain. Then came the understanding that I returned his interest.

His dark brown eyes melted like a chocolate chip baking in a cookie. "Perhaps not."

"Look, Daddy! Anudder mouse!"

I was about to correct Matt for the six hundredth time on the meaning of "Daddy" as I turned to see him holding the dead mouse by the tail.

"Matt! No! Put that thing—"

Win caught me from rushing over. "It's okay."

"Those things are nasty!" I insisted.

"He's a boy. It comes natural," Win said. "You can wash his hands afterward. That's a good lesson for him to learn, too."

"But—"

"Do *you* want to pick them up?"

I shuddered.

"I didn't think so. Go over there and praise Glinda while I show Matt what to do with it. Then we can get down to work."

I tuned out what was going on in the bathroom as I sat on the bed and patted it.

Glinda jumped up immediately, excited that she was asked.

I petted her. "You sure are cute with your little Yoda ears."

I scratched behind them and she leaned into the caress. *Harder, Mama. Harder!*

𝕸𝖔𝖘𝖘𝖞 𝕮𝖗𝖊𝖊𝖐 𝕲𝖆𝖟𝖊𝖙𝖙𝖊

VOLUME VII, NO. SEVEN   MOSSY CREEK, GEORGIA

The Bell Ringer

Booster Club Plans Fundraiser To Catch A Coach

by Katie Bell

In the big leagues, sports teams lure winning coaches with perks like bonuses, houses, private box seats for the whole family, stuff like that. Here in Mossy Creek we hold bake sales!

The new Mossy Creek High School Booster Club is swinging into full coach-bait mode with a big schedule of moneymakers to pad the pure-t embarrassing salary being offered in the search for the school's head coach. Since a certain local poohbah who shall remain nameless (Dwight Truman) is blocking a decent wage for the position, (kinda makes this Bell Ringer wonder if Dwight continues to be way too cozy with our rivals down in Bigelow), Win Allen and other local business folk are leading the campaign to raise money.

No word yet on whether the fundraisers will include that ever-popular carnival moneymaker, the dunk tank.

Your Bell Ringer votes to put Dwight on the dump seat. A sure-fire way to raise a million dollars in a day.

"I love cats because I enjoy my home; and little by little, they become its visible soul."

—*Jean Cocteau*

Sandy Has Faith

"Your BP's still high. Are you sure you feel like going to work today? Maybe you should take a few days off," Jess said. My big old Teddy bear of a husband pulled apart the Velcro closure of the blood pressure cuff that encircled my arm.

I reached up and cupped his face in my palms, smoothing the worry lines out of his forehead with my fingers. "You're very sweet to worry, but I'm fine. Besides, what are the people of Mossy Creek supposed to do without Officer Sandy Bottoms Crane to make the streets safe?"

Jess didn't even smile. "You know what Doc Champion said yesterday. You probably have preeclampsia. If anything happened to you or the baby . . ."

Doc Champion wasn't an OB/GYN, but he'd delivered me and had been our family doctor all my life. I trusted him and had insisted he deliver our baby.

I put my fingers against his lips. "There'll be none of that kind of talk. Me and little Faith are going to be just fine."

Jess smiled and gently rubbed my baby bump. "I love that name, Babe."

"Me too. Of course, she picked it out herself, so how could we name her anything else?" On the night my husband told me I was pregnant I'd first dreamed of my little girl with blond ringlets and a cherub's smile. The second time I dreamed of her, she told me her name was Faith.

"Have you dreamed about her lately?"

The question made me a mite nervous. I was a little more concerned about the gestational hypertension than I let on, but I believe in keeping a positive attitude—in having faith—so I just shook my head. "She's been shy lately. I think she's just waiting for her big entrance."

"She'll be here when she's ready. Have a good day. I'm going out to the construction site after work to see how the house is coming along. When I get home I'll give you a nice foot massage."

"When do you think we can move in?"

"It's going to be a race to see which gets done first—the new house or the baby." Jess handed me a brown paper bag. "Here you go. I packed you a special lunch. No more Bubba's Bodacious Burritos for you until after the baby comes."

I peeked into the bag. "Baked chicken and salad," I said, trying to sound enthusiastic. "Yum."

"Salt free," Jess said proudly.

"Thanks, Hon. You are a wizard with that George Foreman grill."

I kissed Jess good-bye and waddled out the door. Doc Champion was on a soapbox about salt, and I could understand why. Besides the blood pressure, my feet were swollen so much my brothers Mutt and Boo had taken to calling me Big Foot. Ha ha, flippin' ha.

I had reached the stage in my pregnancy where I was getting uncomfortable and so grumpy I'd even been snapping at poor Jess now and then, even though he'd been taking great care of me. The extra thirty-five pounds I carried on my petite frame made me look like a bowling ball with a badge.

I was one of those women you hear about who was way far along before realizing she was pregnant. That made the swelling and weight gain seem sudden.

I'd barely got the cruiser cranked when my cell phone

rang. It was my brother, Boo, who's a firefighter and paramedic. "Sandy, Addie Lou Womack's I've-fallen-and-I-can't-get-up transmitter just went off. Since you're closer, could you go and see about her? Give us a call if she needs anything other than her usual upending."

"Ten-four," I said.

Miss Addie Lou had a body like a bowling ball too, but not because she had a bun in the oven. She just happened to be built that way, and since she was no longer a spring chicken, she lacked the strength to get herself up when she fell down, which was frequently. And when Miss Addie Lou was down for the count, she was about as helpless as a beetle on its back, all arms and legs flailing, and unable to right herself.

Her older sister, Miss Inez Hamilton Hilley, was forever trying to get Miss Addie Lou to attend Tai Chi classes with her down at the senior center to strengthen her core muscles. But Miss Addie Lou wasn't having any part of what she called 'Eastern mumbo jumbo.'

"Mind your own core muscles," Addie Lou had said.

Inez had responded with, "Go ahead and flail around like a Betsy bug, then, you old heifer." And that was that.

When I got to her house, sure enough she was lying on her belly right beside her garden shed working her arms and legs like a tortoise on a hot skillet. "How can you help me up in your condition?" she asked when she saw me.

"I've got an idea." I went into the shed for her wheelbarrow. I backed it up right in front of her and helped her grasp the handles one at a time so she could pull herself up.

"I always said you was a right smart girl," she said when she was finally on her feet.

"Thanks. How'd you manage to fall anyway?" I handed Miss Addie Lou her cane.

"I didn't fall. I got down on my knees to get a better look at *her* and forgot I can't get up by myself. When you get old like me you forget what you can't do no more." She pointed to a little burrowed-out place under the shed.

"Her?" Although I wasn't completely sure I could get back up myself, I knelt down to look under the shed and found myself staring into the wide green eyes of a small grey cat who made a pleasant little trilling sound when she saw me.

The kitty marched in place for a couple of steps with her front feet and gave me the slow eye blink that meant she trusted me on sight. "Aww," I said. "She likes me."

"She's fixing to pop, too," Miss Addie Lou said. "When I first saw her go under there, I noticed that her belly was practically dragging the ground. She's looking for a place to have some kittens. She must be the one who's been putting presents on my doorstep."

"Dead mice?" I guessed.

"Yep. She's a good mouser. I think she's about gotten rid of the ones that took up in my root cellar."

Having to deal with dead mouse carcasses on your doorstep was gross, but it was kind of touching that a little animal liked you enough to bring you a gift of food. It was just so neighborly.

"Is she yours?" I asked.

"Nope. I imagine somebody put her out because she's pregnant."

Normally, I'm not the weepy kind of woman, but with my hormones all atwitter, I just about boo-hooed looking at that poor, sweet homeless cat. "Poor little thing," I said, and put out my hand to her. She looked like she wanted to come to me so bad, but she was afraid.

"She looks kind of scrawny, except for the gut." As if the town gossip in her just couldn't resist, Miss Addie Lou lowered her voice. "I wonder who the father is."

The critter did look downright hungry. "I'll be right back," I told Miss Addie Lou, and went to retrieve my sack lunch from the cruiser. I shrugged off my guilt at giving away the lunch Jess packed for me, pulled out the baked chicken and tore it into shreds with my fingers.

I reached underneath the shed and put a small piece near the kitty cat, who sniffed at it delicately and then proceeded to scarf it down. I placed each subsequent morsel of meat closer and closer to the outside until she was eating in the open, completely untroubled by me and Miss Addie Lou being there.

"She's a pretty little thing," Miss Addie Lou said. "I wish I could keep her, but I'm just not able."

I nodded my understanding. Miss Addie Lou couldn't risk falling on her face every time she leaned over to fill a pet's food and water bowl. Her center of gravity was just too out of kilter. Not to mention how it would tax the resources of the fire department.

When the kitty had eaten her fill, she padded over to me and rubbed her body against and around my legs in fuzzy figure eights that covered my uniform pants in grayish white fur.

Braced on her cane, Miss Addie Lou bent over gingerly and rubbed the little creature's back, making the kitty purr loudly. The old woman started leaning like a willow in a stiff breeze and I helped her right herself before she went on over and balled up like a roly-poly bug.

"Thanks," Miss Addie Lou said. "Well, I guess I'll go and call animal control."

I pictured the poor little thing behind bars, peering at first one passerby and then the next, just waiting for someone to take her home, and I almost teared up again. Spring was kitten season and the county animal shelter would already be overrun with furry babies. I picked up the cat and held her in my arms. She fitted herself on my shelf of a stomach and laid her head against my shoulder.

"I'd dearly love to have her myself," I told Miss Addie

Lou. "But with the baby coming, us building the new house, and Jess working two jobs—at the newspaper and finishing his second book—I just don't know how we could take care of a pregnant kitty."

"Lawsy, I know, Hon," Miss Addie Lou said. "It's a responsibility. You have enough on you right now."

"I'm taking her to Doc Blackshear's," I said. "Maybe they'll be able to find her a home."

"Good idea. I tell you what. I'll get a shoe box and an old towel and we'll make the kitty a bed for the ride to the animal clinic."

With the critter ensconced in the old lady's San Antonio Shoemakers' box in the front seat of the Crown Vic, I waved good-bye to Miss Addie Lou. "You're coming to my shower tomorrow, aren't you?" I called before squeezing myself behind the wheel.

"Wouldn't miss it for the world," she assured me. "I'll be there with bells on."

When I got to the animal clinic, Casey was behind the desk helping out. She greeted me with a big grin, but as soon as she saw the kitty in the shoebox she said, "Uh-oh." Then, when she got a better look at the cat's condition, she amended her greeting. "Double uh-oh."

I sighed. "I was afraid you'd say that. Is Hank around?"

"No, he's out vaccinating livestock. Please tell me that cat is yours."

"'Fraid not," I said apologetically.

Casey reached out and stroked the kitty between the ears. "She's a sweetie. Where'd you find her?"

I told her about Miss Addie Lou and the shed. "I'll have to give Miss Addie Lou some of my upper body exercises. That will help her get up when she's down." Casey flexed her well-toned biceps. Although she was in a wheelchair, Casey was still an athlete, both coaching softball and keeping up with a toddler.

"How far along do you think the cat is?" I asked.

Casey gently rubbed the cat's abdomen. "I'd say she could give birth anytime."

"Any guess as to how many kittens are in the litter?"

"Hank could probably tell, but I don't have his expertise, I'm afraid."

I steeled myself for the next question. "Do you think you can find the cat and kittens a home?"

Casey sighed. "I don't know. The county animal shelter just farmed out some kittens to us today. They do that when they're running over with homeless pets and we have a little room to spare. I'll see what we can do, though. We can at least take her until she has the kittens."

I didn't want to think about the possibilities if nobody stepped forward to adopt her. "I'd appreciate that. Meanwhile, I'll ask around," I said. "Maybe I'll run into someone who wants a pretty little cat like that. What do you call this coloration anyway?" I stroked the kitty's fur backward, revealing snowy white under coat beneath the longer grey guard hairs.

"She's a blue cream," Casey said, bending over to rub noses with the cat. "Say, I have an idea. We could give her away as a door prize at the shower tomorrow."

I laughed. I had made Inez and Lucy Belle promise not to play any of the silly games that usually get trotted out at bridal and baby showers. "That's not a bad idea. Maybe one of the guests will want her."

It was hard to say good-bye to the kitty, even though Casey promised that she would take good care of her. I picked her up and held her again, rocking her back and forth as if she was a baby herself instead of an expectant mom like me.

"I can't wait for your baby to come," Casey said. "You're going to be a great mom."

"I'll be happy if I'm as good a mom as you," I said. "How is Li HaiKui?"

"Perfect," Casey said proudly, handing me a picture of the beautiful little black-haired girl. "Have you picked out a name for your baby yet?"

"Faith."

"I love that," Casey said.

I returned the cat to her box with a final pat on the head. I felt like I'd bonded with the little kitty, especially since we were both about to give birth. For some reason, I just wanted to protect her. I said good-bye to Casey with a final backward glance into the sad green eyes of my new fuzzy friend.

I couldn't get the little animal off my mind as I continued on my shift. I asked each and every citizen I met that day if they wanted a beautiful and affectionate little cat. There were no takers. I even tried to bully my brothers into adopting her, but they resisted me. I must be losing my touch.

By the time I got home to Jess that evening I was downright depressed and more than a little cranky. As usual he was pounding the computer keys so that he could meet the deadline on the second horror book in his publishing contract.

His job at the *Mossy Creek Gazette* was demanding enough with its long and crazy hours. Sometimes Jess would barely have time to come home for supper before he had to set off again to cover a city council meeting, a zoning board hearing, or a high school sports game.

As soon as he got home from covering all those stories, he'd sit down at the kitchen table and work until past midnight on his book.

"I'm home," I said on entering the house.

"How was your day?" Jess asked, not looking up from the keyboard.

"I found a pregnant stray cat," I said.

The keyboard sounds stopped and my hubby looked up from his laptop. "Please tell me you didn't bring it home with you."

Tired an irritable, I snapped. "No, I didn't bring it home. I just really, really wanted to."

"You always want to take care of everyone and everything. But if your blood pressure doesn't improve, you may be entering a high-risk phase in your pregnancy. Have you been lying on your side for four hours every day like Doc Champion told you?"

I made a face. "More or less."

"Sandy . . ."

"It's sooo boring, lying there with nothing to do for four whole hours. Especially when I feel fine!"

"I just don't want you to overdo it."

"Oh, all right," I said, not liking the peevish tone of my own voice. I went to the refrigerator. I must've really been getting contrary because I didn't realize how much I wanted that cat until Jess said I couldn't have it.

"Leftover chicken for supper," Jess said. "Salt free."

"Great," I said.

That night I dreamed of the blue cream kitty. She wandered the streets of Mossy Creek looking for food and a safe, warm place to sleep. She couldn't hear me call and was always just beyond my reach. I woke up tired, frustrated and ornerier than ever.

It was Saturday morning, and Jess was already gone— off to cover baseball spring training down at Bigelow High, where our Creekite kids attended. We were all looking forward to next spring, when Mossy Creek High would be open and we'd have our own teams. He had left me a breakfast of a boiled egg and carrot sticks and a note that said, Have a great time at the baby shower.

I got myself ready, using half a tube of concealer to cover the dark circles under my eyes. As I pulled on my best maternity pants suit, I couldn't get the mama kitty off my mind. Surely someone at the shower would be interested in giving her a home.

When I waddled into the Mount Gilead Methodist Church fellowship hall, my oldest friend and former babysitter, Lucy Belle Hamilton Gilreath, met me with a corsage of pink carnations.

"Hello, sweetie," she sang out. "You look beautiful."

"You're a good liar," I said. "But thanks." Lucy Belle and her grandma, Inez Hamilton Hilley, were giving me this shower on account of them being as close to family as any women in town. Miss Inez was fussing with the tablecloth where the refreshments were laid out, trying to get it even on both sides.

"A chocolate fountain!" I exclaimed. "Y'all shouldn't have gone to all that trouble."

"It's no trouble a'tall," Miss Inez said. "We got it to experiment with having a chow-chow fountain, but the chow-chow was too chunky and it was—"

"It was gross is what it was," Lucy Belle finished. "There was just something unappetizing about seeing chunky chow-chow cascading down those tiers in hunks. You need something smooth like chocolate."

Miss Inez looked out into space like she had gotten a brainstorm. "Chocolate chow-chow . . ."

"Oh, me," said Lucy Belle. "Grandma's getting one of her ideas. That can be dangerous."

I thought I'd passed the stage of morning sickness, but the thought of chunky chocolate chow-chow might be enough to make me backslide. Lucy Belle had given up a lucrative career as a computer programmer to go into the condiment business with her Grandma. One of their secret ingredients—moonshine whiskey—in their signature chow-chow was the worst-kept secret in town.

"Don't worry," Lucy Belle said, misinterpreting what I'm

sure must have been a right bilious look on my part. "We washed the fountain out real good. The chocolate won't taste a thing like vinegar and peppers."

I oohed and ahhed over the refreshments and decorations. They had a great big sheet cake with white icing and each piece decorated with pink flowers and a little plastic baby. All my favorites were there too. Lucy Belle remembered how I love butter mints, so she had made a whole bunch in all pastel colors. Then there were the cheese straws and sausage balls I love so much. I couldn't eat many of them, because they have a lot of salt, but there was plenty of fruit to dip in the chocolate.

Miss Inez had made my favorite punch—the one from her family recipe with the pineapple juice, ginger ale and citric acid from the drugstore to give it that extra kick. They even froze some in a bunt pan to make a nice little ice ring to float in the punch bowl.

"Y'all are just too good to me," I said.

"Nothing's too good for our Sandy," Miss Inez said.

I grabbed some of the cashews and popped them in my mouth. "Y'all like cats, don't you?"

"Love 'em," Lucy Belle said. "But we already heard about the stray that Aunt Addie Lou found. And I'm afraid that the health department wouldn't look kindly on a cat living cheek by jowl with the chow-chow operation."

"I'm sorry, darlin,'" Miss Inez said. "You know my philosophy is a little cat hair never hurt anybody, but not everybody is that open-minded."

Rainey Cecil arrived early to fix my hair, clucking and fussing over me like a hen. Then other guests soon began to arrive—it looked like the whole town turned out—and I asked them every one if they could give a poor little cat and her kittens a home. Everyone had a great excuse why they couldn't. I nervously munched cashews and sausage balls, hoping that the next person who came through the door would want a cat.

I tried not to think about my animal woes as I opened the lovely presents everybody brought. Miss Addie Lou hand-crocheted a receiving blanket. Hannah Longstreet made me a Dutch Doll quilt. Ora Sue Salter had Nancy Daniels sew the baby a beautiful dress from one of her favorite patterns. Ida Hamilton Walker and her daughter-in-law gave me a changing table from the department store. Eleanor Abercrombie gave me one of her specially bred rose bushes.

"Plant this on the day the baby comes," she said, "and they'll grow up together."

Josie Rutherford gave me a Feng Shui kit for the nursery. And Jayne Reynolds—bless her heart—gave me a six month free pass to her new and improved coffee house.

Rainey wrote down the name of each guest and what they brought so that I could write my thank-you cards without missing anyone, and saved the bows in a big old zip-lock bag. Waste-not, want-not are words to live by.

After I'd opened the presents and thanked everyone for coming, Miss Inez and Lucy Belle served the cake. I mingled with my friends and neighbors and thanked them again for their gifts.

"What are you naming the baby?" Maggie Hart asked between swills of pineapple punch.

"Faith," I said. "It came to me in a dream."

"It's bad luck to name the baby before it comes," warned Maggie's mother, Millicent Hart Lavender. She had a handful of plastic babies which she had collected from the other guests' cake.

"Oh, Mama, stop being crazy," Maggie said. "That's just an old family wives' tale. Don't pay her any mind, Sandy. You know how she is when she gets too much sugar."

Millicent certainly was crazy all right. I wouldn't be surprised to see her throw those plastic babies onto the floor and try and read their signs and portents like a voodoo mambo casting bones. Even though she was certifiable, her warning gave me the creeps just the same.

I saw Casey rolling her wheelchair by the refreshment table, balancing her plate on her knees. "Thank you so much for the bath set," I told her. "I just love those bath towels with the bunny ears. Uh, speaking of animals, how's the kitty cat?"

"She went into labor right before I started over here," Casey said. "I'm afraid she was having some trouble, but Hank's with her, so I'm sure she'll be fine."

My heart sank. "What's wrong?"

"I'm not sure, really. Hank just said she was having a hard time."

"The poor little thing," I said, feeling a bit dizzy as I remembered my dream. My heart sank. "I wish there was something I could do for her."

"Sandy, you don't look too good. Maybe you should sit down for a while."

"Oh, my," I moaned. "I forgot about the salt in all those cashews. Not to mention the sausage balls."

"How do you feel?" Casey asked.

"I'm getting a headache to tell you the truth," I said. When I looked around the room I realized my vision was blurring. The last thing I remember is hearing myself say, "Uh-oh."

I came to on a stretcher while my brother Boo was squeezing my arm with a blood pressure cuff. He was as worried as I've ever seen him, which made me a mite nervous, because he's normally a pretty cool customer.

"Your BP's way too high," he said. "You're going to the hospital."

"Whatever you say," I said. I wasn't about to argue with a professional, even if that professional was my little brother and arguing with him came as naturally as breathing.

Lucy Belle squeezed my hand and said, "You're going to be fine, Sugar. Just be good for Boo and relax. Mutt is going by the high school to tell Jess and take him to the hospital to meet you."

"Okay then," I said. While Boo was rolling me out, I called out to Casey, "Let me know what happens with the cat and her kittens."

"Don't worry," she said. "I'm sure they'll be just fine. You worry about you and the baby."

By the time I arrived at the hospital Jess was already there. He grabbed my hand as they wheeled me into one of the little stalls in the emergency room.

He had about a thousand questions about how I felt and what happened at the shower when I got sick. He and Boo and Mutt stood around my little bed discussing, speculating, hand wringing and telling me to calm down.

After the nurse had taken my vital signs, Doctor Champion came in with a clipboard. He asked me lots of questions about how bad my lower back and right shoulder hurt and whether I was having trouble catching my breath. For some reason I found all the questions oddly confusing. When he tapped my knee to test my reflexes, my leg jerked back hard.

"We're going to have to do an emergency C-section," Doctor Champion said.

"Is the baby developed enough?" Jess asked.

"We think her lungs and other organs are mature enough, yes," the doctor said. "If she needs help for the first few days, we'll keep her in an incubator until she's strong enough to go home."

My brothers kissed me on the forehead and murmured words of encouragement. Jess kissed me and said, "I love you a bushel and a peck, Babe. You hang in there, you hear?"

"You bet I will. I love you too," I said.

They wheeled me into the operating room and that's about the last thing I remember until I woke up with a yelling, wriggling, pink little blond baby lying across my chest. Jess was there with tears on his cheeks and a disposable camera someone had given him.

I had told him I didn't want a movie camera in the delivery room, but a regular still one was fine as long as it was pointed with discretion.

"Are her lungs as good as they sound?" I asked the doctor.

"Indeed, they are," Doctor Champion said. I could see his eyes crinkle into a reassuring smile over the top of his surgical mask.

"How about the rest of her?" I asked, touching my baby's smooth, moist cheek for the first time.

"She's fine," the doctor said. "Small, but she'll make up for that in no time. We're going to keep you in the hospital for a couple of days to make sure you're a hundred percent. We'll keep Faith in an incubator for a week or so more until we're certain she's strong enough to go home."

Jess snapped a picture of me and the baby. "Ora Sue said I could take the month off starting today. A whole caravan of women from the baby shower are out in the waiting room. I'm going out to tell them the news that you and the baby are going to be fine," he said.

After I'd nursed the baby and she'd cleaned us both up, the nurse took Faith back to the incubator. The women from the shower came in to see me two-by-two after they'd peeked through the viewing glass at Faith. They declared her to be perfection itself and made rosy prognostications about her future.

Lucy Belle had boxed up the cake and plastic plates and was handing out refreshments in the waiting room while Jess gave away cigars to anyone who wanted one.

Later, when Jess was asleep in the chair across from my hospital bed, I counted all my blessings—a beautiful, healthy new baby, a wonderful and thoughtful husband, a great job and a brand new dream house almost ready to move into.

I was so very lucky and grateful. But as I drifted off to sleep I just couldn't get the homeless, trusting mama kitty off my mind. Would her babies be as healthy as my baby was? I sure hoped so. I drifted off to the remembered sound of her gentle purring.

🐾🐾🐾

The next day little Faith was doing fine and my blood pressure was almost normal. Jess left early to go and check on the construction project but promised to come back by lunch time. I had several visitors, including my boss, police Chief Amos Royden, and Mayor Ida Walker. As soon as I had a moment to myself, I crossed my fingers and called Blackshear Veterinary Clinic to get an update on the kitty cat.

Hank came to the phone. "She's fine, Sandy. She had a pretty little girl just like you did."

"Just one?" I asked.

"Yes," Hank explained. "The reason she had problems is that instead of a whole litter, she had just one really big kitten."

"I'd love to come by and see her on the way home from this hospital if that's okay," I said.

"That won't be possible. One of my vet techs found her and the kitten a home. Isn't that great news?"

"It certainly is," I said. "Thanks so much for helping her, Hank."

"You're welcome," he said, "and kiss that new baby for me."

As I hung up the phone I said little prayer of thanks

that my fuzzy friend and her baby had found a home. I felt sad realizing that I wouldn't see her again, though. I felt like the little animal and I had a sisterhood of sorts over the motherhood thing. Whoever adopted both her and her kitten so they could stay together deserved a special place in heaven in my book.

🐾🐾🐾

Monday morning, while I was slowly walking laps around the nurse's station to get back in shape, Doctor Champion stopped by on rounds and declared me to be in excellent health. As soon as he'd signed the release papers, we packed up to go home for awhile. I planned to spend most of my time at the hospital with Faith until she was released.

As he'd settled me into the car, Jess asked, "Do you feel like driving out to the new house or do you want to go home and rest?"

"Are you kidding me?" I asked. "I've been resting for the last two days. I want to see how the house is coming. What have they done since I saw it last?"

"It's a surprise," he said. "I got all inspired and put in a new feature all by myself just yesterday that I think you'll like."

On the way to the house we talked about our future, our hopes and dreams for our little girl and plans for our life in our new home.

When we reached the building site, I noticed the shutters and all the new trim that had been added since I'd seen it last week. "It looks like a real house now," I enthused. "When can we move in?"

"By the end of the week, I would think," he said. "But remember, when it's time to move, you're not lifting anything heavier than that baby."

"Whatever you say," I agreed. I carefully dodged pieces

of spare lumber on the way to the door.

"Ordinarily I'd carry you over the threshold, but since you're convalescing, I don't want to take a chance on dropping you, so I'll wait," Jess kidded.

"Where's this new feature you're so proud of?" I asked.

"Come with me," he said.

We walked all the way through the house to the back porch. I'd always wanted a house with a wraparound porch, and the back part was screened in so we could enjoy sitting by the babbling brook without getting eaten up by the skeeters in the summertime.

I walked through the door to the screened-in porch and saw that one end had a maze of two-by-fours suspended from the ceiling and painted in all the colors of the rainbow. The little ramps and ladders connected with each other and veered off in all directions until they wound up with the end of one plank resting on the porch floor.

"What in the world?" I marveled.

"It's a catscape," Jess explained. "Look right over here."

Jess led me over to a big cardboard box I hadn't noticed in the sunny corner where some leftover building material was stacked. I looked over the side and saw the fuzzy mama kitty peering up at me from where she lay curled up next to her sleeping kitten.

"How do you like your housewarming present?" Jess asked.

"Oh, Jess! It's the best gift ever! Hank told me they found a home for the cats, but he didn't tell me who adopted them."

"I swore him to secrecy. In exchange I had to promise that we'd bring them in to get spayed when the mom is ready and when the baby is old enough. Oh, and I also promised we'd always keep them indoors so they'll be safe and to never have them de-clawed. That's what the catscape's for. They can climb and play out here as much as they want when they're not in the house with us."

I petted the gray kitty, who stretched her sleek neck upward to meet my touch. Then Jess very gently lifted her baby onto my palm. "They say you should handle kittens early and often so they'll bond with humans."

"Hank said you don't have to wait until their eyes are open like they used to say when we were growing up."

The fuzzy baby squirmed and mewled in my hands. Jess took her and set her back down against her mother's side. "Jess, I couldn't be happier. But what made you change your mind about us adopting the cats?"

"I did some research on the internet," Jess said. "I found out that just holding a pet can make your blood pressure go down. Did you know that?"

"No, I didn't, but I do know one thing," I said. "I have just about the smartest husband in the world."

Jess bent down to kiss me. "And I have most sensible wife in the world. But hey, tell me this—what are you going to name these cats?"

I thought a minute about how lucky we were to have a healthy baby with what we'd just been through and how it was only right to share our good fortune by giving a home to two of God's beautiful creatures.

"We'll name them Hope and Charity," I said. "What else?"

Mossy Creek Gazette

VOLUME VII, No. EIGHT   MOSSY CREEK, GEORGIA

Birth Announcement

This week the stork dropped off a pink bundle of happiness at the Crane home. (Yes, storks deliver to cranes.) Mossy Creek Police Officer Sandy Bottoms Crane and *Mossy Creek Gazette* reporter Jess Crane are proud to welcome their first nestling, Faith Crane.

Faith came a few weeks early, weighing in at only 5 lbs, 3 oz., but Doc Champion is taking good care of her down at Bigelow Regional. She'll be in an incubator for awhile, but should be home inside a couple of weeks.

Faith is said to have her mother's curly hair and her father's way with words. Jess swears she is already saying "wah" for "water." Since "wah" is the only sound she makes so far, impartial observers are a little dubious.

The Cranes plan to move into their new house next week with their bundle of joy. Joining them and Faith to complete the family are a mama kitty and her baby, who Sandy has named Hope and Charity.

Congratulations, you two! And kudos for repopulating Mossy Creek with both a people baby and a kitty baby!

The Mice that Roared

Part Nine

Win

"I'm heading back to the bar." Michael Conners extended his hand. "I've got to see what trouble Regina and Buddy have gotten O'Day's into during the last two hours."

I laughed and shook his hand at the door to The Naked Bean & Buns. "Knowing those two, I guess you'd better. Thanks for coming."

Michael nodded and pulled on a baseball cap against the gentle spring rain falling outside. He only had a block to walk, since O'Day's Pub was just up the square, next to town hall. "Restauranteurs need to stick together. I'm glad you're running. I've had about all I can handle of Dwight."

"If I had a nickel for every time I've heard that sentiment tonight . . . well, I could finance my campaign."

"Charge 'em!" he said with a grin, then stepped into the night.

I turned back into the nearly empty coffee shop and took a deep breath. It was half past nine. I'd made my big announcement at 7:30 sharp, but the crowd, which had been larger than I'd imagined it would be, had stuck around to encourage me and to visit.

Across the shop, Ingrid was just coming back in. She'd gone upstairs an hour earlier to put little Matt to bed.

Bob and Glinda followed on Ingrid's heels. The two dogs

had become bosom buddies, although Glinda had quickly disabused Bob of the notion that she had any romantic interest in him.

Glinda had done a swift and thorough job of cleaning up the nest of mice that had been plaguing Jayne. Whether they'd been killed, decided to relocate or had been intimidated enough so they didn't show their ugly faces anymore, they were no longer a problem.

The Naked Bean & Buns' Grand Opening last Saturday had been a rousing—and rodent-free—success.

Spotting Jayne, Glinda ran over to her and poked her nose into Jayne's leg, as if to say, *I'm back*. Jayne absently bent to pick her up, settled the tiny dog into the crook of her arm as if she'd been doing it for years, and went back to her conversation with Jess Crane, who was covering the "big news" for the *Mossy Creek Gazette*. The proud father was here alone tonight. Sandy and their daughter, Faith, were not supposed to be out and about much for a couple more weeks. But Sandy had sent me her blessing.

I grinned, feeling proud of my role in Jayne's conversion to the joys of dog ownership, and grabbed a sugar cookie off the tray Betty Halfacre was returning to the bakery side of the shop. "I haven't had one of your delectables all night."

"Busy talking. You're a politician now." Betty didn't talk much, but when she did, it was to the point. "Talking's your job."

I winced. "Good grief. I've always thought that 'politician' is one of the dirtiest words in the English language."

She shrugged and moved on. "Your choice."

Yes, it was my choice, and I was more happy about it every day. I loved my adopted town of Mossy Creek, and I had lots of ideas on how to run things better. And since town council was as far as I planned to take my political career, I could avoid the label 'politician,' at least in *my* head.

I moved across the room to another choice of mine, and discovered that Jayne and Jess weren't discussing the town council but Faith, Jess and Sandy's two-week old daughter who had just come home from the hospital.

Jayne smiled at me as I joined them and made a comment that made it obvious she'd been by to see the newest citizen of Mossy Creek.

I knew that, of course. I'd dropped by the Bean every day since I introduced Glinda to the Reynolds family. I'd always had a reason, of course, either to discuss tonight's party or to see how Glinda was doing in her mouse hunt. The excuses were flimsy, and Jayne knew it. It was like our own private joke. I not only enjoyed the joke we shared, I enjoyed the fact that we shared it.

I hadn't asked her out yet. We'd both been too busy, what with the Grand Opening and tonight's shindig. But I intended to remedy that as soon as we chased everyone off.

That took another half hour. I helped with the clean-up, though Ingrid tried to shoo me away. Betty only regarded me with her black, knowing gaze.

A little after ten, it was done. Jayne walked her three helpers to the door where we said our goodbyes.

I lingered after Ingrid and Betty had disappeared down the street.

Jayne looked tired, but regarded me patiently. "Is there something else?"

I nodded and leaned against the door she held open. "Yes. Would you like to have supper Friday night?"

Her eyes twinkled. "I usually do have supper on Friday nights."

I chuckled. "Okay, Ms. Literal, would you care to dine with *me* on Friday night?"

"You're asking me on a date?"

"Sounds like it."

"It's about time."

I chuckled again. "You're right. It is."

"Were you chicken?" she asked.

"No, just biding my time."

"Josie will be glad to hear that. She's been angsting over it."

"I know. You're not the only one Josie's been haranguing."

"Good to know."

"*You* could've asked *me*, you know."

She shrugged. "I know. Josie pointed that out more than one time. I guess I'm a little too old-fashioned for that, especially for a first date."

I picked up her hand and caressed the back of it. "I kinda like old-fashioned girls."

"Then my chastity belt won't throw you," she said.

"If you mean the kid asleep upstairs, then no. He won't throw me. He's growing on me." I felt my voice lower. "You are, too."

Her breath caught, and I felt a tiny thrill that I could make her nervous.

"So?" I asked.

"So?"

"Will you go on a date with me on Friday?"

"Yes. Where? Oh my, if we go anywhere in town, we'll be all over the *Gazette* next week."

"I thought we'd go eat fish down on Lake Lanier."

"Sounds good."

The conversation was complete, but I didn't want to leave. "You said 'yes' awful quick."

"Oh, stop being so smug. Would you rather I vacillated? I can Southern Belle with the best of them, if that's what you want. But I'd rather have an honest relationship."

"I insist on it. Honesty, that is."

"Me, too."

"Noted."

I gave her hand a squeeze, then let go. "Good night, then. I'll see you tomorrow, I'm sure. I'm rapidly becoming addicted to your mocha lattes."

"Good night, Win," she said softly. "I'll see you tomorrow."

I watched her lock the door behind me then cross the shop. She turned at the light switch beside the door to her apartment, smiled, then flicked the switch.

"I'm rapidly becoming addicted to your smiles, too," I told the darkness, then I turned toward home.

*"You think dogs will not be in heaven?
I tell you, they will be there long before any of us."*

—Robert Louis Stevenson

The Heart Knows

Possum lumbered off the paved two-lane outside of Mossy Creek and headed along the paved pathway that ran from the Blackshear Veterinary Clinic past the back porch of Ed Brady's farmhouse. He stepped carefully, avoiding the tiny rocks that speared feet no longer calloused from running through pastures where generations of retired rams—the mascots of Mossy Creek High School back in the day, before the school burned down—had grown old, died and were not replaced—until now.

Had Possum been human instead of canine, he would have applied for the job as mascot at the new high school. If heart had been the only requirement, he would have won, hands down. Make that paws down.

But Possum wouldn't apply. Like his master, Ed, he was too old.

The new school was complete and would open in the fall. The band uniforms were new. The instruments polished to a lightning shine. But there was no ram ready to carry on tradition, at least not one in Ed's pen.

Possum paused, sat back on his haunches and took a deep breath.

Nothing would be the same. Change came, like a thief, taking time and chewing it into airborne flecks of nothingness.

Possum released his breath slowly. It was time for him to take up his self-appointed chores, beginning with round-ing up Ed and leading him back to Magnolia Manor, where they both now lived.

The nursing home was divided into three sections: Individual Apartments, Assisted Living, and Medicare patients who were primarily confined their rooms. The staff had long ago given up on keeping Possum outside or Ed inside.

Miss Irene, the oldest resident of the Manor at age ninety-seven, had threatened to lead another protest march if Possum wasn't allowed free run of the place. And though it was becoming more difficult each day, Possum made it his duty to spend a few minutes with every patient there. They looked for him, waited for him and made certain that Ed didn't leave the Manor without his dog. Lately though, Ed had been leaving Possum behind. Possum couldn't keep up with him.

The erratic beat of his heart was becoming harder and harder for Possum to conceal. But he didn't try to fool himself. His final rounds were coming to an end. Not today, but soon.

His daily trek always allowed for a quick moment with Li HaiKui, Casey and Dr. Hank's black-eyed little Chinese daughter. Right after naptime, Casey took Li HaiKui on an outing that passed the spot where Blackshear Clinic's large-animal-recovery pasture joined the tip of Ed Brady's land. Today was no exception.

Though his canine eyesight was failing, even Possum could see LiLi's face light up when she caught site of him.

Possum made the effort to wag his tail and waited for Casey's motorized scooter to reach his spot.

Today, Dr. Hank walked with them. Casey had LiLi sitting in front of her, leaving the scooter's large wire grocery basket vacant for Possum. The child was beautiful, quiet and gentle, never pulling at Possum's ears or poking stubby fingers in his eyes. But she was too quiet, and though he was only a dog, Possum sensed that Casey was as concerned about LiLi as he was about Ed.

There was a time when Possum would have dashed across the field, announcing the intruders with three short yips for play pals and an anxious howl for the unknown. Now, he walked slowly, his tail drooping as if he hadn't the energy to hold it up.

He reached the scooter and reared up, placing his feet gently against the metal braces on Casey's legs. He stood very still, waiting for LiLi to giggle like other children did. Rippling his skin beneath her touch, he waited for some response. LiLi did nothing except draw tentative little circles on Possum's head.

Dr. Hank lifted Possum into the wire grocery basket attached to the front of the scooter. She had placed a small pillow on the bottom. Possum nestled in the padding and leaned toward LiLi.

There was no touching. No peal of laughter. The doctors had found no reason for LiLi not to speak more than a few words. "She'll talk when she gets ready. We just have to be patient," they said, just like they said about Casey's lifeless legs. But even Casey's father, Dr. Champion, seemed less certain.

Possum twisted around to lick the arm holding LiLi.

Casey squeezed the dog and whispered, "I know, old boy. This is the cripple mobile. I have no working legs, LiLi doesn't speak, and you're fooling yourself about your abilities." Casey cranked the electric motor and pulled onto the path. She'd give Possum a ride back to town today, as she did more and more often.

"When will you know, Hank?" she asked.

Hank said. "They'll fax it to me. "I'd go with you, but I'm going to wait on the report."

"Have you seen Ed this afternoon?" Casey glanced at her watch. Ed managed the short trip to his old home every day, returning to Magnolia Manor at night. He still considered himself a working farmer.

Hank shook his head. "Call me when you find Ed, and I'll come pick you up."

Casey nodded and increased her speed.

Ed wasn't at the holding pen constructed for the new ram mascot arriving next week. Police Chief Royden and the city council had all agreed that even though the new stadium wouldn't be ready for another year, the appearance of their mascot would build school spirit, and spirit was important since the new Mossy Creek football team would have to play its first season's home games at the stadium of Mossy Creek's biggest rival, Bigelow High.

"Let's look for Uncle Ed here," Casey said, tousling her daughter's hair as she came to a stop in front of Ed's house. "I bet he went inside for a drink of water."

Possum managed to climb out of the basket with Casey hoisting his rump from behind. He lumbered into the house. But Ed wasn't inside the cold, dark kitchen of the house where he and his Ellie had lived for so many years.

Possum trudged back to Casey's scooter, his heart thumping hard with worry.

❧❧❧

By the time Casey returned Possum to town, a late afternoon wind picked up, ruffling the brown grass of the square's still-dormant lawn. Soon the square would be green with new growth. Possum leaned his neck across LiLi's knee and licked her leg good-bye. What would the little girl do when both he and Ed were gone? She couldn't talk and made no effort to try. Stoic and wooden, she was content to sit wherever she was placed.

"She's happy," everyone claimed.

But Possum wasn't certain.

That afternoon, not only could Ed not be found, but Miss Irene had disappeared as well. Since the two of them were notoriously independent, Casey didn't call Chief Royden and launch a search. With Possum perched in the scooter's basket, she prowled all the shops to confirm Ed and Miss Irene weren't there, then finally drove her red scooter across her namesake, *Casey's Bridge*, outside the library. She came to a halt beside Hank, who was leaning back against his battered old treatment van. He was holding a blue-edged sheet of paper, a faxed lab report. Hank rarely had the lab fax their findings. Today he had.

"How bad is it?" she finally asked. She lowered her voice as if Possum might overhear. Possum, however, just kept gazing sadly at LiLi, who gently stroked his head.

"Bad. All the results aren't in yet, but the radiographs are pretty clear." Hank glanced down at the file he was holding.

Casey shifted LiLi Kui from one knee to the other. She hadn't mentioned to anyone that she'd begun to feel an occasional twinge in her right leg when she tried to walk with her braces and crutches. Today the twinge was especially strong where the two-year-old sat on her lap. Casey was afraid to voice the words: Was it possible she might regain some sensation in her paralyzed legs?

"So?" Casey asked. "Are you going to tell me what it says, or do I have to put on my doctor's greens and read the diagnosis myself?"

Hank tapped the folder in the palm his hand. "Possum is an old, old fellow. We know that. He was full grown the first time he followed Ed home after Ed rounded up that old ram he boarded for the school."

"The last one? After the high school burned down?"

"Yes. The last school mascot. That was twenty years ago."

"That ram was a legend."

Hank nodded. "Mayor Ida told Dad that the ram seemed to truly believe he was the last hope for the spirit of the Mossy Creek football team. As if he had to keep up the fight for our pride and independence. So once a month or so, he managed to open the pasture gate and let himself out. Possum would round him up and herd him back to Ed's pasture."

Casey nodded. She'd been a girl then, a girl who still had an athlete's body—before the wreck that took away any dream of competing in the Olympics. "Now, instead of a ram, Possum herds Ed back to Magnolia Manor in time for supper. It's as if Possum realizes that Ed represents the last of his kind, too." She glanced up at her husband. "How bad is it, Hank?"

Reluctance thickened his voice as he said, "It's bad. The big C, Casey. Don't know how Possum's managed to follow Ed around as long as he has."

Casey took a deep breath, nuzzling LiLi, who watched Possum intently. "I'll tell you how. He's stubborn. Just like Ed. Can you do anything for him?"

"I can keep him from being in pain, but that's about all. Ed's going to have to stop striking off on his own. What's going to happen to him when Possum isn't around to find him?"

Casey nodded. Everybody looked after Ed when cataracts almost blinded him. But now they couldn't reason with him. "It isn't his eyes. It's his mind. More times not, Ed loses track of where he is, and Possum has to get him home. What are we going to do, Hank?"

"Will you talk to him, Casey? You can do more with both of them than I can."

"Yeah. Just because I'm some kind of miracle on leg braces, people feel sorry for me so they let me rattle on like I carry a fence around with me."

"Fence?" Hank frowned.

"Yeah, the kind of fence people lean against and gossip. Speaking of fences, we didn't check in the back of the pasture, but Sandy just called on her cell phone and said that Ed is probably down there working on the holding."

"He wasn't there earlier. We checked."

"Maybe he's there now."

Casey handed LiLi to Hank, drove her scooter onto the lift at the side of the van, and hit the *Retrieve* button. As she, LiLi, Possum and the scooter were lifted slowly toward the van's open door, Casey asked, "When does the new mascot arrive, Hank?"

"Next week."

"Let's hurry and get the new paved pathway poured. If I can get to the barns and holding pen I can give Ed more of a hand with the ram. Without a paved path this scooter will bog down in the high grass."

"More of a hand with what?" Hank asked as he lifted Casey into the van's seat and buckled LiLi into her child's seat. Possum continued to watch them from the scooter's basket, his jowly, hound-dog face seeming to grow longer, older, sadder.

"Well," Casey stalled. "I just thought I should keep an eye on Ed while he's out there with that wild animal."

Hank laughed. "You can't help Ed train the ram."

Casey lifted her chin and gave an, *I'll show you*, look that Hank had seen before. When Casey's girls' softball team took the state championship *again* last year, Casey's success as a coach who happened to be a partial paraplegic had been on the front pages of Georgia's newspapers more often than Ham Bigelow's re-election as Governor.

"Look, Wonder Woman, you've accomplished a lot, but you still have a physical handicap, and you don't speak *Ram*."

Casey chewed her tongue. She had a way with animals as well as people. When she'd taught Possum to sit quietly in the basket on her scooter as they went to ball practice, Hank hadn't been surprised. Nor when Ed accepted the position of team "mother" and coaching assistant. As gruff as Ed was, he always looked after the little ones, whether they be human or animal. But that was before Ed and Possum got old.

Hank leaned inside the van and gave Casey a hug. Nobody knew better than he how hard Casey had worked in the years they'd been married. Learning to walk with braces, learning to drive his mobile vet wagon, and traveling to a foreign country to adopt their daughter were milestones that made people forget about Casey's handicap. Most believed Casey was just like everybody else. But helping Ed train a three-hundred-pound ram about which they knew nothing was not only dangerous but reckless.

Hank didn't know quite what he was going to do about his headstrong wife. Once Casey took on a challenge, she wasn't likely to give up. So far she was dropping hints of wanting to adopt a second child and taking flying lessons, and now she wanted to help Ed during his training sessions.

Hank scratched his head. She could drive a car, true, but flying a plane was demanding in a very different way. In any case, if Casey was going to take lessons he was going to have to bring in bigger bucks. A country vet operating the kind of second-generation practice Hank's dad had set up made friends, not money. He hoped he could convince Casey that the Blackshears are four-legged animal people, not people who needed wings.

Casey's gaze swiveled past Hank. "There they are. Thank goodness."

Possum watched Ed and Miss Irene slowly walk up the sidewalk. Ed looked so old, so sad. *Like me,* Possum thought. Once Ed caught sight of the child, he perked up, but Casey shook her head.

"Oh, Possum," she whispered, turning to lay a hand on Possum's head. "What will we do without Ed? And what will we do without you? I know you don't understand lab reports, but I do."

Possum nuzzled LiLi and gave Casey's hand a lick. He'd been wondering the same thing. What would they do without him?

Ed had to train a replacement for the Mossy High School mascot. Who was going to help him? Who was going to chase the new ram back to the pasture when he escaped?

And Casey's leg had feeling coming back. When Possum had reared up and put his paws on her legs he could feel her muscles jerk. She'd need someone to lean on as she learned to walk again.

And LiLi *could* learn to talk, but how could she do it by herself?

The answer was, none of them could. That meant Possum had a job to do before he left. He had to train a replacement for *himself*.

But where would he get one smart enough? And did he have enough time?

🐾🐾🐾

Two days later, Possum encountered a chubby little white dog wearing a silk nightgown—a dog he'd never seen before. In a private conversation in dog-talk, Possum learned that her name was Polly and she was about to give birth.

Polly was a King Charles Spaniel who'd run away from home down in Bigelow because her owners planned to sell her puppies. People think animal mothers don't grieve for their babies, but they do. Polly wanted—no, *needed* to keep her babies.

Besides, as soon as the puppies were born her owners

would discover that the father of this litter was not the champion Spaniel whose services they'd bought, but a charming hillbilly Polly met during a family camping trip. The puppies would be worthless mixed-breeds. They'd end up at an animal shelter. So Polly wanted to keep her babies, and she would disappear into the mountains and live in the wilds, if that's what it took.

When Possum heard her story, he made an offer that would solve all their problems—but it was an offer he had no idea how to implement. If he pulled it off, Polly could keep her babies, Ed would socialize the ram, LiLi would begin to speak, and Possum would have the replacement companion Ed would need when he was gone.

It would take careful planning to make his scheme work. For now he had to convince Polly to return home—wherever that was. Then he had to contact Professor Sagan's amazing bird—the one who appeared and disappeared in some mysterious way that nobody understood. Normally birds and non-flying creatures didn't communicate, but this was an extraordinary bird . . . and Possum needed some extraordinary help.

It was midnight when Possum carefully tip-toed down the carpeted stairs at Magnolia Manor and through the doggie door to the outside. Half an hour later he was standing at the base of Colchik Mountain giving his best rendition of a creature alert.

One eerie call after another echoed up the mountain. Bird to bird. Coyote to raccoon. Owl to fox. Squirrel to rabbit.

Then suddenly a large, white, mythical creature soared silently across the moon and came to rest on a fence post. It cocked its head toward Possum, and he moved hesitantly toward it.

"What can I do for you, my friend?"

Possum explained what he needed, and the large,

ghostly bird nodded.

"I'll see what I can do." He flew away.

Possum shivered in the coolness of the springtime mountain air, but he waited patiently for the bird to return. Nearly an hour later, he saw the lovely creature approaching.

"I made an agreement with the ram," the bird said. "The ram will allow Ed to teach him. Not obviously. You know how sheep are. They have to keep up their ornery reputation. But he won't give Ed too much trouble, and he will proudly represent the spirit of Mossy Creek."

Possum lowered his head in gratitude. When he looked up, the bird was gone.

Now there was a button-eyed child with sad vacant eyes who needed to know she could speak. How could a dog that couldn't speak teach words to a child who couldn't talk?

"Don't worry, my friend," the whisper came through the gauzy sheet of fog that drifted down from the mountain. "You'll work it out."

For the next week, Possum spent at least an hour with Ed and the ram, marveling at the presence of Sagan's white bird—hidden, but always nearby.

One morning, Ed went out on his old front porch and dropped into the swing.

"You know, Ellie, old girl," Ed said to the spirit of his dead wife. "I'm not sure I'm going to be able to finish what I promised."

Possum put his front feet on Ed's knees and whined. When Ed helped him climb into the swing, Possum laid his head on Ed's knees, crying softly.

🐾🐾🐾

An hour later, Casey left the veterinary clinic for her daily scooter drive to the square. When she saw Ed on the swing at his old farmhouse, she stopped.

"You okay, Ed?" she called.

"Just feeling a little low today," he answered and struggled to his feet.

"What are you doing? You're going to fall." But her words were too late.

Ed crumpled against the porch rail.

Casey screamed for Hank and started to cry.

Possum howled.

By the time Hank ran down the walk and reached Ed's house, Casey had used her cell phone to call Doc Champion.

"Con sarn it," Ed swore when Hank tried to help him up. "I been going up and down these steps since the war." He grabbed the rail and attempted to pull himself up. "The big one. Got through that all right, and I reckon I can stand up without your help."

But he couldn't.

Possum watched in dismay. His heart played a drum roll in his chest.

As the EMTs, led by Sandy's brother, Boo Bottoms, were about to load Ed into the ambulance, he called, "Stop! Where's Possum?"

Boo picked up Possum and placed him on the gurney beside Ed.

After much poking and x-raying at Mossy Creek's small emergency clinic, Dr. Champion stood between Hank and Casey and frowned down at Ed. "I've been telling you that you have to slow down. Now I'm ordering you to. If you plan to play Santa in this year's parade, or anywhere else, you have to do what I say."

He turned toward Possum and shook his finger. "And that goes for you, too, you old hound dog."

Both patients reluctantly agreed, though Possum didn't want to.

How was he going to fulfill his promise to bring Ed

another dog?

🐾🐾🐾

Near midnight, a shrill keening sound echoed through the mountains that overlooked Mossy Creek.

Sagan's bird.

Possum struggled to his feet and made his way downstairs to the porch at the back of the Manor. The bird flapped transparent wings and hovered overhead until Possum understood he was to follow the bird out of town.

After Possum made his way into the countryside he heard a pasture gate open at Ed's farm, and soon the ram joined them. The ram knelt down and allowed Possum to ride on his back. Then they followed the bird up the mountain.

After a few minutes, they reached a cave hidden by a large rock. Sagan's bird perched on a fallen tree limb. From inside the cave came a weak, mewling sound.

Possum dug through debris hiding the entrance and found Polly weakly cleaning a tiny white ball that seemed almost lifeless. Her baby. She hadn't gone home like he'd asked her.

As Possum watched, Polly worked to clean her pup, but looked as if she could barely manage.

Moments later, the pup squirmed from its birth sac, squeaking impatiently for it's mother's attention. But it wasn't to be.

Polly rested her head on the cave floor and shut her eyes. Possum saw that giving birth alone had not been her best idea. She'd had trouble and wasn't going to make it. She was trusting her baby's future to an old hound dog.

Now all Possum had to do was get Polly's baby safely to Ed. But how?

The ram leaned inside the cave and knelt down for Possum to climb back up on his back. Possum gently took the tiny pup into his mouth before slowly climbing up.

Sagan's bird perched on the ram's neck and spread its wings like a cloak to keep the pup warm.

They hurried back down the mountain.

🐾🐾🐾

At dawn Casey Blackshear sat on her back porch watching the sunrise as she held her daughter in her arms. "Oh, my darling, LiLi," she whispered. "I love you. If I could only hear you say you love me, too."

Then she saw it—the most curious sight she'd ever seen. From the direction of Ed's house came a white animal, its antlers alabaster in the light of the sun.

LiLi stirred, making a sleepy sound.

Casey turned and called through the backdoor screen, "Hank?"

"I'm here," he whispered, stepping onto the porch. "I see it. Lord have mercy. If that doesn't beat all."

It was Ed's ram, gently opening the gate with one horn before walking toward the porch. Possum rode on its back.

"Possum's carrying something, Casey."

Hank hurried into the yard, reached out gingerly and lifted Possum off the ram's back. The young sheep moved away as if he did this kind of thing every day. As Hank set Possum on the ground, Possum gently dropped the tiny pup into Hank's hand. It cried softly.

Hank carried the tiny pup to his wife and daughter. "Look, LiLi, it's a puppy. A baby dog, LiLi. Possum has brought us a puppy."

LiLi smiled and reached out toward the little pup. "Possum's baby," she said in wonder. "Ed's Possum's baby."

Casey and Hank gasped. LiLi had never spoken like this before. Through tears of joy they beamed down at her daughter. "Yes, LiLi. That's right."

Hank looked the pup over carefully. "Newborn. I'd say in the last few hours. Seems healthy, though. Wonder where it came from."

"I don't know what's happening here," Casey said, "but let's take the baby to Ed. I feel that's what Possum means for us to do."

"Give me a minute to clean the pup up, then I'll drive," he said.

A few minutes later, he helped Casey into the van and fastened LiLi into her car seat. Possum stretched out on the back seat, breathing heavily. Casey cuddled the pup on her lap.

At the nursing home, Casey spotted her father's car. She knew without being told that Doc Champion was there for Ed. Possum whined.

"We'll get there in time, Possum," she murmured.

Hank unfolded Casey's wheelchair and guided her into it, then settled LiLi into her mother's lap. The pup nestled in LiLi's lap. Hank lifted Possum from the van and carried him as Casey rolled her chair by the wheel guides. They started inside.

"Hurry," Miss Irene called from a hallway, her thin blue hands clutching the front of her robe. Her eyes glistened with tears.

Dr. Champion told them somberly that Ed was almost gone. Hank laid Possum on the bed beside him and guided the old dog's head to Ed's shoulder. Casey gently placed the pup on Ed's barely moving chest.

LiLi let out a joyous laugh. "Possum's baby," she said.

Words, Possum thought as he settled into his master's arms for the last time. *From a dog who can't talk to a child who now can.*

The adults didn't notice as shadows crossed the sky outside a window. But LiLi saw, and nobody argued when years later she swore that she'd seen an old man, a little white dog and a happy hound following a big white bird with wings that reached toward the mountain top. Possum's puppy mewled as Ed's chest stopped moving beneath him and Possum's last breath warmed his face.

Possum's baby knew that love lives on.

And so did LiLi.

Mossy Creek Gazette

VOLUME VII, NO. NINE　　　MOSSY CREEK, GEORGIA

Mossy Creek's Beloved Santa and His Four-Legged Elf are Gone

Edward Alton Brady, Sr., one of our most revered Creekite citizens, has died. Ed's well-known hound dog friend, Possum, has died as well, as if knowing that Ed and his wife Ellie need him to chase the rabbits out of their garden in Heaven.

Ed Brady was a proud war veteran, an esteemed farmer, a respected volunteer fireman, a loving if grumpy husband, neighbor and father, and a loyal friend. He married Ellie shortly after WW II and they set up housekeeping at historic Brady Farm, one of the oldest farms in Mossy Creek. Ed is survived by his son, Ed Brady Jr., a successful computer game inventor who moved back to Mossy Creek in recent years. The reunion brought Ed and Ed, Jr. together after a long period of estrangement, and we're happy to report that they became very close.

Ed is perhaps best known for playing Santa in the Mossy Creek Christmas parade every year since 1952. Creekites young and old have fond memories of skinny Ed in a padded Santa suit, perched atop a fire truck as it crept up Main Street. He tossed candy to all the children and, it was suspected, gleefully tried to pelt some of the naughtier kids (and adults) on their heads. Adele Clearwater will never forgive him.

Creekites will always remember Ed's devotion to Ellie. After a stroke confined her to Magnolia Manor Nursing home, he arrived every morning to feed her breakfast. Although Alzheimer's darkened Ellie's mind, Ed found ways to break through to her memories of their years together. Her response to Ed's "ugly Christmas tree" is but one of many heartfelt times the couple shared despite Ellie's failing health.

Continued on next page

Continued from previous page

Ed never quite recovered from her death a few years ago, but still managed to cause an occasional ruckus. After the state revoked his driver's license due to poor eyesight, Ed turned to his old John Deere as transportation. During one of his more notable drives into town, Ed and his tractor were run into a ditch by Governor Ham Bigelow's limousine. Ed suffered a broken leg but, happily, was soon able to afford cataract surgery thanks to the much-harassed governor's grudging settlement. We applaud Ed for adding his name to the long roster of Creekites who have merrily tweaked Ham Bigelow's pompous pride.

Ed was rarely seen without Possum by his side. They were a team. Possum had a strong intuition for those in need, most of all for Ed, who prized Possum's friendship despite a sometimes rocky relationship due to both of them being independent and stubborn. Possum leaves behind a son who will be raised with great love by Hank, Casey and Lili Blackshear.

We'll miss Ed and Possum every day of the year, but especially at Christmas. It's sad but fitting that they left this earth together. We're sure Ellie was waiting for them with open arms.

Rest in peace, Ed and Possum. We know the two of you will watch over Mossy Creek from Heaven, keeping an eye on your old friends, both the people and the critters.

300

The Mice that Roared

Part Ten

Jayne

Ed Brady's funeral was tomorrow. Another icon of Mossy Creek gone. And Possum—how I'd miss that sweet old hound. He would be buried alongside Ed.

I put down the *Gazette* and stared out my back window at the azaleas blooming riotously along the banks of the west branch of Mossy Creek. Their pink, purple and white flowers intertwined into a colorful mosaic painted by Mother Nature. They reminded me of my metaphor about life. It *is* a mosaic, every bit as colorful, every bit as fragile, every bit as fleeting as the mosaic right outside my window. The flowers bloom, they're beautiful for a week, maybe two, then they fade and fall off.

I add pieces to my mosaic all the time. Ed Brady was one, and he'll be remembered every time I see the shiny piece of glass he placed there.

"Ginda! Ginda!" Matt screamed with delight as the small dog chased him through the apartment, barking gleefully.

I couldn't help but laugh. The little dog was a shiny new piece, as well. Smart and funny and opinionated and passionate.

How had I ever amused my son before she came? They ran each other to exhaustion, then collapsed in a heap of jeans and fur to sleep until their next adventure.

The day before, I'd sat on a bench on square, enjoying the warm, sunny spring day as they chased around the park. Glinda never left Matt's side when we were out. She guarded him as if she'd given birth to him herself. She wasn't vicious about it, but she stood on alert every time someone approached that she didn't know. It wouldn't be long, however, until she knew everybody in town.

Mossy Creek was like that. The people here were friendly to people passing through but very protective of their own, If you passed through and decided to stay, then you became one of their own and were sheltered every bit as much as someone born here.

I had first-hand experience of that. And so did Win. Win.

My smile deepened down to my toes.

Our date had gone very well. We'd driven down to a fish house on a north finger of Lake Lanier and lingered over trout, dessert and coffee until the manager cleared his throat and announced they were about to close. We hadn't even noticed the time passing, we'd been so deep in conversation, so deep in each other.

It'd been a long time since I felt that way— tingling with knowing something was just so *right*. I'd had the same feeling when I first visited Mossy Creek, which boded well for the relationship.

And I knew Win felt the same. Not only had he told me, but he'd been by the coffee shop every day since. Our next official date was the funeral tomorrow. Tonight he was catering the wake.

I had a sneaking suspicion Win Allen would be another bright shiny piece of glass in my mosaic. Perhaps even a gilded one.

Some people count their blessings. In Mossy Creek, I count my pieces of glass.

Recipes from
Bubba Rice

Teasel's Tuna Brownies
(for dogs and cats, if your cat will actually eat a treat!)

Ingredients:

2 six-ounce cans of tuna in oil

2 eggs

1½ cups wheat flour (use rice flour if your pet is
   allergic to wheat)

1½ tsp garlic powder (do not use garlic salt)

Grated parmesan cheese

Directions:

1. Preheat oven to 250 degrees F.

2. Drain tuna and mix with eggs, flour, and garlic powder
   in a large bowl.

3. Form into a doughy ball.

4. Spread 1/4 inch think on a greased cookie sheet.

5. Sprinkle with cheese.

6. Bake 25-30 minutes or until golden. Cut into small squares.
   Size the squares so the treat is just right for your pet's
   size. Store in an airtight container in the refrigerator, or
   freeze some for later.

Clay's Summer Treat for Dog
(makes a yummy cool treat
for those dog days of summer)

32 oz vanilla yogurt

1 mashed banana

2 Tbsp Peanut Butter

2 Tbsp Honey

Blend together and freeze in either 3 oz paper cups or
ice cube trays.

And you know, kids probably won't turn their nose up at these
either. Increase honey to taste.

Butler's Apple Pie Cookies for Dogs

1 cup Unsweetened Applesauce

1 tsp Cinnamon   ½ cup Powdered Milk

1 cup Cold Water   2 Large Eggs

½ cup Vegetable Oil   2 tbsp Honey

5 cups Whole Wheat Flour

Preheat oven to 350 degrees. Combine all of the ingredients and
kneed together. If mixture is too stiff, add more water. (Word
of warning—this is a sticky dough!) Roll out dough to desired
thickness and use heart or bone shaped cookie cutter to cut
out. Dogs don't actually care so you can just cut up the dough
into squares. Bake 20 – 25 minutes until browned.

For dogs with a wheat allergy, use rice flour. If you keep Goat-
A-Lac on hand for nursing orphaned puppies and kitties, that
makes a dandy substitute for powdered milk!

This recipe will yield a lot of cookies so you may want to start
with a half-recipe to gauge the yield using your cookie cutter
size.

Bubba's Dry Rub

This one's for people, folks!

This rub works well with just about any kind of pork barbeque. I've used it on ribs, shoulder and roasts.

Ingredients:
¼ cup dark brown sugar (packed)
3 tbsp smoked paprika
1 tbsp coarsely ground black pepper
1 tbsp kosher salt
1 tsp cumin
1 tsp dried onion flakes
½ tsp cayenne pepper

Preparation:

Combine the ingredients in a food processor or a coffee grinder and blend. This should be enough rub for about 2 – 3 pounds of meat.

Marinate the meat for at least one hour, then rub it down liberally with the dry rub before putting the meat on the grill. Remember, the secret to a good barbeque is "LOW (heat) AND SLOW (cooking)."

Bubba's Shrimp Alfredo Sauce with Roasted Red Peppers

This is quick, pretty simple and very flexible recipe. If you're feeling adventurous, try replacing the shrimp with sautéed chicken, fresh sea scallops or crawfish and it works just as well.

Ingredients:

1 pound 41-50 count shrimp, peeled and de-veined

¼ pound butter

4 tbsp extra virgin olive oil

1 pint heavy whipping cream

8 ounces fresh grated parmesan cheese

1 – 12 ounce jar of marinated roasted red peppers

1 bunch of green onions, rough chopped

4 cloves garlic, smashed and diced

1 tsp kosher salt

Preparation:

Melt the butter in a large, non-reactive skillet on medium heat. Add the olive oil, onions and roasted red peppers. Sautee for 10 minutes, then add the garlic, salt and cream. When the sauce reaches a light boil, reduce the heat to medium low and add 4 ounces of parmesan cheese. Stir until the cheese has fully melted and is blended into the sauce. Simmer for 10 minutes, then add the shrimp. Stir until the shrimp are fully covered by the sauce. Cook for another 3 – 4 minutes, then remove from heat and pour over pasta and top with the remaining parmesan cheese.

Prep time: 10 minutes
Cooking time: 25 minutes
Serves 4

Big Fat Critter
Spaghetti Sauce

Ingredients:

3 lbs.sweet Italian sausage — open the casing and form the sausage into balls, then brown in a skillet and set aside to drain off grease

4 lbs. ground beef — browned and drained

Mix the ground beef (but not the sausage balls) with:

2 Tablespoon olive oil

1 Large garlic clove, crushed

1 Large onion, chopped

2 Teaspoons oregano

2 Tablespoons basil

2 Big cans tomato paste

2 Bay leaves

1 Quart canned tomatoes, blended

1 Pint thick, sliced mushrooms

1 Cup white wine (the kind you drink, not cooking wine)

Preparation:

Lower heat and simmer 1½ hours. Add sausage balls near the end. If more liquid is needed, add wine.

The Cart Before the Corpse

A Merry Abbot Carriage-Driving Mystery in Mossy Creek
Fall 2009

Fans of the long-running Mossy Creek Hometown Series will gallop to bookstores for this spin-off equine mystery series by veteran Mossy Creek author Carolyn McSparren, a nationally known novelist and expert carriage driver, who owns and shows carriage-driving horses in her home state of Tennessee.

Open your barn doors and fasten your (buggy's) seatbelts for *The Cart Before the Corpse.*

Internationally famous carriage-horse trainer Hiram Lackland, a handsome Southern widower, dies mysteriously after retiring to a farm outside Mossy Creek. His estranged daughter, Merry Abbot, also a horse trainer, arrives to settle his estate. But Merry quickly plunges into bit-chomping dilemmas when her father's friend and landlord, mystery-novel maven Peggy Caldwell, insists he was murdered.

Before Merry can so much as snap a buggy rein, a handsome and annoying GBI investigator, Geoff Madison, is on her case. Then there's the troublesome donkey: Don Qui. Short for Don Quixote. And the fact that Hiram was teaching all of Mossy Creek's lonely women how to—ahem—drive his carriage.

Can Merry rein in the truth? What kind of horse play was her rakish dad involved in, and why would someone want to giddy-yup him into an early grave?

Stay tuned for the answers in this first episode of, "As the Carriage Wheel Turns."

www.BellBridgeBooks.com

The Mossy Creek Storytelling Club

(In order of appearance)

Jayne & Win.................................Martha Crockett

Peggy & Dashiell.....................Carolyn McSparren

Ida .... Deborah Smith

Amos ....Debra Dixon

Nancy & Eileen........................Maureen Hardegree

Louise.......................................Carolyn McSparren

Sam .... Pam Mantovani

Hermia..Michele Hauf

Lil Ida.............................Kathleen Watson Hodges

Sandy.. Susan Goggins

Ed & Possum ....Sandra Chastain

The Mossy Creek Hometown Series

Available in all fine bookstores or direct from BelleBooks

Mossy Creek
Reunion at Mossy Creek
Summer in Mossy Creek
Blessings of Mossy Creek
A Day in Mossy Creek
At Home in Mossy Creek

Other BelleBooks Titles

KaseyBelle: *The Tiniest Fairy in the Kingdom*
by Sandra Chastain

Astronaut Noodle
by Kenlyn Spence

Sweet Tea and Jesus Shoes
More Sweet Tea
On Grandma's Porch

Milam McGraw Propst, author of acclaimed feature film
The Adventures of Oicee Nash

Creola's Moonbeam

All God's Creatures
by Carolyn McSparren

From *NYT* bestselling author **Deborah Smith**

Alice at Heart — *Waterlilies* series
Diary of a Radical Mermaid — *Waterlilies*
The Crossroads Café
A Gentle Rain

P.O. Box 300921 • Memphis, TN 38130
901-344-9024 • www.BelleBooks.com